The
Immortals
of
Myrdwyer

A Mages of Bloodmyr Novel : Book III

by Brian Kittrell

The Immortals of Myrdwyer is registered with the
United States ISBN Agency using the following designation:

ISBN-13: 978-0-9829495-6-6

First Edition

The work is published by:

Late Nite Books
P.O. Box 321
Brandon, MS 39042

email: publisher@latenitebooks.com

United States of America

Cover design by Brian Kittrell with some artwork/art elements (commonly known as "brushes") used from Obsidian Dawn (http://www.obsidiandawn.com). It is with great appreciation and admiration that I was allowed to use these assets for creating part of this cover. Rights for reuse granted specifically by Obsidian Dawn (or their representative) in the form of licensing terms found on DeviantArt at
http://www.redheadstock.deviantart.com/journal/12379986.

DEDICATION

This book is dedicated to

Jacob

my son

❧ CONNECT WITH THE AUTHOR ❧

You can easily reach author Brian Kittrell by the various methods described below.

On Twitter:
    @Brian_Kittrell
    http://www.twitter.com/Brian_Kittrell

On Facebook:
    http://www.facebook.com/author.BrianKittrell

On the Web:
    http://www.latenitebooks.com

On YouTube (author interviews, discussions, and more):
    http://www.youtube.com/user/LateNiteBooksDotCom

Through eMail:
    brian@latenitebooks.com

Through the Mail:
    Late Nite Books
    Attn: Brian Kittrell, author
    P.O. Box 321
    Brandon, MS 39042

BOOKS BY BRIAN KITTRELL
RELEASED AND COMING SOON

THE MAGES OF BLOODMYR SERIES
THE CIRCLE OF SORCERERS
THE CONSULS OF THE VICARIATE
THE IMMORTALS OF MYRDWYER

THE SURVIVOR CHRONICLES
THE DYING TIMES
THE WAR OF THE DEAD
PRISONER AND SURVIVOR
A WORLD FORSAKEN

THE PANACEA SERIES
CURE
STASIS
BLIGHT

❦ Table of Contents ❧

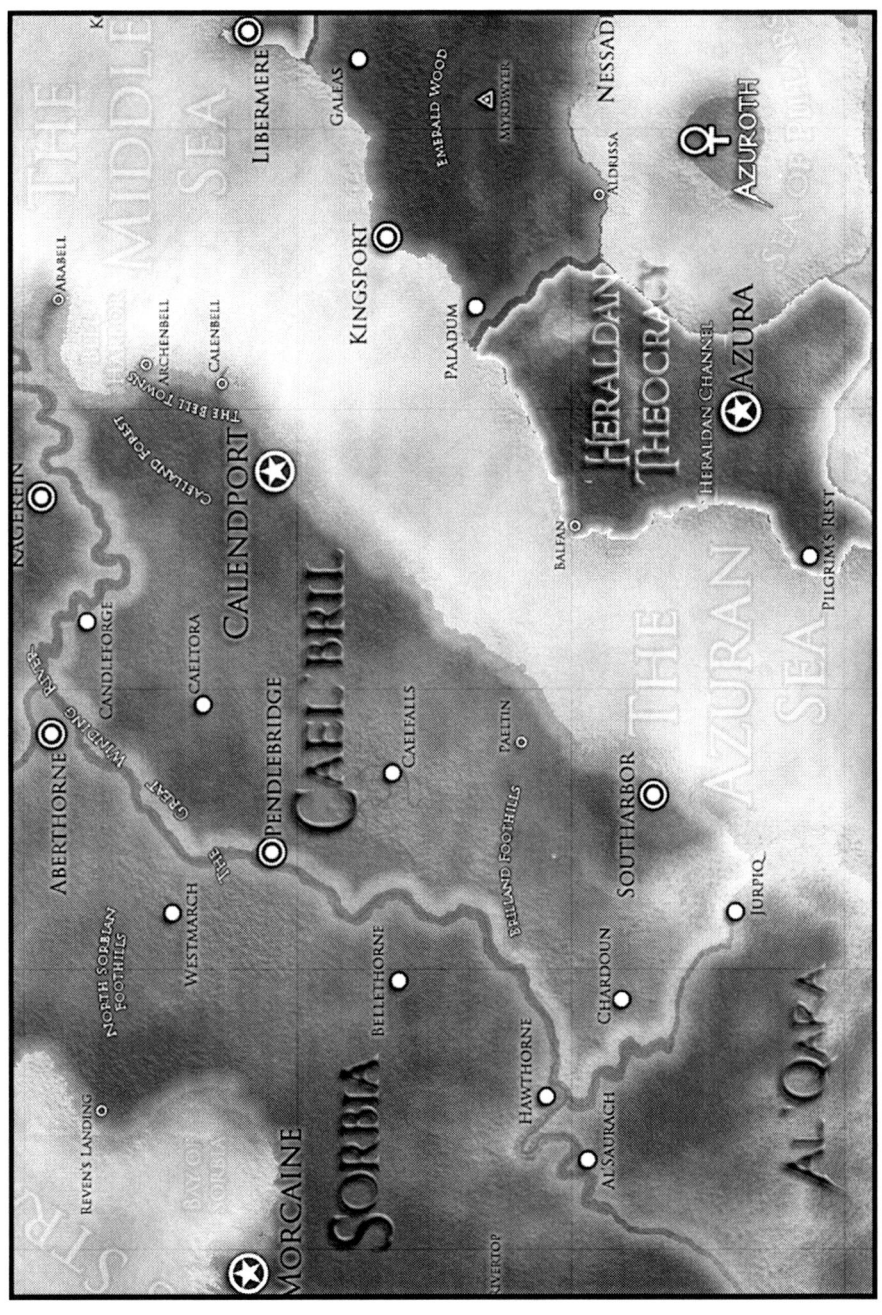

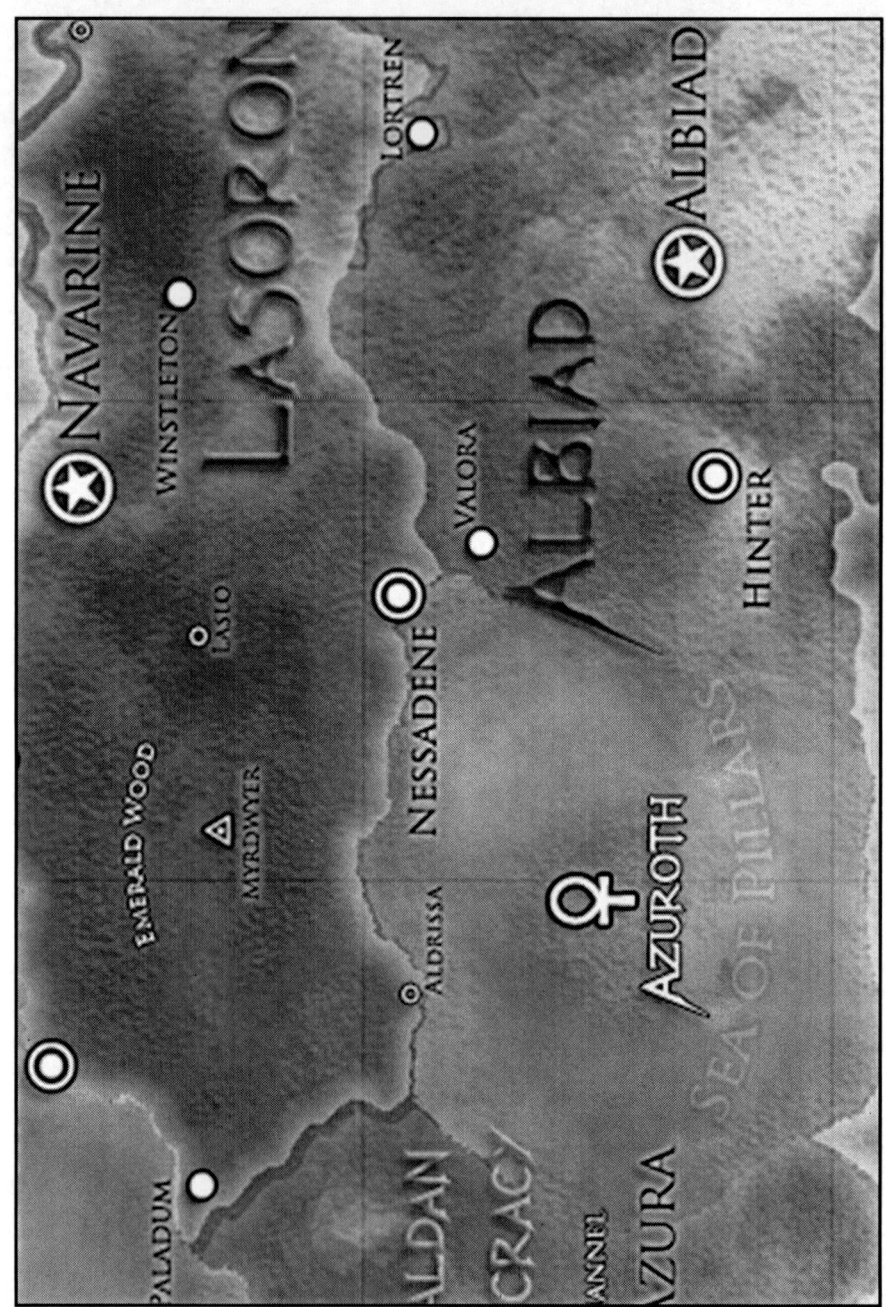

THE IMMORTALS OF MYRDWYER

FIRST EDITION

PROLOGUE

The reign of Grand Vicar Tristan IV has come to a violent end, and an unlikely peace settles over the Bloodmyr Isles. Aldric Jurgen is declared Grand Vicar of the Heraldan Theocracy and anointed as Petrius III. In his first act as leader of the church, Jurgen proclaims that priests shall no longer hold disdain for sorcerers, and he arranges for the city of Azura to celebrate the deeds of Laedron Telpist and his friends, the heroes responsible for ending the war and wresting power from the Drakars.

From Sorbia to Gotland, from Falacore to the Qal'Phamet Empire, voices are heard whispering the story of a young mage and his party who have defeated the Zyvdredi in the Heraldan lands. Some voices speak of these happenings with joy and celebration, while others tell tales of murder and intrigue against their brothers and sisters.

With their work finished in the Holy Land, Laedron, Marac, Brice, and Valyrie depart for Lasoron, a land of vast forests. Laedron seeks The Bloodmyr Tome, an artifact of untold magical power, and the secrets of someone named Farrah Harridan, one of which he hopes will provide answers for his peculiar condition.

❧ Chapter One ❧

The City of Nessadene

Laedron went to the forecastle of the ship and gathered his companions. "We're close to Nessadene, and we'll soon disembark on these foreign shores."

Marac nodded. "Right. Once we get everything together, we'll meet you outside."

Laedron returned to the top deck with his bag in hand, then waited for the crew to tie off and lower the gangplank. The ivory faces of the buildings gleamed by the glow of fire in the street lanterns, and he thought they were constructed from limestone by their unblemished appearance. By the time he could step off, Marac, Brice, and Valyrie had joined him.

"Have you ever seen a city like Nessadene?" Brice asked, taking a long look at their surroundings.

"Quite different, I must agree." Laedron pointed at the distant buildings as he walked down the plank. "Smooth stone and painted—or stained—stark white."

Hearing a peeling sound at each step and smelling

turpentine, Laedron reckoned the pier had been constructed of pine timbers and the boards had recently been replaced. *Pine is hardly the sturdiest of woods from which to construct a pier. Perhaps it's in abundant supply here?* Even some of the roofs and walls of buildings had been built with pine, a feature Laedron noted as they passed along the road. When he heard the flapping of cloth in the wind, he looked up to see the Lasoronian flag—two bars, one green and one white, with the symbol of the griffin, the mythical winged lion once thought to inhabit the forested lands of Lasoron.

"We'd better find lodgings first. Somewhere to rest our heads," Marac said, casting a wary eye on the strangers who walked near them. "How about that one? Looks like an inn."

What about the heads that need no rest? Laedron turned to see the building Marac had indicated. In front of the two-story structure, signage—a carving of a bed and a moon—had been hung near the street. Laedron nodded. "As good as any, I suppose."

Unlike the other nearby buildings, the inn had both pine shingles and walls. *Looks like only the larger buildings are made of stone. Maybe it's too great an expense to waste stone on a hostel.*

He followed Marac through the door, past a dining table with seating for twenty or so people, and approached the innkeeper, a burly man clothed in black, who stood behind a counter of pine. "What's your rate for four rooms?"

"Four? We don't have four rooms available, I'm afraid."

"How many do you have?" Laedron asked, then looked up to see a number of well-made steins painted blue, purple, red, and green on a shelf above the bar.

The man flipped through his ledger with his fat fingers, then picked at his beard. "Two."

Laedron glanced at Valyrie, then returned his gaze to the man. "We'd have to double up, but we can manage."

"Fine. How long will you stay? One night?"

"Better make it two. The morning after the second, we'll let you know."

"Two silvers, then." The innkeeper extended his hand, received the coins from Laedron, and offered two brass keys in exchange. "Up the stairs and down the hall. Four and five."

"Thanks." Laedron gestured at the steins. "By the way, who made all of those?" Laedron gestured at the steins.

"When I have nothing else to do, I'll work on a new one."

"You did them all?"

"It's a hobby of mine, and the customers sit and stare for hours. Good for business, you see?"

Laedron nodded. He kept one key and gave the other to Marac, then led the way upstairs. Valyrie followed Laedron to the door marked with the numeral four, and Brice went with Marac into Five.

Before Marac closed his door, Laedron called out, "Get some rest. In the morning, we must sort out our plans to find this Farrah Harridan."

Laedron opened the door. The room was hardly worth the silver piece demanded for rent. The curtains did little to provide privacy, and he wondered if they were capable of stopping any sunlight whatsoever during the day. *No matter. 'Tis but a room, a room I don't plan to inhabit for long, but some creature comforts would have been nice.* The bed seemed to be comfortable, and he didn't feel awkward at seeing one bed in the room, as he had felt when he had traveled with Ismerelda. Observing Valyrie, he noted that she seemed comfortable with the furnishings, as well.

Never again. He snatched the wand and scepter from his bag before sliding it under the bed with their other luggage, remembering how he had left his casting implements in a room the last time he had really needed them. *I'm keeping these in my boot.*

He walked around the bed, peered through the dirty glass of the window, then turned to Valyrie, casting uneasy glances between her and the bed. "I don't expect—"

"No need to be silly, Lae. We've slept next to one another before. Why would this be any different?"

He nodded.

"Besides," she tossed her bag onto the bed, "it was you who stopped things from becoming too serious the last time, if you don't recall."

"I just wanted to be clear, to put you at ease."

She laughed, then shook her head. "Nonsense."

"Well, that's settled." He sat on the edge of the bed and pulled one of his spellbooks from his pack. "I suppose you'll want to get some sleep. Will my reading keep you awake?"

"Actually," she said, falling on the edge of the bed, "I'd much rather learn a little about magic. You said that you could teach me, right?"

"Yes, but it's late, and you'll need to be fresh for the morning."

"Can't you fix that?"

He furrowed his brow. "Fix that? Fix what, exactly?"

"My tiredness. Use a spell to restore me, to make me feel as if I've slept."

"Well, yes, I could." He folded his arms. "What makes you want to learn magic, anyway? I can't deny its allure, but what specifically?"

"What? I cannot be curious?" she asked, smiling. "When I met you, I saw an opportunity to learn how to cast those spells I read about in my books. Will you teach me?"

"Very well, but it's not something to be undertaken lightly. So long as you realize that, we can proceed." He reached into his boot and handed her his beginner wand. "This is a wand, the most basic of casting implements."

She ran her fingers along the shaft, examining the intricate carvings of runic symbols. "What's its purpose?"

"To hold your attention while you concentrate. To prepare and cast a spell, you require concentration, an utterance, and an implement like a wand. All of those things come together and manifest into an event—a spell."

She stood. "What will I learn first? Fire? Lightning?"

"Not so fast." He chuckled. "You must learn to crawl before you can walk. First, I shall teach you of the dreaded vibrancy illusion."

"Dreaded?"

He laughed. "My sister hated it. I can still see the look on her face when I last practiced with her—a grimace of disdain for the simpler aspects of magic."

"Did you train her?"

"No, not exactly, I merely tutored her in addition to my mother's teachings." He drew his scepter from his boot. "The vibrancy illusion is nothing more than the conjuration of harmless light. It's mostly useless, but it is a spell you must learn and master."

Raising the scepter, he chanted the words and swayed the rod. A pale green light dripped from the ruby. Maintaining the spell, he drew shapes in the air that briefly remained before fading away. Her eyes lit up at the spectacle, then he released the spell. He repeated the incantation several times until she could vocalize it without his help.

Nothing happened when she said the spell—not a spark, glimmer, or glint. She shook the wand violently. "Why isn't this thing working?"

Laedron dodged out of the way of the wand. "It won't work on its own, for a wand is only a tool; the user must be skilled in its use."

"What am I doing wrong?"

"You're not concentrating."

"I am."

"You're not," he insisted. "Introversion. You must go within yourself, to the depths of your very being. Summoning magic is the act of going against reality to affect change."

She nodded, then started again. He paced in circles around her while repeating the incantation until she could say the words without his help. As a sparkle of light appeared at the end of the wand, he smiled.

She gasped, her face full of excitement, but she must have lost her concentration because the light faded away. "I did it! Did you see?"

He felt as Ismerelda must have upon seeing a student succeed. *The apprentice has become the teacher.* "Yes. Very good. Now, again."

She took a deep breath and exhaled, then extended the wand. Chanting the words, she waved the wand to and fro. A glimmer of light appeared just beyond the tip. He noticed her face turning red, the veins in her neck tensing beneath the skin, and a sway in her hips. *The headache's coming on strong now, but she resists.* Watching her, he became amazed at how fiercely she fought the urge to end the spell. *Such vigor. Good.*

"Let go," he said. "Let it go before you lose consciousness."

Releasing the spell, she fell to her knees, dropped the wand, and grabbed the sides of her head with both hands. "Unbearable!"

He crouched beside her and put his hand on her back, a move that Ismerelda and his mother would probably have frowned upon had they seen it. '*A mage must suffer in solitude. Otherwise, he will never learn to cope,' Ma had said. Can I not show her some compassion? Some understanding? Is there only one true way to instruct a student?*

Though obviously in pain, she smiled at his touch. "I can only imagine what you must feel when you conjure your spells, the ones far greater than this."

"It gets easier." He helped her to her feet. "With practice, you build up a tolerance. While you continue your learning, that tolerance becomes a resistance, and you learn to forge through the pain."

"How long does it take?"

"After a few weeks, you'll learn to anticipate the headaches and stop before they grow too intense, and as you go along, you'll find the pain easier to bear."

"Weeks?" She lowered the wand.

"Does that disappoint you?"

"I only mean to say that we may need to take it slow. The pain is greater than any I've ever experienced."

"'Tis only the beginning." He opened his spellbook and tore away the pages with his writing, leaving only the blank ones. "Take your notes in this. You need it more than I do." Lifting the cover of one of Ismerelda's spellbooks, he slid his old notes inside.

* * *

With the morning light pouring through the disheveled curtains, Laedron cast a spell to reinvigorate Valyrie's body, then exited into the hall. He found Marac and Brice coming out of their room at the same time. "Let's see about getting something to eat."

Descending the stairs, Laedron detected the scent of steamed oats and fresh-cut fruit—apples, pears, and peaches, if his nostrils and memory did not betray. Upon reaching the base of the stairs, he turned and walked over to the innkeeper. "Do you offer meals for your renters?"

"Indeed. A breakfast of porridge comes with the room, but we have other things if you don't care for the stuff."

"Porridge?" Laedron asked, glancing at the others joining him before returning his gaze to the innkeeper. "What's that?"

"Boiled oats."

Laedron wrinkled his upper lip. "What other things do you

have?"

"Whatever you'd like," the innkeeper replied, gesturing at the long table. "Over there."

Laedron nodded, then walked over to the table, sat, and retrieved three apples from a bowl. He wasn't able to make out much of the inn the night before due to the dark, but he could tell that the innkeeper cared more about the tavern than the lodgings. The curtains didn't have holes, the linens were clean, and the chairs and tables were in far better condition than the beds and dressers in the rooms.

Marac inspected the fruit bowl, then selected some pears. Valyrie and Brice joined them, each with a bowl of porridge in hand. Brice took the sugar, milk, and spices right after Valyrie, as if he didn't know how boiled oats were best eaten and was merely following her lead.

Laedron unfolded the scrap of paper Jurgen had given him just before their departure from Azura. "We passed this street on the way here. Twelve Pinecrest."

"A house?" Marac asked.

"Your guess is as good as mine, but Jurgen looked through old church ledgers and discovered that address to be the source of the books."

"Better place than any to start," Brice said.

"Finish up. I'm going to see if I can find anything out about the place." Laedron rose and walked over to the innkeeper. "Are you familiar with this address?"

The innkeeper read over the scrap of paper that Laedron had produced. "Aye. A left from here, then your first right. About halfway down that street, you'll find it."

"Do you know what lies there?"

"Twelve Pinecrest," the innkeeper repeated aloud, scratching the scruff of his neck. "The bakery? No, that's nine or ten. Oh, yes. I remember now. A shop of books and paper goods. It's been there for quite some time."

"Ever been? Met the owner?"

"No, lad, not I." The innkeeper scrubbed an old stain refusing to release its grip on the wooden counter. "Never been one for books, if I'm being honest."

"My thanks," Laedron said, folding the paper and returning to the table.

"What'd he say, Lae?" Brice asked through a mouthful of oats.

"From his recollection, it's a bookseller. Not much else."

"Come on, Thimble." Marac stood. "You look like a fool eating that."

"Do not."

Driving his companions out of the inn like a shepherd, Laedron led them through the door and down the boulevard.

✍ Chapter Two ❧

Of Bookstores and Spellcrafting

J ust as the innkeeper had directed, Laedron found the shop along the wide avenue, and unlike the stone buildings surrounding it on every side, the bookstore, from the base to the roof, had been built of pine timbers. The dark brown panels of its exterior stood in stark contrast to the white faces of the other buildings, and years of disrepair were evidenced by the patchwork of lumber covering holes and weak spots. Laedron reached the wooden gate fronting the property and studied the sign, a wooden oval painted with a black field behind a golden moon and stars. He knew that such placards often decorated the shops and establishments of mages. *Lasoron isn't known for its sorcerers. Perhaps it's just a coincidence.*

"Something bothering you?" Marac asked.

Laedron gestured at the sign. "Strange to see that here. Regular merchants rarely use such symbols to mark their shops."

"Maybe it's customary here in Lasoron." Marac nervously scratched his arm. "Or maybe they're mages."

"Be ready for anything," Laedron said, passing through the gate. First onto the porch, he peered through the window and saw only dim shelves full of books and the glimmer of a small fire in the hearth. He pushed open the door and immediately caught the scent of old tomes and dust mixed with the smoky aroma of the fire pit. Then, his eyes met those of the man behind the counter.

"Greetings," the man said, closing an old volume on the counter in front of him. He had hair similar in length, color, and style to Marac's, a sandy brown, trimmed short. "I'm Shanden Grey, proprietor of this establishment. Might I interest you in a book?"

Laedron held out his hand to Valyrie. "The book, please." After she handed it to him, Laedron walked over to the proprietor and slid the book across the counter. "I was wondering if you knew anything about this. We came across it in Azura, and its contents are a curiosity to me."

Shanden opened the book and fixed a pair of spectacles on his nose. "Can't say that I do, unfortunately."

Laedron produced from his pocket the ledger that Jurgen had given him, then pulled out the sliver of paper noting the origins of the book. "It came from your shop."

"Truly?" Shanden closely examined the book from back to front, then the ledger. "Strange. I've never seen it before."

Laedron studied the man and noted that the bookseller seemed rather young compared to the presumed age of the Farrah Harridan novel. "Have you always owned this place?"

"It's been in my family for quite some time. If you would care to, you could return with it tomorrow, and I'll ask my mother to come along and see about it."

"No way to see her today?"

A concerned demeanor draped Shanden's face. "She's elderly and infirmed, I'm afraid. She has her good days and her bad days, and this is one of the bad ones. To be honest, I fear that she may have few months left in her."

"Then, tomorrow?"

Shanden nodded.

* * *

"Another night's stay?" Marac sat on one of the long benches in the inn's common room. "I hoped we'd be on our way by now."

Laedron joined Marac at the table. "Little we can do. The only lead we have is this Shanden's mother."

"I can think of worse places to spend the night," Brice said, sitting across from Laedron. "An old, abandoned church in Azura readily comes to mind."

"You can say that again." Valyrie sat next to Laedron and snatched an apple from a fruit bowl. "I only spent one night there, and my back still aches when I recall the bedding."

"Mine still aches from it," Marac said, reaching back and massaging the base of his spine. "The fight with Andolis and our time on the ship didn't help, either."

Laedron reached for his wand. "I can—"

"No, no. It'll be fine."

"Why do you stop me? With the wave of a wand, I could take all of the pain away."

"And leave me with nothing but pleasant feelings?" Marac asked, hovering over a loaf of bread. "A little pain is good for you, my father used to say. Reminds us that we're still alive. Keeps us fighting."

Laedron tilted his head in confusion, but who was he to force Marac to do one thing or another? "As you wish. You need only tell me if you change your mind."

* * *

Having finished his evening meal, Laedron stood and said, "We'll meet here in the morning."

"What will you do?" Marac asked. "The night's young."

"I thought I might work on my new spell—"

"The one where you appear and vomit?"

"That's the one."

Marac glanced at Valyrie. "Maybe you can convince him not to do anything dangerous."

"It'll be fine." Laedron reached the bottom of the stairs. "I've considered things, and I believe I have a solution."

Marac shook his head. "Please, take care. The more you meddle with new magic, the more nervous I become."

Without another word, Laedron ascended the stairs, and Valyrie followed him to their room. Once the door was closed, he retrieved his old notes that he'd tucked into one of the Zyvdredi spellbooks and reviewed what he'd written of his traveling spell. He was unable to purge his thoughts of the nausea that had accompanied it; the sickness quivered in his belly at the idea of uttering the incantation again, but to leave the spell tucked away would mean its end, as if he'd never invented it in the first place.

"Anything I can do to help?" Valyrie asked.

"Keep practicing your vibrancy illusions." He picked up a quill, dipped it in ink, and perused his notations.

Holding the wand before her, she chanted, and the spell flickered. Her words and motions faded into the background as he concentrated, searching for a way to improve his spell and to rid it of the negative side effects. For a moment, he felt how he thought a regular student of magic might, the death, destruction, and underhanded dealings swept away and only spellcraft remaining. Try as he might, he was unable to forget the reason that he found himself in a strange, foreign land, hundreds of miles from his mother, sister, and everything familiar.

There must be a way to prevent the spinning and tumbling, he thought, scratching some notes on the back of the paper. Then, it hit him like a flash-bolt. *Encasing.*

He imagined manipulating the space around the target of the spell instead of affecting a person directly. *Like the shell of an egg. A protective barrier, with calm and serenity within. The shell travels, carrying the contents inside.*

He barely noticed his tongue poking through his lips at the corner of his mouth, an almost involuntary reaction to deep contemplation. He wrote faster. Like a madman, he scrawled line after line until the page had been filled. Throwing the papers aside, he shot up from the bed.

Valyrie spun around with a look of surprise, her spell fading from existence. "What's gotten into you, Lae?"

"Sorry. I think I have the answer to my little problem."

"This time, I'm going with you." She returned the wand

to its sheath at her belt.

"No, you can't—"

"Yes, I must. If Marac expects me to keep you out of trouble, I go where you go."

"It might not be safe."

"I didn't agree to come with you because it was safe, Laedron Telpist."

He nodded. "Right. Stand close, then."

With a wave of his wrist and a chant in Uxidin, a spinning sphere of energy formed around them. He closed his eyes and focused on the destination.

* * *

When the swirling energy dispersed, Laedron scanned the immediate area. Finding that no one had seemed to notice their sudden appearance, he took Valyrie's hand. Thankfully, he had not been afflicted with the nausea and dizziness he experienced the last time he had cast the spell. *The change worked.*

Her crystal blue eyes met his, then she turned to the sea before them. "Why this spot, Lae?"

"I've always liked being at the seaside." He looked out across the waves. "It's not much different from my life, really. We both—the shore and me—sit between two worlds, and we're not truly a part of either. For the bank, it's the land and the sea, but for me, it's the magical and the plain."

"I don't understand. You're a sorcerer, so aren't you a part of the magical world?"

"Only to a point. I never completed my training. I've

come far, but I haven't learned the secrets or the traditions. It's like being a sparrow living with chickens; you can fly, which is spectacular to the others, but you're still an outsider."

"What would make things better?"

He shrugged. "I don't know if anything can. The academy and my teacher are gone, the sorcerers usurped and scattered, and little is left of the old ways. I—" He choked and looked away.

"What, Lae?" She put her arm around his shoulders.

"I don't even know if Ma and Laren are still alive." He took a deep breath, trying to steel himself. "No need to be burdened with that right now. Ma used to tell me not to worry unless I had something to worry about."

"She would be correct. Wise words." She stared at him, then looked all around. "Are we still in Lasoron?"

He pointed over his shoulder. "Nessadene lies behind us. I noticed this spot when we sailed into the harbor."

"The city seems so far from here. How far do you think we could travel with that spell?"

"Difficult to say."

"Across seas?"

"I wouldn't want to risk it. A spell can last only as long as the caster can concentrate. If I lost my focus, we could land in the middle of the ocean."

Stepping down onto the beach, she pulled him along behind her. "And what, mighty sorcerer, will you do once you're through with adventuring?"

"What do you mean?" He sat beside her on the sand.

"You said something about returning home. To Sorbia?"

Having occupied his mind with crafting his spell, he had almost forgotten what his home looked like. "I haven't considered it, to be honest. I suppose that returning home will be the reward, if I make it that long."

"You don't think you will?"

"If I knew how long this last piece of our journey will take, I might be more optimistic. We have no way of knowing."

She took his hand in hers once more. "Yes, but what about after you return home? You have no plans for the future?"

"Of course." He looked down at her hands massaging his and felt a tingle crawl up his arm.

"Well?" She smiled. "It's difficult to talk to a man who won't speak."

"Before all this, little care was ever given to what I thought."

"You don't have to worry about that now. Like it or not, the world's opened its eyes and ears to you, Lae."

"Sometimes I wish more than anything that the world would be blind and deaf to me again. What good is an audience when they watch you only to see you suffer?"

"Good things have happened, too. Or do you deny that?"

"Good things, yes. Plenty of bad, too."

Her reaction to his words spoke volumes. Her face told of her pain, her anguish at losing her father, but he also saw hope in her eyes.

"I need not tell you that. You know of the bad things just as I do."

"I can only hurt so much before I need to feel joy," she said, inching closer. "For the first time in a long time, I can honestly say that I feel happy. I only ask what you see in the future because I want to share in your hopes and dreams."

He stared at the water, the wind pushing the surface just enough in some places to cap the waves with white foam. "Someone will have to bring back the things that once were."

"The things that once were?" She hugged tighter to his arm.

"From the ashes of the magic academy, a new one must be built. New mages must be trained to carry on our traditions, our ways."

"Does the task lie at your feet? Did no one else survive?"

"Victor. Perhaps he would be best suited for the job."

"I remember the name, but I cannot place him. Another mage?"

"Yes. He took me in when I had lost my way. When I was in Morcaine, I tried to join the army—"

"You?"

He straightened his back and puffed out his chest. "Something wrong with that?"

"You don't seem the type."

"Suppose I don't feel the same way?" He tensed. "You don't think I can stand up and fight for what I believe?"

"No, Lae," she said, wrapping her arm around his back and squeezing him. "From the moment I laid eyes on you, I didn't think you were that kind of man. I couldn't see you fitting into the uncompromising lifestyle of a soldier, and I still can't."

He relaxed a little. "At the time, I saw no other way. I

wanted to help in any way I could, but it took Count Millaird to guide me. He arranged my passage to Westmarch, where I came under the care of the Order of the Shimmering Dawn and Victor Altruis."

"And from there, your adventure led you to Azura. To me."

He grinned. "Yes."

"I'm glad we found each other."

"Me, too." He sat quietly in her embrace for a few moments before asking, "What do you see in the future?"

Her eyes shifted. "Well… I keep thinking about what you said. That you cared deeply for me."

He nodded.

"What did you mean by it?"

"Just what I said. I care deeply for you."

"Love?"

He tried to swallow the lump in his throat to no avail. His lips quivering, he said, "Yeah." When he turned to look at her again, her lips met his. Her hand slid across his shoulders, and he was lost in the passion of her embrace.

Snapping back to reality, he heard voices and bustling past the woods above the shore. "Come, let's go back to the inn. Others approach."

She nodded, and by use of his traveling spell, he returned them to their room at the inn, then cleaned the sand from their garments with the flick of his wrist. With Valyrie's arms wrapped tightly around his back, he took his lips from hers only long enough to blow on the candle and extinguish the flame. He guided her to the bed, then sat once she had crawled to the other side. Lying down, he pulled her alongside, and she rested her head on his chest, locked in a loving embrace.

With some hesitation, he said, "I didn't want to mention it, but I must. This is too important to hold my tongue. You know, we won't be able to do much of this once on the trail."

"Why not, Lae?"

"The others… and the task at hand. We must remain focused on the goal, and until we accomplish what we've set out to do, we'll have to treat each other like we treat Marac and Brice. If we don't, we risk everyone."

She slid her cheek against his shoulder. "Why must we be so cold? We've had no problems thus far."

"I think it's best."

Sitting up, she looked down into his eyes, her black locks mantling her face. "I don't understand this. Why can't we be close at the same time?"

"It will put us at risk." He put his hands behind his head. "If we can't think clearly, we'll end up making mistakes."

"I don't know about you, Laedron Telpist, but I thought I *was* thinking clearly." She lit the candle, and Laedron could see that she was flushed with anger. "You think this is just one big mistake?"

"No, not at all." He sat up when she folded her arms. "I only mean to say that we have to keep our minds on the task at hand."

"Forgive me if I'm smart enough to think about more than one thing at a time. After everything we've been through, the love we've shared, you say this now? You expect me to put my feelings—my love, my heart—on hold so that we don't risk offending anyone?"

"I—"

"You'd better not say anything else."

He stood. "I wanted to say that I was sorry."

"I'm sorry, too." She opened the door and gestured for him to leave. "Perhaps, when you think you can handle things, we can talk like adults. Until then, good night."

"Val, I—"

"Good night."

Walking out into the hallway, Laedron tried to look at her once more, but she closed the door before he could. After standing for a while amidst his regret, he turned to the door across the hall. *Oh, Marac's going to get a good laugh over this one. And no more rooms for rent means I have no choice but to stay with him and Brice.*

He knocked, and shortly afterward, Brice answered. "Yes…? Oh, Lae."

"Mind if I stay here?"

"Something wrong with your room?" Brice asked, stepping aside.

"You could say that." Laedron sat on the chair in the corner, then opened the bottom dresser drawer and propped his feet on it.

Marac stared at him.

Probably trying to think of some smart remark. Laedron asked, "You have nothing to say?"

"What could I say? These things, in the course of love, happen."

Not quite what I expected, but I'll take it. "She needs some time to… cool off."

"I hope she gets there soon. We have no time for games on the road," Marac said, then crawled into the bed and rolled onto his side. "Goodnight."

After Marac and Brice had fallen asleep, Laedron sat awake in the chair staring at the ceiling and wondered if his instincts were correct, if he would better serve them in the end by keeping his distance from her. *I can choose no other way at this juncture, for all other paths seem to lead inexorably to fault and defeat. Damned Fates, if only I could sleep, if only I could have a rest from these thoughts.*

ᓥ Chapter Three ᶇ

Tracking Farrah Harridan

Laedron glanced at Valyrie as they walked back to the bookstore the next morning. *She hates me. I just know she does, and I won't be surprised if she takes the first ship back to Azura.* He felt love—true, unstoppable adoration—for her, but for the sake of everyone's safety, he couldn't indulge those feelings. *I care for her. That's all that should matter now, but we can't endure if we don't maintain our resolve. Being open and acting however we might like could weaken our coherency and put us all in grave danger. Later, when all of this is done, when we're safe to do whatever we please and live the lives we choose for ourselves, things will be different. I only hope that it won't be too late to rekindle what we have—what we* had.

After passing through the gate and entering the

bookstore, Laedron locked eyes with an elderly woman seated near the fire.

Shanden said, "Ah, you're back."

"You're the boy who's found one of my books, are you?" the old woman asked, eying his every move. "Come to discuss Far'rah Harridan, have you?"

Far'rah. Is the emphasis at the end important? "Yes, madam. Well, my friends and I—"

"We should speak in private. Come along, young man." With the aid of an oaken cane, the woman rose and proceeded to go into a room in the back of the store.

Laedron turned to Shanden. "My friends can't come with me?"

"My mother—Callista, to you—demands privacy."

"Why? Anything that she says will be relayed to my companions anyway."

"You're the sorcerer, aren't you?" Shanden wiped the counter with an old, dusty rag, his frankness striking to Laedron.

"Yes." For a moment, he wondered if he had entered some sort of secret coven of mages, its existence hidden from the watchful eye of the Heraldan church. *Only by hiding their natures could sorcerers survive in Lasoron. The church's grip on these lands is too tight for it to be otherwise.*

"Then, she will speak only with you," Shanden said, pointing over his shoulder toward the back room. "She doesn't like to be kept waiting."

Laedron wanted to say, "And I don't like to be apart from my comrades, especially in circumstances such as these," but he didn't. Reluctantly, he took the book from

Valyrie—after she handed it over in a rather aggressive manner—and approached the door leading to the rear chambers of the structure. He took a deep breath, then entered through a red curtain.

Two fireplaces in a shop this small? he mused, taking in his surroundings. The old woman had already claimed a plush chair at the fireside, and a blanket was draped over her lap. Beneath her straight silver locks, a large emerald adorned a golden pendant at her breast, and she wore the necklace over a long-sleeved shirt with a tight collar and a floral print.

"You've brought a book for my examination, young man?" Her voice reminded him of the kind, elderly ladies of Reven's Landing, but she spoke with more strength, an underlying authority.

He handed the book to her. "Yes, madam. We seek answers—"

"Answers? Or power?" Callista leaned forward and filled her cup to the brim from a teapot. "Care for any?"

"No, thank you."

"Why don't you have a seat?" She gestured at the other chair.

He sat, but leaned forward in anticipation of what she might reveal. "You were saying? Power?"

"He's hungry." She laughed. "Perhaps you're not the one *they* seek."

"They? What do you mean?"

"We'll get to that in due time." She eyed him as if inspecting prey just before the kill. "Tell me, what do you know of Far'rah Harridan?"

That emphasis again. So strange. "Know of her? Well, I—"

The old woman erupted with laughter. "Nothing, I see. Will it be for the best, though? We shall see."

Frustrated, he sat in silence.

"Good."

He raised an eyebrow.

"It would seem you are willing to listen. I've met many sorcerers, young man, and before now, I figured them all for fools." She must have taken the tea down the wrong pipe because she choked, coughed, and covered her mouth with a frilly napkin. "Drunk with their own ambition, they were unwilling to listen to a wise word from an old woman."

"I think you'll find me quite atypical of most mages."

"I *hope* that is the case." Despite the apparent danger of doing so, she sipped her tea again, then placed it on the table next to her. "So, this book. A wondrous thing. A dangerous thing."

He watched her while she rubbed the blank cover, her eyes closed tight, her face exhibiting a sort of longing. *I've seen mages obsess over spellbooks before—Ma was the world's worst—but I can't recall anyone feeling this strongly about some regular old book.*

"A transcribed history," she said, opening her eyes and peering at him. "Well, as close as one can make a transcription without the original. A book of rituals and magic. A cry for help."

He furrowed his brow. "A cry for help?"

"Indeed."

"How so?"

"To attract those seeking out the secrets of which it speaks, to draw them here, to me, and only the ones clever enough to find me can proceed." She exchanged the book for her cup and sipped more tea. "The allure of everlasting life, of limitless magical power. Attractive, is it not?"

"No," he replied flatly.

She spit the tea back into her cup, the liquid dribbling down her chin. "No?"

"The greater the power, the more men seek to possess it. If I were ever to find it, I would do best to be rid of it."

"Interesting." Dabbing her mouth and chin with the ruffled cloth, she set the teacup aside. "If you mean what you say, you would be the first."

"Then, I might be the best to help you. What do you mean by 'a cry for help'?"

She looked around the room as if the answer were written somewhere on the walls. "We have time, and we'll get to that."

He leaned back in the chair.

"The best place to begin would be with your questions. What are they?"

At the present time, I'll be careful about what I reveal. I'm still unsure of this woman's intentions. "This book speaks of an ancient ceremony, of becoming a wizard, and a font—"

She closed her eyes. "'He would take on the qualities of magic itself; he would be restless, impervious to toxins, and needing little sustenance. Flowing through him like water in the river, magic would embody his existence.' Yes, I know the passage well."

Remarkable. She can recite the tome as if reading straight from the page. "What does it mean?"

"Exactly what it says, young man."

"Are you a sorceress?" He studied her for evidence of sorcery, but she had no wand, spellbook, or anything else that mages usually carried. "You must be."

"You confuse memory with ability." She smiled, and although she probably meant no harm, the grin was unsettling. "No, I'm not a mage myself, but I've known quite a few. Did you have any other questions?"

"I've been troubled by restlessness lately."

"Go on."

"My appetite has been easily quenched, and no matter how much ale I consume, I feel nothing."

She rubbed her chin. "It would seem that you've been dabbling in things not meant for mere mortals, Sorcerer."

"It was done *to* me. I had little choice in the matter."

"Nonetheless, it would seem that you've been put on the road to becoming a wizard. What you do next will determine your ultimate destination."

"And what choices lie ahead?"

"You speak as if they've already been made for you."

He sighed. "Enough of these games."

"The choices are simple: become a wizard or do not."

"That's it?"

"In essence, yes. I merely point out the way to both, and in the end, you decide."

He raised an eyebrow. "And what lies along the way?"

"Many things." She glanced away. "The village of Laslo shall be your first stop. From there, head west until you come upon a road in disrepair, an ancient highway."

"And after that?"

"Follow it to its end, and if you were meant to, you'll

find the choice you seek."

"What's out there?"

"*Myrdwyer.*" She spoke the word with perfect Uxidin inflection.

"Meer—dwai—ur?"

"The lost land of the Uxidin, young man. An old forest in which secrets may be learned from the voices that have gone silent."

"What does that have to do with the cry for help that you spoke of?"

"Everything." Taking the oak cane in hand, she stood. "Now, off with you. I've told you all that you need to know."

He shot up from his chair. "You've told me nothing."

Stopping at the curtain, she looked over her shoulder at him. "It'll have to be enough, for it's all I know." She paused as if trying to make a decision. "It's been a number of years since anyone's come asking about the Uxidin or that book, young man. Be careful in the ruins."

He knew she was lying about not knowing more, but he saw nothing to be gained by pushing her. Joining his friends near the gate outside—they had apparently tired of waiting in the shop—he said, "We must head north to the village of Laslo, then west to a place called Myrdwyer."

"What? Where?" Marac asked.

"A lost settlement of the Uxidin."

Valyrie blinked rapidly. "A lost one? As in, no longer populated?"

At least she will speak to me. "That's what the old woman —Callista—said." Laedron started toward the inn.

"But that's crazy," Brice said, catching up to him.

33

"What's the point of going somewhere with questions if there'll be no one to answer them?"

"Your guess is as good as mine, but it's the only lead we have. I must know what's happening to me." He sighed. "If she thinks I have a chance of learning more in the ruins, then to the ruins I must go."

* * *

Laedron and the others picked seats around a small table situated in the corner of the inn's common room. Each ordered a meal from the serving woman.

Once they had received their food, Laedron asked, "Any thoughts as to when we should leave?"

Marac glanced at the nearby window. "Only a few hours of daylight left, and we still need to gather supplies for the journey. First light in the morning?"

Although Laedron would have preferred to leave sooner, he couldn't argue with the fact that they would need provisions. "Good. The morning, then."

Brice nodded, then turned to Valyrie. "You know anything about this area?"

"A little," she said. "What is it that you'd like to know?"

"How to get to… where are we going, Lae? Myr…"

"Myrdwyer."

Valyrie shook her head. "I've never heard of such a place. It's not on any of the maps I've seen."

"We'll ask the innkeeper," Laedron said. "Marac, you and Brice should see about some horses." He several gold coins across the table while being careful to conceal them with his hand.

After Marac and Brice had gone, Laedron and Valyrie walked over to the innkeeper's counter, and Laedron handed a silver coin to the man. "It appears that we'll be staying one more night."

"Fine," the man said, pocketing the coin.

"Might I ask a few questions?" Laedron asked.

The innkeeper nodded.

"Are the roads dangerous in these parts?"

The man stopped wiping the counter and leaned closer to Laedron. "Aye, a bit. Some of my guests refuse to take to the roads, what with the war, the army heading east, and everything else. Highwaymen, young man. Running rampant."

"Why is the army heading east?" Valyrie asked.

"I hear tales," he said. "Lots of stories about the dead walking out from the swamps."

The Almatheren Swamp? Yes... I remember hearing about that. "Have you ever seen one of these... walking dead men?"

The innkeeper paused. "Aye."

"Well?"

"It isn't pleasant. The meat hanging off of them, the dead stare of their eyes. Murderous beasts. Best cut off the head quick lest they take yours."

"They come after the living? Why?"

"Hard to say. If I was one of them, I'd say it was an insatiable envy, a want to be alive again, and a hatred for those who have what I did not. A curse of the Necromancers who've made them, I'd say, or a command to do whatever evil they can before being returned to Syril by the edge of a blade. Their souls are eternally tormented in the dark rituals of the evil mages, or so it seems." He paused when Laedron's breathing hastened. "You needn't worry about that, though; the army's off to send them back to the hells. You should keep your concern on the roads that have gone unchecked."

"No one's left to guard the routes?"

"They've little choice, for the undead are numerous and do not negotiate. The army's always patrolled the roads, and with the soldiers gone, the bandits have come out of the woodwork. Open season on traders and couriers, or anyone braving the highways."

"When would be the best time to travel?"

"During the day. Harder for them to sneak up on you that way. Of course, some might still attack; a bandit's motivation lies in two places—his stomach and his purse—and the emptiness of either guides his decision-making."

"Thank you for your help."

"Think nothing of it. As a purveyor of fine liquors and not-so-fine lodgings, I'm obliged to help my customers. It's part of my job, really. If a little information might help them, well… a client who stays alive might come back and be a client again."

Laedron returned to the table. "Looks like we'll have to keep a sharp eye while on the road."

"He spoke of bandits. That doesn't worry you?" Valyrie asked.

"Shouldn't be any more trouble than we've already faced. Robbers tend to be disorganized, and not many are a match for a sorcerer in the company of knights."

"Suppose they're well-organized and have a sorcerer of

their own?"

"Don't worry, Val. We'll prepare for any possibility." Laedron turned to the door when it opened and saw Marac and Brice returning. "And, Val, about last night—"

"Think nothing of it. The mission, remember? Nothing is more important than that," she replied, a certain nonchalance about her. *She doesn't mean that. If she's trying to make me feel guilty, she's doing a damned good job of it.*

Holding up a scrap of paper, Marac grinned. "Four geldings, and they've given us a deal since few are seeking horses for travel these days."

"Good. We depart at first light," Laedron said, reading over the receipt when Marac passed it to him.

* * *

Night fell across the city, the white walls of the stone towers darkening with the setting sun, and Laedron retired to the room with Marac and Brice. He wanted to say something before Valyrie closed the door to her room, but he didn't. *Things are so delicate between us that I'd rather give her space. No, I'd like to be in her arms this last night, but I should have thought about that before I said what I did. I've been such an idiot.*

"She'll be all right in the end, Lae," Marac said, plopping onto the bed, his tone making him seem almost sympathetic to Laedron's plight. "You'd better get some sleep. We have a long way to go in a short time."

Nodding, Laedron sat in the corner chair, hung his shirt over the back of it, grabbed a bed sheet, and closed his eyes, trying to force the remorse of his many mistakes and failures from his mind. *I couldn't help Ismerelda. I was barely a match for Gustav, and Andolis nearly killed me. I've driven the only woman I've ever loved away, and only the Creator knows if she'll ever forgive me for that. Damned spells! Damned magic! If only I could sleep away these thoughts.* He shifted his weight to get comfortable and quickly realized that if being a wizard meant never sleeping again, he wanted no part of it. He'd drive himself insane long before the usefulness of his power became apparent.

❧ Chapter Four ❧

The Highways of Lasoron

Laedron pulled the sheet over his bare chest, his skin prickled by the cool air. Then, his eyes shot open at the drowsy feeling. *Have I slept?* The inky darkness of night had dominated the landscape, and the last thing he remembered was staring out the window and watching the nightlife of Nessadene. *Can it be so? Is the spell losing its power over me? Am I cured, or shall I die by its fading?*

Not wanting to disturb Marac and Brice, he rested his head on the pillow. For a moment, he wondered where the pillow had come from, but the thought was fleeting. The night sky like a weight on his eyelids, Laedron once again fell asleep.

* * *

"Good morning," Marac said. "Sleep well?"

Laedron shifted in the chair, his back strained from the position in which he'd slept. "Surprisingly I did."

"Maybe it's a good thing."

"I hope so." He scooted to the edge of the chair and put on his shirt. "If it's not, it's a very bad thing."

"No need to worry about it until we know otherwise." Marac strapped his belt about his waist.

Brice came through the door, a towel wrapped around him. "They've got hot water for the bath here. Down the hall, opposite the stairs."

Laedron nodded, put his feet on the floor, then staggered through the hall, ending up at the tub. Leaning against the lip, he struggled to keep his balance; it was as if all of the energy had been leeched from his body. *Looks like the sleeplessness has finally caught up with me. Oh, I can't get atop a horse and go slogging across the countryside in this condition. Perhaps I can convince them to stay here one more night. No, I'll have to get through it. Maybe the bath will help.*

Slipping into the water, he rested his neck against the cool edge of the tub, and after a while of soaking, his muscles felt reinvigorated by the heat.

He couldn't tell—and he didn't really care—how long he had spent in the soothing water. But when it began to cool, he stepped out of the tub, dried himself, and dressed.

Meeting Valyrie on the way downstairs, Laedron caught the familiar scent of the inn's breakfast foods, but he desired nothing to eat. Though he had recovered somewhat from his morning fatigue, he didn't want to weigh himself down with a heavy meal. *A handful of nuts and some fruit should suffice.*

Marac and Brice, having already started their meals, greeted Lae with a nod when he reached the bottom. Valyrie apparently didn't want to slow them down because she, like Laedron, took a few things from the fruit bowls and headed toward the door, and Laedron returned the keys to the innkeeper. "Thank you for your hospitality."

"Take care on the road," the innkeeper said, waving as Laedron exited.

Laedron turned to Marac once they all had joined him outside. "Where's the stable?"

"Up along this road." Marac pointed to the right. "It's on the north end of the city."

"Lead the way."

* * *

Across from the stable, a rather strange, fenced compound had been built, and the area was unlike anything Laedron had ever seen. A great pile of stones sat at one end of the lot, and two mounds, one of white powder and another of blackened sand, were on the other. In the center of the heaps stood a wooden structure with unfamiliar machinery, and he could see workers mixing the ingredients and pouring the substance into carts bound for the boulevard.

"What do you make of that, Marac? Anything like a mill?"

Marac glanced at the place. "I asked the stable master about it yesterday. He said they make something called *concrete* there."

"Concrete?" Laedron asked, the foreign word twisting his tongue.

"Yeah. It's what they use instead of stone since the country hasn't any good quarries." Marac gestured at the nearby structures. "All of these buildings are made of the stuff. The streets, too. Everything not made of wood, anyway."

"And it holds up?"

Brice nodded. "He said that it has to dry first, but yes. Once it's set, it stays."

"Marvelous." Valyrie stared up at one of the tallest towers in the skyline, but she shied away from Laedron when she smiled, as if unwilling to share her happiness, no matter how brief.

Approaching the stable, Marac exchanged a few words with the stable hand, then the boy left and returned several times until he'd brought out four horses.

"Just a minute," Laedron said, watching Marac mount his gelding. "I want to get some of that stuff."

"The concrete? But why?"

"Might be useful back home if we ever get there."

Brice stopped him. "But Sorbia's rich with stone, Lae."

"Stone that can be formed into any shape so easily? I think not." Laedron walked briskly across the avenue and approached one of the men. "Could I buy some of that?"

"What?" the man asked, apparently befuddled at Laedron's question.

"A handful of each pile. How much would it cost?"

"I don't know." The man arched his eyebrows and rubbed his chin. "A gold piece, I suppose."

"For the lot?"

"Surely."

Laedron fished out a sovereign and tossed it to the man. "Does that include a sack to carry them?"

The man nodded, collected a handful from each pile, and put the samples into separate burlap bags. "Here you are, young fellow."

"Thanks." Laedron returned to his friends, slipped the sacks into his saddlebag, and climbed atop his horse. "Laslo, then?"

"Yes, but do you know the way?" Marac asked.

"North, I suppose."

"Best get a map." Marac turned his horse so he could see the stable master. "Know where we can acquire a map, my good man? Nothing fancy, but enough to get around this country."

"Where are you going?"

"Myr—"

"North," Laedron said, stopping Marac. "For a while, at least. Then, west of Laslo."

"The Ore and Timber Guild. That way. Ask for a surveyor's

sketch."

"I'll get it, and I'll see what extra food I can pick up. Just meet me at the north gate," Marac said, taking off down the boulevard.

* * *

Once Marac arrived at the gate, Laedron nodded to the others, then led them down the road. *Looks like they waste few resources on the roads outside of town*, he mused, observing the dirt and gravel mix beneath the horses' hooves. Not long into the journey, he could no longer ignore the sun beating down upon his neck and his clothes moist with sweat. In the city, a constant breeze seemed to flow from the sea, between the buildings and onto the people in the streets, but such luxury was not to be had the farther inland he went.

Marac took a deep breath, then exhaled even louder. "This is what I love. The countryside, the fresh, free air. Nothing like it."

"I know what you mean." Brice came up alongside Marac. "The flowers and the birds chirping. Can't be replaced."

"Keep sharp," Laedron said, studying the distant tree line. "We're turning westward, toward the forest. If we're to find brigands, we'll likely find them there."

Marac reached out and patted Laedron on the shoulder. "Fret not, my friend. We're behind you every step."

Even though Marac's words had been spoken playfully, they gave Laedron some comfort; he couldn't think of anyone else he'd rather have at his side. Then, he glanced at Valyrie and felt as if he'd made a mistake by bringing her and leading her on a dangerous path into the wilderness. *She's grown, Lae,* he thought, remembering Marac's advice. *She's grown enough to make up her own mind. But am I grown enough to make her happy? To win her back when this is over?*

"Let me see the map," he said, opening his hand to Marac.

Trying to steady himself in the saddle, he brought the parchment sketch near his eyes to see the finer details. "Myrdwyer isn't listed here."

"I asked the surveyor about that. He told me to stop dreaming of lost civilizations and buried treasure." Marac took a stout pull on his canteen. "I hope we won't end up chasing ghosts amidst the tall Lasoronian pines."

"It's there. Callista said it would be there, and we'll find it."

Marac narrowed his eyes. "What makes you trust the old woman?"

"The things she says and the way she says them. Somehow, I know her words to be true."

"I hope you're right."

"We should keep our voices down for now," Laedron said. "No way of knowing who might be listening."

Nearing the tree line, Laedron took in the colors and shapes of the trees, and like all the others in Lasoron, the pines made him feel foreign to the land. They were nothing like the familiar oaks, birches, hickories, and dogwoods of his native Sorbia, and the evergreens were covered in needles of green or brown, a stark contrast to the forests of his home, which had leaves of every shade of rich green, brown, and red.

Though dark, gloomy, and daunting, the forest's interior gave some shade from the summer sun, but it had a way of keeping in the humidity. The occasional bird fluttering through the woods put Laedron on edge, but he relaxed little by little the deeper they went, becoming accustomed to the ambient noises. Farther into the wood, the road worsened into a patchwork of holes, dirt, and loose gravel, causing the horses to stumble in places. The tree limbs grew closer to the ground as they traveled, and honeysuckles— their sweet smell penetrating his nostrils—reminded Laedron of Reven's Landing, of home.

"We'll have to slow up a bit," Marac said, running his fingers through his horse's mane. "Can't risk an injury, to ourselves or to our horses."

"We've been riding for a while now. May need to walk them for a while." Brice gripped the reins and slowed to a halt. "Besides, we could pick up the pace a little if it weren't for all these branches hitting me in the face."

Laedron nodded, climbing down from the saddle, and the others did the same. He led them for another hour or two until the trees thinned enough—and the horses seemed rested enough—for them to mount up and ride again. Before climbing onto his gelding, he studied the ground. *It's nothing more than a lightly treaded trail at this point. Will we be able to find an ancient highway when the time comes?* He decided to keep his thoughts to himself, for he saw no need or benefit in sowing doubt in his companions.

The trees and shrubs of the wood had a way of easing the passage of time, for Laedron found them far more interesting to observe than the open plains and cloudless sky. Much to Laedron's dismay, the wind that had kept the humidity somewhat at bay had ceased. He picked the burs off of his clothes, but for each one he discarded, another one seemed to appear. A mixture of sap and sweat dripped slowly down his cheeks and neck, and annoyingly, his skin itched everywhere the stuff had accumulated.

Each step became accompanied by ever-taller grass, which he knew to be a sign that the path had seen few travelers in the recent months. After turning at a sharp bend in the road, he stopped at the beginning of an old stone bridge spanning a gentle brook.

"I wonder how long this has been here," he said, then cleared his throat. He hadn't said a word for over an hour, and his voice crackled from dryness and breathing the pollen from the pines.

Brice climbed down from his saddle and walked over to the bridge. Crouching, he said, "Old, but strong. It's seen little upkeep, but it's seen little traffic, too."

"What about the other side?" Laedron stood in his stirrups,

trying to get a better vantage point to see across the creek.

Marac, being a bit taller than everyone else, scanned the tree line beyond the stream. "It's thick over there. There's an opening near the bridge, but the trees have grown in tight."

"Can we not rest here a while?" Valyrie asked. "I'm unaccustomed to riding such distances. I could use a break."

Laedron nodded. "I wouldn't normally want to stop, but we could benefit from fresh water near camp."

"I think we should keep going for a while." Marac turned to Laedron. "We'd be safer inside the woods. Better concealment and more cover. Out here, we're in the open. Sitting ducks."

"What if we make camp just behind us?" Laedron pointed at a rise above the water. "Less cover than the thickets, but faster access to the river if we need water."

Narrowing his eyes, Marac studied the ridge. "Right. The height advantage will make up for the cover if we're ambushed. Easier to defend the high ground."

"Good." Laedron pulled on his reins, steering his horse toward the bluff. "I hope the air runs cooler up there, too."

* * *

Leaning against a pine, Laedron peered into the distance and watched the sun set behind the trees. He heard the rustling of leaves over the chirping of crickets and glanced over his shoulder to see Valyrie coming up behind him.

"I never thought you'd be one for sunsets," she said, folding her arms.

It's good to hear her voice again in a kind way, a tone I thought was lost to me. "No?"

She shook her head.

"Even sorcerers should appreciate the true beauty of the world. Spellcraft is only one facet of life, and to spend your entire life pursuing it—and nothing else—would be a waste."

"Sounds as if you have made your choice."

"Choice?"

She came alongside him. "To which world you will belong. Between the magical and the plain, it seems you would rather be part of the magical."

"I have little choice now." He turned to her. "I must complete the journey I began with Ismerelda."

"Must you?"

He nodded. "If I don't, I'm merely a curiosity, a strange and out-of-place vagabond. No, I cannot turn back now. Neither can you."

Her brow wrinkled, but she said nothing.

"You've started along the path, also. Opened a door not easily closed." He glanced at the wand sheathed at her hip. "Once you've felt the touch of magic, you'll never be quite the same." His heart filled with desire, hungry for her embrace.

She took a step back and gestured toward the camp. "They sent me to fetch you." *And withdrawn, once more, out of reach again. Damn my fool mouth. I should never have said anything.*

Returning to the camp, Laedron grinned. Marac and Brice had staked the tents in a circle around a proper campfire, and they had unpacked the horses. *Incredibly efficient,* Laedron thought. He'd only been gone for an hour at most. "Where'd you learn to prepare a camp?"

Marac pulled taut the strap on his pack, then buckled it. "Do you think Meklan Draive would have cut us loose without a handle on survival?"

"No, probably not, but I never expected anything like this."

"The knights taught us much of combat, but we picked up a few other things." Marac dragged a fallen log near the fire and sat on it. "How do you take your salted beef?"

Laedron's stomach rumbled. "How salted?"

"I was assured that they smoked it first, so they would have gone lighter with the salt."

"Pink, then."

"You?" Marac asked Valyrie.

"The same."

Brice poked the fire with a stick. "Should be hot enough now."

"May want to add to the pile." Laedron reached for a thick limb.

"No, we have to keep it low." Marac waved his hand. "The bigger the fire, the more likely we are to be noticed up here."

"Are we not alone?" Laedron asked.

"I'd rather not find out. We'd be best to take every precaution." Marac retrieved some metal rods from his pack and poked a few forked sticks into the ground at the fire's perimeter. Then, he carefully placed the rods across the open flame, creating a makeshift grate.

Laedron said, "Never seen anything like that before."

"I thought about it on the ship from Azura." He grinned. "Better than trying to cook on the end of a stick."

Brice laughed. "I bet you'll get less of a wood flavor, too."

"I can't wait," Marac said, plopping the beefsteaks over the fire, then he gleefully rubbed his hands together. "It'll be a welcome change from a handful of nuts here and there."

Laedron leaned over and inspected the glowing embers. "How long do you think it will take?"

Marac stretched out his legs, crossed them, and leaned back on his log. "Hard to say. When it's done, it's done."

"I should have time to visit the creek, yes?" Laedron asked, the itching inside his shirt insatiable.

Marac shook his head. "No one should go off alone."

"I thought you weren't worried. 'Fret not,' didn't you say?"

"That was before we got into the forest proper." Marac tossed a twig into the fire pit. "Now's the time to be careful."

"I'll go with him," Brice said. "I'd like to get a drink."

After searching through a nearby backpack, Marac tossed him a metal canteen. "Drink from that one. When you're done, fill it up and bring it back. It'll need to be boiled."

Laedron led the way down the hill. At the stream's edge, he could barely see a random flicker from the campfire, and he felt safer knowing that a bandit would have to come close to their shelters to suspect their presence. He removed his shirt and used handfuls of water to wash away the sweat and dirt from his skin.

Brice dipped his towel into the water, then carefully balled it up. Noticing Laedron watching him, he said, "For the morning. I prefer to bathe before the day begins."

"Good idea." He dunked his shirt in the water, saving it for later.

The smell of sizzling steak hit him like a wall when he reached the top of the hill, a kind replacement for the musty scent of pine needles and earth. Coming between two of the tents, he heard a metal scraping sound. "It's just us," he warned.

Marac took his hand off the hilt of his sword. "Sorry. Just a bit on edge." He sat on the log.

Laedron joined him at the fire. "I hope you won't be too high strung to sleep."

"I thought you might like the honor." Marac nudged Laedron with his elbow, glancing back and forth between Laedron and Valyrie. "You've had nothing to keep you up all night of late."

Letting out a deep sigh, Valyrie shot up from her seat and headed toward one of the tents. "Despicable."

"I wish you hadn't said that." Laedron tossed a pebble into the fire.

Marac exchanged a concerned look with Brice, then gazed at Laedron again. "Why not? I was just having a bit of harmless fun, Lae."

Laedron watched Valyrie disappear into the tent. "When we reach the end of our journey, I fear that she may not return home with us."

"If that's the case, it wasn't meant to be," Brice said, lighting a twig by the fire.

"Oh, and you're some kind of expert in the matter, Thimble?" Marac rapidly shook his head. "I've heard it all now."

"Just watch what you say. Please, do it for me." Laedron, not waiting for a response, went to his bedding and tried to get comfortable.

"Looks like I'm first up on watch," Marac said.

❧ Chapter Five ❦

Onward to Laslo

Like the others, Laedron took his turn on watch, then slept until the morning rays woke him. He joined Marac by the fire and took some jerky when it was offered. "Should we wake up Brice?"

"Not just now." Marac turned to look at Brice. "He was the last to sleep, and we can do the packing while he rests."

Laedron nodded, and he glanced at Valyrie as she emerged from the tent. "Sleep well?"

"I suppose." She stretched her back, rubbed her side, and sat next to Marac. "It'll take me some time to get used to sleeping on the ground. Feels like I slept on a root."

She's taking this a bit too far, Laedron thought, watching her sitting at Marac's side. *Is she trying to irritate me, or does she desire a change?*

Marac stood, then began taking down his tent. "According to the map, we can make Laslo by nightfall. If they have an inn, you'll be spared the discomfort."

After helping Marac dismantle the tent, Laedron did the same to the other, then carefully packed his belongings onto his horse. With all the commotion, Brice woke from his slumber, dagger in hand, as if he'd had a bad dream. He quickly returned the knife to its sheath, then rose.

"Antsy?" Laedron asked, looking over at Brice while strapping his bedroll to his horse.

"Noises in the night. I never worry about them when I'm behind a locked door, but out here, every creak and rustle puts me on edge." Brice cleared his throat and straightened his clothes, then worked on packing his own gear.

Once the horses were loaded and the campfire had been stamped out, they mounted up and followed Marac to the road. Seemingly without a second thought, Marac took off across the bridge, leading them over the stream and into the thick wood beyond. Although the sun had risen and taken its place high in the sky, the canopy over the road made it seem like dusk. To Laedron, traversing the bridge and entering the wood seemed like crossing over into a whole other world, a place of danger and unknowing.

Like the previous day, Laedron heard little more than hoof beats on the trail, for he and his party didn't speak. With the little survival training he'd had, he knew that engaging in conversation would dull their wits, making them less alert to their surroundings, and give away their position to anyone nearby who might be listening. It made the traveling harder, though, and they rode until noon without as much as a word between them.

"Whoa," Marac whispered, pulling on his reins to stop his horse. He leaned forward in his saddle, squinting at the path ahead.

Laedron stopped next to him. "What do you see?"

"Something blocking the road. Either that or it turns suddenly. Hard to tell."

Closing his eyes, Laedron listened to the forest, trying his best to ignore the horses' idle stirrings. *The fluttering of wings. Chirping of birds.* "We can only go forward from here. 'Tis the only road to Laslo."

"Keep your eyes and ears open," Marac whispered, turning to Brice. "Be ready for anything."

Like Marac, Brice pulled the shield from his back and affixed it to his arm, then Marac inched forward, peering at either side as he went. When they reached the block in the road, Laedron climbed down from his horse. A huge pine several feet in diameter had fallen there, prohibiting passage beyond that point.

"It's recent," Marac said, pointing at the limbs. "The leaves are still green."

"Maybe we can find a way around. Surely there's a way through." Brice glanced at the trees. "There, to the right. An opening."

Laedron walked alongside the tree to its trunk and found scratches and cuts at the base. *Fresh cuts. Sap flowing from the nicks.* His eyes widened, and he drew his scepter. "Too recent!"

Marac and Brice drew their weapons. When he raised his shield, Marac jerked his arm from the impact of an arrow strike. He hopped to the ground. "Down! Down! We'll not withstand them on horseback."

Laedron leaped from his horse. "Val, through there! Get out of here. We'll find you after."

Without a word, she snatched the reins and rode hard northeast. Laedron watched an arrow fly past her and strike a tree. He breathed a sigh of relief when she reached the cover of the woods. Brice landed on the ground, scurried to Marac's side, and hid behind his shield. "A steep hill to our left. I saw an archer atop it." Marac shoved Brice. "Why didn't you tell me, Thimble? Want to see my head taken off?"

"I didn't see it until you jumped down. Quit pushing me!" Brice shoved him back.

"Both of you stop it, or we'll be killed for sure," Laedron said, peeking over them.

Another arrow struck Marac's shield. He stared at the point mere inches from his eye. "We've got to do something."

Laedron couldn't tell if Marac bore contempt or fear in his eyes. *Probably both*.

Another arrow dinged against Marac's shield. "Damned bandits. They'll hit us eventually."

"I think they *are* hitting us," Brice said.

"You know what I mean, Thimble."

Laedron clenched his jaw and sneered at them. "Enough. What are our options?"

"Advance on their position." Marac braced his shield arm with his other hand. "It's uphill, but we can't stay here and do nothing."

Presenting his scepter, Laedron said, "Or escape."

"What's the plan?"

"Keep your shields up, and I'll set a fire."

Marac sighed. "You'll burn the whole forest down that way."

Brice dropped to his knees, and an arrow sailed over his head. "Better to lose the forest than our lives. Do it, Lae."

"Wait," Marac said, his eyes shifting, a plan clearly forming in his mind. "Can you summon a winter storm?"

Laedron took his head in his hands. "It's unlikely to harm them. We don't have time for theatrics."

"Yes, but it'll get them off of us. Summer suddenly turning to winter? It'd make me second-guess attacking whatever could do that."

"If you like, but it'll make things harder to burn if they keep shooting." Laedron readied his scepter. "It won't take them long to figure out that there's a sorcerer over here, either."

"I don't care if they know we have a sorcerer. I don't care if they think Azura herself has come down from on high." Marac gritted his teeth. "Do it. It's better than setting fire to half of Lasoron."

Standing up halfway to see over his shield, Laedron pointed the rod toward the woods and chanted a spell of wintertime. Marac and Brice crowded in front of him, doing their best to shield him from the oncoming barrage. From the large ruby, silver and blue light erupted, draping the trees and the ground all around them with ice. Even though he could see little through the canopy, he noticed the sky changing from a vibrant blue to a somber gray. *Snow clouds*, he mused, waving the scepter from side to side.

Fewer arrows came their way the longer Laedron held the effect, and after a while, the snow flurries were the only things flying around. He strengthened the blizzard with his finishing words, then took hold of his friends by the shoulders. "Best get moving now. It will last a while yet, but not forever."

Barely on his horse, Laedron yanked the reins to the right and took off in the direction he'd sent Valyrie. He drove the horse onward until its hooves flung dirt and pine straw, the cold air replaced by the hot summer haze beyond his spell's reach. When he cleared the trees, he felt the sting from the branches that had struck him in the face and the wetness of the blood on his skin. *Funny. I hadn't noticed them hit me on the ride here.* His thoughts were cut short when he spotted her horse.

Riding over, Laedron first realized that Valyrie was nowhere to be found. The cliff was the second thing he noticed. He climbed down from his horse and ran to the ledge. If it weren't for his eagerness to find her, Laedron could have spent hours staring at the breathtaking landscape, the rolling hills in the valley and the lush green treetops extending to the horizon.

"Val!" His voice echoed into the distance. "Valyrie!"

Marac and Brice emerged from the woods, and Brice stopped just short of the drop, his horse obviously riled at being so near the cliff.

"Help me find her." Laedron held his hand over his eyes to shield them from the sun. "Val. Where is she?"

"I hear something... over here," Marac said, scurrying to the ledge and falling to his knees. "Look, down there."

Laedron ran to the edge, then dropped next to Marac. Never before had Laedron seen the kind of fear that Valyrie had in her eyes. Clinging to some exposed roots, she didn't make a sound, as if even a muffled scream might cause the roots to give up their hold.

"We're going to get you up. Just hold on." He pulled out his scepter and chanted a levitation spell.

Before he could finish the incantation, he heard a snap. With a shriek, she fell.

Laedron's instincts took over. Stepping off the ledge, he heard Marac shout, "Lae, no!"

His clothes flapping in the breeze, Laedron forced the incantation past his lips. *The fear will have to wait. I must save her. I must.* He stretched out his hand, the tops of the pines below fast approaching. *Closer. Only a little closer. Reach, dammit!*

Once their hands touched, Valyrie pulled at him, then wrapped her arms around his chest and climbed him in a frenzy.

"I can't—" He struggled to get his mouth free, to finish the spell and save her, but her arm coiled around his head and neck like a snake constricting on its prey.

He pried at her arms with his free hand. "Va—" He knew that they must be close to the ground, but he couldn't see. He tried to speak again. The words came out like a muffled scream. Peeling her arms over his head like a wet shirt, he broke loose long enough to shout the last word a few feet from the ground, slowing their descent.

Landing, he took a deep breath, but his knees buckled. He sat, then he lay on his back and tried to calm his nerves. Although he couldn't see their faces, he imagined the looks Marac and Brice were giving one another at the top of the cliff. He turned his head to see Valyrie, her breathing panicked and her hair frizzled. "All right now?"

"All right?" She clenched one hand into a fist while snatching briars from her hair with the other. "We could've been killed."

"But we weren't."

"I can't catch my breath!" Grabbing her chest, she collapsed to the ground, using one arm to keep herself from falling flat.

He crawled over to her. "Just breathe. Take it slow."

"Do you do this sort of thing often?"

"What, jumping off a cliff to save someone? No, not really, but in your case, I decided to make an exception."

She gazed into his eyes. The look could have been anything—relief, happiness, or something else—but he was relieved that it was something other than anger and resentment. *At the very least, it got her to relax.*

"Ready to go back up?" he asked.

She nodded.

Waving the scepter in a circle around them, he wrapped his arm around Valyrie and cast his spell. His feet lifted off the ground. Ascending, he stared at the majestic beauty of the valley, the river and its rapids flowing south, and the deer running between the trees. He reached the top and saw Marac with a scornful glare on his face. *Oh, dear. I'm going to hear it now. Perhaps I should've stayed down there a while longer.*

"The next time you decide to jump off a cliff," Marac said, his arms folded, "I'd appreciate a little warning."

"Sorry." Laedron released Valyrie once they had landed. "It's what sorcerers—"

"Don't give me that 'it's what sorcerers do' bit. You scared the hells out of me with that stunt."

Brice stepped between them. "All things considered, he *did* save her from the fall."

"Oh, don't you start now."

Laedron put his arms around both of them, herding them away from the edge. "Friends, don't let this drive a wedge between us. Marac, I'm sorry, but I had little time to explain."

Marac nodded forcefully. "I just don't want to lose you again. I can't."

"You won't." Laedron smiled, then gestured at the horses. "Shall we?"

"Yes, but we're not going back to that damned road." Taking hold of the reins, Marac climbed onto his horse. "If the trees grow away from this cliff the whole way, we'd do better to follow it to the village."

"Agreed." Laedron helped Valyrie onto her horse, then mounted his. "And hopefully no more bandits."

With the open ground between the cliff and the woods, Marac quickened his pace at the lead. The rapid beating of hooves and the valley's rim took them all the way to the end of the depression, and in the distance, Laedron spotted palisade walls. *Laslo. It must be.*

❧ Chapter Six ❧

The Middle of Nowhere

Approaching the village, Laedron kept a sharp eye on his surroundings. The wooden spikes, the high walls, and the barricades, all of it was meant to bar entry to outsiders and all fashioned from the fresh-cut pines. *Is that what I think it is?* he thought, staring at the black substance coating the tips of the spears. *Old blood, the blood of dozens of battles. Who would charge against layers of spikes? Surely brigands are not that foolish.* The village seemed like an enclave of civilization placed exactly in the middle of nowhere.

When he reached the front, the gates were shut, and a man stood atop the wall, a bow in his left hand and an arrow nocked in his right. His tunic—half green and half white—was emblazoned with a black griffin. *A soldier of Lasoron. Perhaps too far to call to the Almatheren?*

"You don't look like bandits," the soldier said. "What business have you in Laslo?"

Laedron pulled on his reins, bringing his horse to a halt beneath the wall. "We wish to stay for a night. Nothing more."

"And what will you do after that?"

"Move on. To the west," Laedron said, imagining the cross expression the guard was probably giving him behind the plated helm.

"The road doesn't lead west, boy. You plan to travel through open country to Kingsport or even as far as Paladum?"

"Not so far as that, no."

"I suppose I should keep this gate closed to you, then." The guard returned the arrow to his quiver. "Laslo has no need of madmen seeking to wander the wilderness. Why not get an early start and leave now?"

"Please, let us in, for the sun's low in the sky. We have the coin to pay for all that we'll need." Laedron reached into his pocket and held up a sovereign.

The guard tapped the front of his helmet with one finger. "New coin? Could be helpful…"

"We won't be any trouble. I swear it," Laedron said.

"Very well, young man." The soldier turned a crank, and the gate opened. "Tie your horses with the rest and meet me inside."

Laedron urged his horse through the opening, and once his friends had passed the threshold, the guardsman closed the gate, then climbed down a ragged wooden ladder.

"I'm Sir Paldren, protector of this city." The man extended his hand to Laedron once he had dismounted.

"Laedron Telpist of Sorbia."

"Sorbia? You're a long way off from home, aren't you?"

"Indeed."

"What would a Sorbian want in the deep woods of Lasoron?" Paldren removed his helmet, revealing a salt-and-pepper beard and green eyes.

If I'm untruthful, will he be able to tell? Laedron considered the size of the small village and the remoteness. *Would it matter if I told him? It's not as if he could call upon anyone who might mean us harm from way out here.* "We're venturing to the ruins of Myrdwyer."

"And why would anyone want to go to those ancient grounds?"

"Answers."

"I hope you're good at holding conversation with stones and moss, my strange friend." Paldren gestured for him to follow. "Little remains there beyond broken rubble and old memories, a testament to Uxidin arrogance."

"Arrogance?"

"They tried to build a city to stand forever, but they succeeded only in decorating the forest with broken buildings and overgrown roads. The great empires that remain today learned a lesson lost on the Uxidin: place all of your hopes in tomorrow, and you'll find that the problems of today don't take care of themselves."

Laedron eyed the knight with curiosity. "Have you been there? Have you seen the ruins?"

"Yes, and it's a place I won't soon visit again. Nothing to be gained there. Don't look forward to getting much sleep, either, if you tread that place."

"No?"

"Sounds in the night. Whispers and moans float on the evening breeze like pollen in the spring. Ancient sorrows that never had healed from aching hearts long since forgotten, I'd say." Paldren pointed at a row of small buildings. "The village's families live in those row houses. You'd do best to leave them alone, for they don't abide outsiders."

"Then, you've seen the highway? The path leading to Myrdwyer?" Laedron asked.

"What remains of the road lies west of here. An arrow's shot away from the west wall, you'll find the base of a column made of marble, and what remains of the pavers will take you to Myrdwyer." The soldier continued across the center of town and gestured at the tallest building in the village. "That's the lumber mill, the lifeblood of these people. Next to it is the guardhouse, and then the stores. Brenner, our only merchant, operates the inn and adjoining shop at the end of the line."

"How long has it been since you've been to the Myrdwyer ruins?"

"Oh, I would say ten years or more, but it was still enough to keep me stirring some nights."

"Thank you for allowing us to stay here," Laedron said. "We should make arrangements with… Brenner, you said?"

"Indeed. You can tie your horses to the post outside." Paldren stopped him before he could walk away. "Tell me, did you run into any bandits on your way here?"

"Yes, about a day's travel south."

"Can you tell me what happened?"

Laedron thought about his response, wondering if the knight had any prejudice against sorcerers. "We lost them in the woods. After that, we followed the valley. Why do you ask?"

Paldren glanced back at a long covered wagon. "We'll have a lumber shipment leaving in a few days for Nessadene, and the men from Kingsport are overdue. We'd hoped to send an escort with the wood, but I was wondering if we could do without."

"I would recommend that you not send that cart unguarded. We didn't encounter any other brigands, but that's not to say that there are not more on the roads."

"I appreciate it. The wood can wait, then. Carry on." Paldren walked toward the wall.

Laedron called out to him before he got out of earshot. "Sir Paldren, can you tell me how far the Myrdwyer ruins are from here?"

"A little over a day. Maybe two."

Laedron turned to his friends. "Let's see about lodgings for the night."

"Did you hear him, Lae?" Marac asked. "He's been to Myrdwyer and found nothing."

"And he also said he hasn't been there for a number of years. Are you suggesting that we turn around now? After we've come so far?"

"Of course not. I only wonder what you think is to be gained from this."

"Something's out there." Laedron stared into the western sky. "Someone must be left. Callista seemed so sure of it."

"Forgive me if I don't put much faith into the words of a woman you've only just met. What if she lied?"

"Why would she?"

"Amusement? The crone's probably sitting on a stack of books, laughing at us right now." Marac folded his arms, a sour glare twisting his features. "What reason do we have to believe her?"

"I do, Marac. Everything she's told me rings true. Well, except for the last bit."

"What last bit?"

"She said that she told me everything she knew." Laedron shook his head. "She told me little and withheld anything important."

"So, instead of sending us on a fool's errand, she's more than likely leading us into a trap?" Marac asked. "More the reason to pull up stakes and go home, lest we lose our lives traipsing about the wild lands."

Laedron nodded. "If you don't want to come with me, wait here for the soldiers from Kingsport and hitch a ride with Sir Paldren. I *must* finish this journey, though. I must."

"I only needed to be sure that you're sure, Lae," Marac said, extending his hand. "I'll follow you to the ends of Bloodmyr if you're certain it'll be worth it."

Laedron took Marac's hand in a firm embrace.

"Me, too!" Brice said, and Laedron and Marac laughed.

I can always count on Brice to break the tension. "Good. At least we'll have comfortable beds to sleep in tonight." Gesturing for his friends to follow, Laedron led his horse along the row of buildings to the end, tied the reins to the hitching post, then entered the inn. Everything in the inn had some measure of dust coating its surface, and Laedron could tell at a glance which things saw more use because they were cleaner. The windows barely let in any sunlight, as the panes obviously hadn't been cleaned since installed. On the left, a line of cots had been placed along the wall, and a portly man stood behind a counter on the right. Laedron caught the scent of something awful, then spotted the probable source: a pot had been hung in the fireplace, its contents bubbling. "This is your place?"

The man cleared his throat and looked up from his ledgers. "Last time I checked. Need something?"

Not the usual greeting from an innkeeper. "Yes, some beds for the night."

"The four of you?"

"Yes."

"Two silver."

For this? Laedron gazed at the cots with a skeptical eye. Some of them looked as though they had never been cleaned. "Two silvers?"

The man spit into the receptacle at his feet, and the impact resounded with a ding. "Too pricey for you? I'd suggest the next inn if your purse strings are too tight."

"Very well. Where's the next inn?"

"Go out my door and take a left. Out of the gate and about a week later, you'll hit Paladum, if you're lucky."

"Fine," Laedron said, plopping two silvers onto the counter.

"Now, was that so hard?" The man grinned, revealing jagged yellow teeth. "Welcome to the Brenner's Board House."

Laedron wanted to say, "And what a fine board house indeed, Mr. Brenner," but he resisted. In the grand scheme of things, losing a pair of silver coins to a swindler represented the least of his concerns. Money didn't seem quite as important as it once had. *Is this the way true adventurers regard coin? As merely a means to an end? Pavers along a road leading to a much greater reward? Perhaps it depends upon the adventurer.*

Brenner gestured at the foul-smelling cauldron. "The cot comes with a bowl of my finest pottage. Help yourselves."

Avoiding the stew, Laedron took a handful of jerky from his pack. His friends didn't seem interested in sampling the local fare either because they kept their distance from the filthy stuff. *The man's probably immune to rotten meat and spoiled vegetables by now. Disgusting.*

Marac sat on his cot and pulled his sword from its scabbard.

Brenner threw up his hands. "And what do you plan to do with that?"

"I need to sharpen it."

Laedron shook his head at the innkeeper. "We mean you no harm. We've a long way to go yet, and we have preparations to make."

Brenner wiped his mouth with a stained rag. "Just don't get any wise ideas."

Marac glared at Brenner, then reached into his pack and produced a whetstone. The rhythmic scraping of the stone against the sword's edge made Laedron feel more at ease, as if they were sitting in the Shimmering Dawn chapterhouse, and for a moment, he expected Piers or Caleb to come through the door with news of more plots.

After examining the arrow holes in his shield, Brice laid his sword and dagger on his cot, then stared at Marac. "Mine needs it more. Mind if I get started?"

Nodding, Marac tossed the stone to Brice. "What about you, Miss Pembry?"

Valyrie looked at Marac, and Laedron could tell by her expression that she didn't understand what Marac had meant by the question.

"It may be a good time to arm yourself," Marac said. "We may not always escape our fights. Do you know how to use a weapon?"

She replied, "I can use a bow."

"You think we can get a length of pine here?" Marac asked, turning to Brenner. "Can the mill supply one?"

Before the innkeeper could answer, Valyrie said, "Bows aren't made from pine."

"We'll be hard-pressed to find a staff of oak around here, I'd wager."

"Not that kind of bow." She laughed. "The kind that shoots arrows. A shortbow, preferably."

Laedron raised an eyebrow. "You know how to shoot a bow?"

"Indeed."

"Are you any good?"

"You doubt me?"

Crossing his arms, Laedron examined her. "I only speak to the point that we have no evidence to the contrary. Where did you learn?"

"The university."

"Archery is a part of their curriculum?" Marac asked.

"They train the militia archers there. There's more to shooting than releasing a string and praying that you hit the target."

"All right," Laedron said, waving at Marac. "It would be best to see her in action before we draw any conclusions. We could use an archer."

Marac reached out and took the whetstone from Brice. "Could've used one a while back. Why didn't you say anything until now?"

"For one, you never asked."

Marac pointed at her. "In the future, I would appreciate your volunteering useful information. Keeping secrets puts us in danger, and *no one* is going to travel with us and put us at risk."

"Enough," Laedron said, his neck and ears growing warm. "I won't have you speak to her that way." As soon as he said it, he wanted to take it back, and he saw the irony in the statement. *I thought I was the one who said we should take a break from our emotions.*

"You would take her side? If she'd had a bow, you wouldn't have had to use m—" Marac cut off before he finished the word, shooting a look over at Brenner. "You wouldn't have had to do what you did in the forest. If you two didn't have something going on, you might be able to see—"

"Stop this. She's a part of our group, just as you are." Laedron stepped closer to Marac. "Our relationship has nothing to do with this."

"Doesn't it?"

"He's right, Lae," Brice said, fidgeting with something in his hands. "We've been talking about it."

"So, you and Marac have it figured out, have you? What business is it of yours?" Laedron huffed, his skin boiling.

"It's our business when our lives are on the line." Marac furrowed his brow. "When your attachment is so strong as to be blind, you'll put all of us in danger."

"My attachment?" With little regard for volume, Laedron said, "Do you not see?"

Marac and Brice sat in silence like dogs scolded by their master.

"Meklan Draive put us together. And do you know why? Because men with close bonds fight better. They are more successful. Am I close to Valyrie? Yes, but I am just as close to you, Marac Reven. Through all of this, I've grown closer to Brice." Laedron walked away. *Now I see the truth of what she was trying to tell me, but is it too late to salvage what we had?* "We're not cold, calculating killers. We're friends—nay, brothers. Brothers in arms."

"I only meant—"

"I know what you meant, Marac, but if ignoring my heart is the only way forward, I cannot proceed. We would become nothing better than the Zyvdredi—cold men with no love." Laedron stared at Marac through a long pause. "If I deny my love for her, I must deny my love for you. I won't... can't." Glancing at Valyrie, Laedron saw her stern expression and folded arms, and he felt no warmth from her. *Perhaps it is too late for us. Creator, why have I allowed things to get so far? I will make this right. I must.*

Marac nodded. "What did they used to say about you in Reven's Landing? 'Don't argue with a Telpist. You'll be fighting an uphill battle to win,' I believe it was."

"Aye." Laedron took a deep breath. "That's what they say."

"You're right, Lae." Marac extended his open hand. "Being high in the clouds, it's hard to see where you came from."

"We've all been under insurmountable stress of late, and I can't fault you for your words." Laedron took Marac's hand. "As we've always done, we'll have to forge ahead despite ourselves. I dream of the day when all of this is behind us."

"Ouch!" Brice dropped something that *thunked* against the planks of floor.

Bending down, Laedron picked up an ornate lock, being careful not to stick himself with the barb on the bottom of it. "What's this?"

"Something Caleb gave me in Azura. Damn!" Holding up his hand, Brice displayed a wound on his finger with blood dripping from it.

Laedron stared at the needle protruding from the lock. The end was soaked with Brice's blood, and he wondered how Brice had come to be injured by it. "Were you being careless?"

"I almost had it open, and that point shot out of the bottom." Brice shook his head. "I guess that was the surprise he was talking about."

"He gave you a trapped lock?" Valyrie asked.

Brice nodded.

Marac chuckled. "What a bastard."

Valyrie laughed. "My thinking exactly. Will you be all right?"

"It's just a scratch." Wrapping his fingertip in a piece of linen, Brice sighed. "It'll teach me to look closer at something before playing with it."

Laedron remembered when Ismerelda had shown him the mending spell and how she hadn't stuck him with the dagger. "A good lesson to learn, but there are other ways of teaching it." Pulling the blankets back, Laedron sat on his cot, then pulled up his legs. "The hour's late, and we have a long road ahead. Goodnight."

❧ Chapter Seven ❦

An Ancient Highway

E arly the next morning, Laedron awoke before the others. He sat up in his cot, the sun still not above the horizon, and watched Marac sleep. *What have these travels done to him? To all of us?* The rage he'd observed in Marac's eyes the previous night disturbed him. *Is it fear? The not knowing? We must hold it together. We must.*

Removing the tattered sheet from his body, Laedron stood, being careful not to rouse the others, then ambled to the window. Through the dirty glass, he saw Sir Paldren emerge from what

Laedron assumed to be the man's home. Paldren walked to the wall where they had first met him. *I wonder who watches over the place while he sleeps. Or maybe he doesn't sleep. Maybe he can't.*

Hearing a hideous snort from his right, Laedron scanned the area behind the counter, then sighed with relief. *It's just Brenner.* The innkeeper rolled onto his side, and a handful of dust fell to the floor at the man's shifting. Laedron's chest tightened. *I don't think I've ever met a man so nasty in all my life. I think I kept myself cleaner than that whilst sleeping amongst the refuse in the alleys of Morcaine.*

"No!" Marac shouted. He sprang from his bed, then grabbed his chest and tried to catch his breath.

"What's the matter?" Laedron asked.

"Sorry. Nothing," Marac said, sweat pouring off his face.

Brice sat up on his cot. "Didn't sound like nothing."

Marac wiped his forehead. "Just a bad dream. We were on the tower again."

Laedron sat across from him. "The tower?"

"In Azura, the Grand Vicar's Palace. I dreamed that Andolis killed us all, one by one. He saved me for last."

Laedron smiled and patted Marac on the shoulder. "Thanks to you, he won't be murdering anyone else."

"Thanks to me? No. We all had a hand in that." Balling the damp sheet, Marac dropped it on the floor. "I can go the rest of my days without meeting another Zyvdredi master, though."

"I know how you feel. I even feel the same way," Laedron said, "but we've done a favor for countless innocent people. We stopped Andolis before he could fulfill his plans."

"Is that our job?"

"The Shimmering Dawn sent us after Gustav, and we couldn't leave Andolis to fulfill his plan."

"That's not what I mean, Lae." Marac averted his gaze from Laedron and stared at his bare feet. "In a deeper sense. Are we the guardsmen of the world? Is it our place to save people who will not save themselves?"

"It has always been the way of Circle mages to help those who cannot help themselves."

"Yes, yes. I understand that; help the helpless. But those who won't lift a finger? It's our place to solve their problems, too?"

"Andolis was a powerful sorcerer, Marac, as powerful as they come. Even if they'd tried, they would have failed."

"I seem to remember piercing his back with my blade. He wasn't invincible."

"Yes, you killed him, but not before Brice slashed him and certainly not before I dueled him with magic. You must also take into account the number of militia lost on the steps of the palace, how hard we fought to make it inside in the first place." Laedron bobbed his head. "Had he not been Zyvdredi, the Heraldans might've had a chance, but tales are told of the difficulties that Circle mages have had taking on a Zyvdredi master."

"But they didn't try."

"And why would they try to usurp him? With his silver tongue, he told them what they needed to hear. Old stories of empire and glory drove them to go along with his plans. He used their own pride as a tool to control them, and if anyone had stood against him, they would've been cast out as traitors."

"Precisely, Lae. That's what I'm saying. We stopped him, the three of us, and if people don't want our help because they'd rather go along with it, why should we be bothered to step in?"

"In this case, to help our own people, to end the war, and we had luck on our side. Under other circumstances? You can't save the whole world from itself. At some point, people must make their own decisions, live their own lives, and deal with the consequences."

Marac chuckled. "Funny thing, that. I think this is the first time we've agreed on something."

"It could be." Laedron smiled. "The teachings passed down to us never speak of fixing every problem, but when directly challenged, Circle mages must do whatever it takes to preserve themselves and the traditions."

"You learned much in a short period of time," Valyrie said. "Ismerelda would have been proud of you, I'm sure."

"Ismerelda didn't teach me of the Circle." He turned to her. "My mother did."

"Your mother is a sorceress?"

"Indeed, and a powerful one at that," Marac said before Laedron could answer. "A good woman, though. Kind and generous to our whole village back home."

"I should like to meet her."

"One day." Laedron grinned. "I would like that, too."

"Well…" Brice took a deep breath, his voice cracking. "If you're done making me homesick, I'd love to get on with our journey."

"Of course." Laedron donned his pack. "Westward?"

"There's still the matter of a bow." Marac eyed Valyrie. "If she can do what she says, it could be an asset."

The bow. Yes. I'd completely forgotten about it. Laedron nodded, then looked at Brenner. "Anywhere we could purchase a bow?"

"Nowhere that I know."

"You're the merchant, aren't you?" Marac asked.

Brenner grinned, his teeth not unlike the black-tipped spikes along the town's palisade. "Yes, milord, of course. Allow me to show you our silken robes, golden rings, and fine paintings whilst I'm at it. This is Laslo, if you hadn't noticed, and the people here deal in food and clothes. I can't be bothered to teach you how to run a business right now, but I'll share a little secret with you: to stay in business, one caters to the clientele."

"No need to be snippy about it." Marac sneered. "Where can we find a bow? Nothing too extravagant."

"I'm sorry if I can't help with that. You might ask Paldren, given that it's a weapon."

"Right. We'll see Sir Paldren." Marac turned and walked out of the inn.

"Thank you for all of your…" Laedron eyed Brenner one last time before leaving. "…hospitality, I think."

Laedron, Valyrie, and Brice jogged behind Marac, joining him as he reached the base of the ladder.

"Sir Paldren?" Marac called.

Paldren turned toward them. "Yes?"

"Might you have a bow for sale?"

"What?" Paldren raised an eyebrow. "A bow for sale?"

"We have need of a bow."

"And arrows," Valyrie whispered.

"Arrows, too." Marac put his hands on his hips. "Do you have any we could buy?"

"Well, let me think about that." Paldren climbed down the rickety ladder. "What do you need it for?"

"One of our party is an archer."

Paldren examined Brice. "And he's without a bow?"

"Not him," Laedron said, gesturing to Valyrie.

"A girl?" Paldren sized her up. "What would such a pretty lass need with a weapon?"

"To do my part. Will you sell us one or not?" she asked, a fire behind her eyes.

"I have one, and some spare arrows, too, that I could part with, I suppose. For the right price."

Here we go again. Laedron rolled his eyes. *How much this time? Twenty platinum, a castle, land, and title?*

"Fifty gold coins for the lot," Paldren said, scratching his chin. "A bow and fifty arrows."

Marac's eyes widened. "Fifty—"

"We'll take it." Laedron fished out the coins and handed them over.

"You're mad, Lae!" Marac tried to stop the money from changing hands. "Fifty gold? And before we've even seen it?"

"It's a fine bow, I assure you. Your friend knows a deal when he sees one." Paldren put the sovereigns in his pocket. "I'll fetch it, and to put you at ease, young master, I will return your coin should it meet with your disapproval."

The knight disappeared through the door of his house, then emerged carrying a stringed length of wood about half the height of a man and curved away from the grip on both sides. In his other hand, he held a quiver. He handed both to Valyrie.

"A composite yew bow?" she asked, her eyes wide.

Laedron, though he knew nothing of bows, took her comment and apparent surprise as signs in favor of the bow's quality and construction.

Paldren nodded. "It's lower on the draw weight, but that was the way I needed it. I used that one in the past when I thought I may have had need to shoot from horseback. Since I don't travel much anymore, it's yours."

"Draw weight?" Laedron asked.

"The power of the bow." She pulled the string taut. "The harder it is to draw, the harder the impact of the arrow."

"Perhaps I underestimated you," Paldren said. "Would you care to try it?"

"I'd rather save the arrows if it's all the same."

"Here." Paldren pulled one from his own quiver. "Don't worry about breaking that one. That hay bale is your target."

She nodded, nocked the arrow, and drew, the bow and string creaking under the strain. Releasing the string, she squinted past the bow at her target.

"Not bad," Paldren said, walking over to the bale and pulling out the arrow. "At least you hit it."

"I wasn't aiming at the bale." With the others following, she joined Paldren, then tugged at the string wound around the straws of hay and frowned. "Missed my target."

"It was close, though. Surprisingly close." Paldren examined her, as if impressed by her competence. "How long have you been shooting?"

"For a few years, on and off. Each time the university hosted a new batch of men for the militia, I'd be sure to visit and pick up anything that I could."

"University? What university trains archers?"

"The Arcanists of Azura."

"The Arcanists? My, my." A smile creeping across his face, Paldren gave her the arrow. "Keep that one. And good luck on your endeavors outside these walls."

"Thank you for letting us in for the night," Laedron said. "If you'll be so kind to open the gate, we'll be off."

"One last thing. We used to send smaller shipments of lumber west when requested, but the last one returned and reported that the ancient bridge was damaged. We've sent word to Navarine, to the king, but with the fighting in the east, he's yet to send aid."

"Ancient bridge?"

"The valley makes a sharp turn west of here and has long marked the divide between the east and the west of Lasoron. The Uxidin built a bridge—well, they built most of the ones we still use today—but this particular bridge was quite long indeed, a marvel of ancient engineering by any standards. One of the sections has fallen out, so you'll be forced to find a way across it or travel down the valley and up the other side."

"I think we can handle that. Thank you."

With little more than a nod, Paldren returned to the top of the wall and turned the crank to open the gate. Slamming shut behind them, the gate was a symbol of what Laedron anticipated for the rest of the trip. *From this moment forward, we shall see no security, no shelter, until our journey has concluded,* he thought, glancing one last time at Sir Paldren atop the palisade.

Through sparse forest, they trekked until Laedron spotted the columns the knight had described, two marble pillars that had been there so long that they seemed to have sprouted from the earth. Only pine straw and undergrowth surrounded them, as if the trees refused to encroach upon the columns.

Laedron climbed down from his horse. He crouched beside one of the stones and dug into the ground with his hands. A few inches down, he felt smooth rock against his fingertips. "Here it is."

Marac glared at Laedron from his saddle. "Must we crawl along the ground to find this road? There had to be another way."

Laedron cleared away more of the thick straw-dirt mixture. "No. If I go along and find a few more in a line, we can merely follow the spacing between the trees. The stone's been placed with a tight fit, where trees can't grow up between the blocks." He searched the ground for another piece of the road. Finding one, he smiled and pointed to the west. He mounted his horse, then brushed his hands together, dusting off the bits of pine straw and mud. He pulled on the reins and led the way deeper into the forest, keeping an eye on the spacing between the trees as he went.

Brice slapped his neck, then examined his palm, as if he had killed a mosquito. "How much farther do we have?"

"We follow this highway until its end. At most, two days by Sir Paldren's estimation."

"Two more days," Marac said, then quaffed a mouthful of water from his canteen. "I'll be glad to be done with this damned forest."

They rode on through the rest of the day and came to the start of a stone bridge late in the afternoon. Beneath the bridge, the valley extended deep and long, and Laedron couldn't see the end of the vale no matter how hard he strained. Wide enough for five horses to cross walking side by side, the bridge was a sight to behold, a miracle of the ancient world still standing in the present.

Neither nature nor age had been mighty enough to fell the stonework, but he remembered what Paldren had said about a section missing.

"This should be interesting." Laedron cleared his throat. "Ready?"

Marac stood in his stirrups and stared at the river far below. "Is it sturdy?"

"Only one way to find out."

"Do you think it'll hold, Lae?" Marac asked.

"A bridge that massive and thick? We'll be fine. I'm sure of it."

Reluctantly, Marac and the others followed Laedron onto the bridge, all of them silent, as if even a whisper could rattle the foundations and cause them to plummet into the chasm. The gusts of wind through the trestles and the patter of hooves against stone were the only sounds Laedron heard. He kept his eyes focused on the path ahead. *Don't look down. The simple act of looking down could be enough to pull you over the edge.*

He slowed to a halt when he spotted the break, stopping about a stone's throw away from a huge section of missing bridge. "Hold up here."

"Creator! How can we get across there?" Leaning forward, Valyrie hugged her horse as a child might her favorite toy. "It must be a hundred feet or more to the next landing."

"A little magic goes a long way." Laedron drew his scepter. "I'll send each of us—horses and all—across the gap."

"Do you know nothing of horses?" Marac asked.

"What? I know enough—"

"If you lift a horse off the ground, there's a good chance that it will panic. You may be able to save one, but the other will fall to the bottom. Since we want to lose neither people nor mounts, we'd better come up with a better solution than that."

"A bridge of air, then?"

"Tell me, then: what do horses do when you drive them over the edge of a cliff?"

Laedron shrugged. "They fall?"

"Unless frenzied and ignorant of the edge, they stop, Lae. A bridge could work, but it has to be something that the horses can see."

"Good thought." Scratching his chin, Laedron considered the options. *Conjure air, but change the color? Or summon the illusion of stone? The latter would be more difficult, but it may be safer.* "I'll try to conjure a replacement that looks just like the bridge, but it could take some time. It would be best if I test it before anyone else."

Marac nodded. "Take your time. We have that in abundance."

Laedron hopped down from his horse, crouched, and examined the stonework. *It's almost as if it's woven together magically. Such small stones fitted together in such a precise fashion... one would face some difficulty to find masonry of this quality even in Sorbia.* Crawling along, he tried to find a pattern, something he could duplicate on a scale large enough to cover the gap, but no matter how close he came to finding one, he couldn't.

"Problems?" Marac asked.

"I can't find a common scheme; all of the stones are shaped differently."

"Can't you just create some?"

"For a space that size..." He pointed at the gap in the bridge. "It's easier and safer to have a guide. Far simpler to make a copy than invent something new."

"You might want to give it a shot, Lae. You may never find something you can use, and you might be able to conjure a spell well enough for us to get across without it."

Laedron nodded and climbed back onto his horse with his scepter in hand. Closing his eyes, he imagined long lengths of timber across the span because he had far more experience with wood. *A hundred feet? Almost two hundred?* Waving the wand, he repeated the incantation and concentrated on his spell, then opened his eyes to see the result. Timbers glimmered into existence, bridging the gap. He added another, then another, and more until the space had been completely covered. He counted slowly while maintaining the spell. *I need a count, a measure of how long I can keep it going. Without a count, we won't know how many might cross during each cast of the spell.*

"Sixty... sixty-one..." He clenched his eyes shut and stilled his mouth, focusing on his count and fighting the strain. *Seventy... seventy-one...* He released the spell and fell to his knees. He waited for the ache to fade, then asked, "Do you think that will be enough time to get over?"

"It'll have to be," Marac said. "We have no other choice."

"We could go back. Down through the valley." Brice came alongside Marac, pointing over his shoulder. "It's the safest way."

"And lose a few days of time?"

Brice scoffed at Marac. "What good is time when you're lying dead at the bottom of the valley? Or worse, two broken legs and left suffering and starving until you finally die?"

"Time isn't on our side, Thimble. Laedron's sleep is returning, and I don't take that as a good sign; it could mean the magic—and his life—are fading away. The sooner we get to Myrdwyer, the better."

Laedron gazed at Valyrie. "What do you think?"

She shrugged. "I would have to agree with Marac. If something happens to you before we get there, what need will we have for answers?"

"Oh, we'll still have a need for answers, but it'll be hard to find any without him, I'd say," Marac said. "No one else here has a handle on spellcraft or the ways of magic like Lae."

Seemingly deep in contemplation, Brice rubbed his chin and jaw for a while, then said, "I think we should go one at a time." He pulled a coiled rope from his pack. "This is at least a hundred feet.

Tie one end to the first person and the other to one of the horses on this side. Switch it up as each of us crosses. Keep your feet free of the stirrups unless you want to take two horses with you. If we fall, we lose a horse, but not one of our lives."

"We need the horses. All of them," Marac said.

Brice shrugged. "We need our lives more."

"I'll just have to do it well." Laedron readied his scepter. "Who's first?"

"The slowest first," Marac said, glaring at Brice. "You, then Valyrie, then me."

Before wrapping the rope around his waist, Brice knotted both ends into a loop, then gave the loose end to Marac.

"Why two loops?" Marac asked.

"When you come across, we'll have to tie off to one of our horses." Brice pointed at the far end of the bridge. "Easier to add loops to both ends now than to try throwing the rope."

Marac gestured at Laedron. "It's a sound plan, but what about him?"

"Eh?"

"Once you two have crossed, I'm to put the rope around myself and the other end will be tied to one of your horses. When I go, both ends of the rope would be on that side, and we would have to toss the end some hundred feet or more back to Lae."

"You'll take my horse with you when you go, Marac," Laedron said.

"But you could fall."

"If I do, I stand the best chance of surviving. Have you forgotten when Valyrie fell?"

"If that's how you want it, that's what we'll do. I'll tie this end to your horse since you won't be on it." Marac secured the rope to Laedron's saddle.

Once Laedron conjured the planks to bridge the gap, Brice guided his horse forward. Each impact of the horse's hooves against the wood pressed against Laedron's will, and he fought reality itself to keep his illusion going. Brice looked back over his shoulder with fear in his eyes. *The pressure. Fight it. You can do this.*

Once Brice stopped on solid ground, he untied the rope from his waist. Marac pulled it back, helped Valyrie secure it, and she started across the bridge. She kept a quicker pace than Brice, and the hooves pounding on his illusory bridge made his heart race.

Forty... forty-one... Laedron counted upward, maintaining the spell. Marac, watching Valyrie dismount and secure the rope, hastily tied his end around himself, then he looked questioningly at Laedron.

"Go. Plenty of time."

Keeping his eyes on Brice and Valyrie, Marac urged his horse and guided Laedron's across the bridge. His hands shaking, Laedron watched as the boards bowed and creaked. His will weakened and a headache formed behind his forehead. Just when Marac reached the other side, the planks fell and faded from existence in mid-air. Laedron dropped to his knees. He felt beaten, as if the horses had been trampling his body instead of an imaginary bridge.

Marac called, "Come on, Lae. Get up. You can do it." Brice and Valyrie joined in with his cheering.

One step, then the next. A bit more, and I'll be across this bloody ravine, with my friends once again, and onward to Myrdwyer. Thinking of the name filled him with dread, for he had come to associate that name with the endless road, the broken bridge, and his pain and misery. The name had become a mirage, an illusion no more real than his wooden planks, no more tangible than the answers he sought. *Will I ever discover the truth? Or will this whole journey be for naught?*

He stared across the gap at his friends, all of them apparently eager to see him cross the span and join them on the other side. *I cannot lose faith. Failure is a choice, not an unavoidable end.* He raised the scepter. *I can manage a levitation spell. I don't need a whole bridge.* He chanted. When his feet lifted off the ground, he compelled his body forward. *Slow. Keep it slow. Easier to take. Work through the pain!* Gritting his teeth, he kept his focus on the spell, doing his best to ignore the agony coursing through his veins. He closed his eyes when his speed and balance wavered. His spell was diminishing with every step. When he thought he was close enough, he released the spell and dropped. His chest and head struck the stone, but he felt his legs dangling in the breeze. His head pounded from the impact, and he couldn't tell if he'd broken any bones from the fall. The scepter rolled out of reach, and he noticed sparks flickering within the ruby. Then, the weak stones that had been supporting him gave way.

Slipping over the edge, he reached out and clawed at the little spaces between the pavers.

Marac slid to the edge, then reached out and grabbed Laedron's hand. "Brice! Valyrie! Get my legs!"

Laedron stared into Marac's eyes. *Is this how it will end for me?* Drenched in sweat, his hand was slowly slipping from Marac's grip. Blinking rapidly, he looked down into the ravine, then he saw only darkness.

৩০ Chapter Eight ৩০

What Lurks in the Dark

D*reams. So vivid. Flashing lights. If I can dream, I must still be alive.*

"How long was I out?" Laedron asked, opening his eyes. The camp had been set deep in the woods, and he had been placed on his sleeping bag near the fire.

"Half a day." Valyrie wiped his face with a wet cloth. *Perhaps she doesn't loathe me after all. Marac or Brice might have told her to do this, though. I cannot be sure if it's by her want.*

"What happened?"

"Marac did everything he could to hold on until we could lower the rope."

"Everything's a blur." Laedron rubbed his temples, then his eyelids. "Everyone made it? Marac and Brice are safe?"

She raised an eyebrow. "The spell must've taken quite a bit out of you."

The spell. My rod. Through the pain, he reached down and

searched his body. "Where's the ruby scepter?"

She twisted around and brought the scepter where he could see it. "Here."

Taking it and staring into the ruby at the tip, Laedron wondered if the sparkle he'd seen before he passed out had been real or merely a figment of his imagination. He thought back to the moment when he'd blacked out. *The sudden strain. Like a pile of bricks falling on top of me. What happened?*

"What's wrong, Lae?" she asked.

"I don't know. The spell seemed impossible to maintain, so I released it. When I hit the ground, I saw the ruby flicker." Peering into the gem, his voice cracked. "Everything seemed easier with Ismerelda's scepter. Until the last time, at least."

"But why? Is there something special about it?"

"She never told me."

"Yes, but what do *you* think?"

He pondered his experiences, searching his memory. "Something about it must cause magic to flow more easily, though I know not what." He sighed. "More questions. Always more questions. You'd better let me have the wand back for now, in case the scepter doesn't work."

She handed it to him. "Will you still teach me?"

"Of course. I didn't know if you still desired that."

"You're up. Good," Marac said before Valyrie could answer. He walked over and dropped a few broken limbs between Laedron and the fire. "How do you feel?"

"Like I've been trampled by a stampede of horses. Achy, and my head hurts."

Marac handed him a canteen. "Drink that. We'll have a meal before long."

"Thank you, Marac."

"Don't worry about it. We have plenty of water."

"No, not that. For saving me."

"Ah, you don't have to thank me for that."

"I don't? Of course I—"

"You saved me from Gustav and the executioner, so we'll just call it even. Besides, what else could I do?"

"Thanks anyway." Laedron sipped some water, but his queasiness made him pause before he drank too much. He looked around at the unfamiliar surroundings. "How far until we reach the ruins? Any way of knowing?"

"The ruins? They're all around us." Marac gestured at the worn stones on the ground. "Seems like this is the outskirts of what used to be a great city. This, I think, is your lost city of Myrdwyer."

A blanket pulled tight about his shoulders, Laedron stood and crept toward a half wall of what must have been the remains of a house or some other small building. He stared into the distance where the stones became more numerous and the trees were few and far between. For a moment, he thought he heard the noises of a bustling metropolis. *Probably the wind. It could be nothing else, for this city is long dead and deserted.*

"We had better get some food in our bellies and some sleep if we're to go exploring the ruins tomorrow." Marac fished through the packs, then pulled out his metal rods and started arranging them over the fire. "I'll take watch first, and Brice will cover the other half."

Brice rolled over on his sleeping bag. "I'll eat later, then take —"

"I'll take the second half," Laedron said. "I'm hardly tired."

As Laedron approached, Marac said, "You've been through a lot. Brice can—"

"I said I'll do it, Marac. I'm sore, but I'll manage."

"If you say so, Lae." Extending his hand, Marac offered a metal rod. "Would you mind helping me with the cooking?"

Without a word, Laedron helped Marac build a grate over the

pit, then plopped down on his bedding and rubbed his shoulders. *Sorer than I thought at first. Better not make it obvious.* He helped Marac season the cuts of beef after a light rinse to remove the salt, and over the next hour, they ate supper.

"Whippoorwill, most likely," Laedron said, trying to put them at ease when the others searched the air for the source of a mysterious flapping. "I saw a few on the way here."

"You were awake?" Marac nearly spit out his last bite of meat. "Made us haul you for miles, and you were awake the whole time?"

"No, no." Laedron waved his hands. "I mean, before the spell, before I passed out."

Brice shook his head, searching the night for whatever had made the sound. "Sounds like bats."

"Could be, but no need to worry. Neither will harm us." No sooner had he finished speaking than Laedron heard the distinct sound of wolves howling in the distance. "No need to worry about that, either."

"That's wolves, isn't it?" Standing, Brice scanned the trees. "They sound hungry."

"I'll protect you, Thimble." Marac puffed out his chest and chuckled. "I won't let them get you."

"I'm serious!" Brice said. "They'll sneak in under the cover of night and attack. Maul us to pieces, they will."

Glancing at Valyrie, Laedron detected fear in her eyes, too. "Get a hold of yourself, Brice. We've dealt with far worse than a few wolves. Do you think I'd let them get us?"

"What if there are twenty? Thirty? You're in no condition to cast spells, and the rest of us can't fight so many."

Marac shook his head. "A thousand? Ten thousand? Wolves don't hunt in packs that big. At most, we might see five or six, and that's assuming it's a big pack and they come this way."

"You can fight six wolves at once, Lae? As weak as you are?"

Brice asked.

"Surely. I'm Laedron Telpist." He elbowed Marac. "Master of the elements… and wolves to boot."

A smile crossing his lips, Brice seemed to calm. "All right. I'm going to get some sleep."

"You'd better, too," Marac told Laedron. "I'll come to wake you in a few hours."

* * *

The crackling of the fire stirred Laedron from his sleep, and he rolled onto his side to watch the flames dance above the coal bed. Opposite him, Valyrie seemed undisturbed. Brice displayed an innocent smile as he slept. *He's probably dreaming of cakes and cider, of perfect looming and amazing stitches. How could Marac hold such contempt for him? I've never met a kinder person,* Laedron thought. *Speaking of Marac, where is he?* No matter how hard he strained to peer into the darkness, he couldn't see his friend.

Sitting up, Laedron straightened his clothes and picked up his scepter. He looked again, but Marac was nowhere to be found.

"Marac," he whispered. "Marac!" He stood, stuck the scepter into his belt, and called out again, but the only response was Valyrie's shifting. Not wanting to wake her or Brice, he made his way to the edge of the firelight and peered through the trees. The sudden howling of wolves, seemingly closer than they had been, startled him, but he remained silent. *Where has he gone? Damn! He should know better than to go wandering the wilderness without telling anyone.* Laedron rolled his eyes at the irony of his thoughts, for he was intent on searching for Marac without alarming the others. *Just a quick look around won't hurt. If I can find him, there'll be no cause for worry.*

Careful to be as quiet as he could, he walked into the brush surrounding the camp, squinting at the strange shapes made by the shadows. He repeated the pattern of going a few steps, then searching for any sign of Marac several times before he came to a pile of rotten logs—more like a decaying wall of timber—at the base of what seemed to be a massive pine. *That tree must be a hundred feet through the center. And there's another one!* Growing at varying distances from one another amidst the ruins, the trees must have been ancient, and he imagined that the forest had existed for a long time before the city had been built. He had no way of telling, though, and he could only assume facts about the place based upon his own paltry knowledge of history. Shaking his head, he decided that his amazement with the flora would have to wait. Marac was still out there somewhere, and Laedron was determined to find his friend.

He found footing in the pile of old trunks and climbed to get a better vantage point so he could survey the area. Nearing the top, he hugged the tree and sat perfectly still. The howling of wolves was closer than he'd heard thus far. He peeked through the limbs and saw four gray wolves pouncing upon each other while a larger one sat atop a boulder and howled at the full moon. *They're at play and must not have noticed my approach.*

Though the howling and the proximity of the wolves made the hairs on the back of his neck stand on end, he mustered the courage to ignore his fear and take in the important details of what he was observing. *Five in all. No blood on their mouths, no shredded clothes or bodies nearby. Unlikely that they've killed Marac. No evidence.*

He felt a vibration in the log he perched on, and he froze, his mind first, then every muscle in his body. The wolves stopped their frolicking and paced back and forth in the clearing, as if preparing for a fight. *It wasn't just me. What's causing that?* With a thumping rhythm, the vibration resounded throughout the wood. Then, the noise intensified to pounding, growing louder as it pattered out a beat.

It sounds like... but it can't be footsteps. Too heavy. Too large. His eyes widened when the brush just past the wolves parted, and he was unable to move or make a sound. First, he saw the head of the creature, which appeared similar to a huge, brilliant-cut emerald. The body emerged next as it sprung twenty feet through the air, landing in the middle of the wolves. Snarling, the biggest wolf charged the crystalline beast. What had been a green light swirling inside the creature's emerald structure flashed to a red glow. *A living thing comprised entirely of jewels? Is that what got Marac? Am I dreaming? What in the hells is that thing?*

He watched in horror as the crystal monster grabbed the first wolf and tossed it like a used plaything. The snapping of the animal's spine when it struck the tree was audible to Laedron even from his vantage point a hundred yards away. The beast raised its emerald arms, the glow inside it intensifying. A stream of red and violet light shot from the wolf's body, and the monster seemed to be taking the energy into its own body. *Is that...? It can't be. Impossible. It looked just like the spell Andolis cast on me, the one by which he promised to take my soul.* The remaining wolves bit at the creature's crystalline legs, but Laedron figured they would be more likely to break their teeth than anything else.

Glowing ever brighter, the creature turned toward the other wolves, silent except for the crinkling of leaves and twigs beneath its bulky limbs. The quiet sent Laedron's pulse racing faster, for the creature's silence spoke volumes of its nature, its propensity to kill without apparent malice, its ability to rip flesh in its grisly fingers without screaming out in anger or victory. *A cold, calculating mechanism of death. If Marac encountered this thing, he's surely dead.*

The wolves must have felt intimidated because they inched backward, and when the creature lunged, they fled. Like a dart, the crystal abomination pursued, its bloodlust or appetite apparently not sated. It carved a path of destruction through the forest, breaking through the smaller trees and fallen logs as though they were little more than twigs and leaves in its path.

Creator! Who would make such a thing and loose it upon the forest? Laedron thought, unwilling to accept the possibility that the crystalline beast was a natural occurrence. *It must be the work of mages. Nowhere else in the natural world do gems take on a life of their own. And where evidence of sorcery is found, a sorcerer must be near. The Uxidin? Why would they make something like that? Zyvdredi? I dare not think it. Dammit, where did Marac go?*

He climbed down the log pile and, hiding in the shadows, stalked from tree to tree, keeping an eye out for the monster in case it reappeared. He made his way back to the campsite. The fire had thankfully burned out, cloaking his friends in darkness.

"Val," he whispered, shaking her shoulder. "Wake up, Val."

Swatting at his hand, she rolled over. "Is it morning?"

"Keep your voice down. Marac's gone."

"I am?" Marac asked.

Turning around, Laedron said, "Where were you?"

"Scouting the perimeter of the campsite. What else would I do?"

"What side?"

Marac pointed over his shoulder in the opposite direction Laedron had gone. "I found some tracks that way, followed them for a bit, then came back. They look like footprints, but I couldn't tell for sure."

"Did you see *it*?" Laedron tried to hide his fear, but he didn't think he did a very good job of it.

"See what?"

"The monster."

"Oh, I knew it. I just knew it." Brice, seated on his bedroll, rocked forward with his arms wrapped around his knees, and his voice took on a higher pitch. "What are we going to do? Creatures of the night!"

"Keep your damned voice low if you want to survive this."

"What did you see, Lae? What *exactly*?" Valyrie asked.

"A creature made of crystal, like huge emeralds fused together." He turned to Brice. "It killed that pack of wolves you were worried about. Well, it murdered one and chased the rest into the forest."

Brice quivered with fear. "We've got to get out of these woods. I knew we were wrong to come here."

"Not until we find the answers we seek." Laedron sighed. "We've come too far to turn back now."

"And risk our lives? We should cut our losses and go, if you ask me."

"Well, nobody did!" Laedron, afraid that raising his voice had drawn the attention of someone… or some*thing*, ducked and scanned the trees. "It didn't see me while I watched it. We should be fine as long as we keep quiet and hidden. We keep low, move under cover of shadow, and speak no louder than a whisper."

Clenching his eyes shut, Brice breathed and exhaled slowly. "Right. Yes."

Valyrie stood and took her bow in hand. She slung the quiver across her back and stared at Marac. "Did the tracks you found lead anywhere in particular?"

"No. Unless they make a sudden turn, they go to the west of the ruins."

Brice peered into the darkness. "I'll need to get a look of those tracks."

Laedron crossed his arms. "For what? What could you possibly do about them?"

"To see what I can figure out and to see where they go."

"So you're a tracker now? When did this happen?"

Brice glared at Laedron. "The instructors in Westmarch thought we'd need to know a little more than sword fighting and how to wear armor. On top of that, Caleb taught me a number of things about being a sneakthief, Lae. A little about picking pockets, a bit of picking locks, and even a few things of traps and tracks. While you spent your time in the militia, I spent my time honing my skills."

"Just do it," Valyrie said, pressing her hand against Laedron's shoulder. "Now's not the time to argue. Maybe he can find something of use."

Nodding, Marac led them to the spot where he'd found the tracks.

Brice crept along parallel to the marks. After studying the grass and brush for a while, he picked up something small. "A thread of string."

"Did you go this far, Marac?" Laedron asked, moving closer to see.

"No, I stopped back there, near the horses." Marac crouched next to Brice. "I doubt it's one of ours."

"Impossible to tell, but it's out of place here in the middle of a field." Brice eyed the brush leading away from the camp. "We'd better pack up our belongings before going any farther. We can't afford to get lost without our supplies or our horses."

They returned to the camp, bundled up their sleeping packs and possessions, then put their gear back on their horses. Afterward, Laedron followed Brice back to the suspicious patch of grass.

"You see how the weeds lay like this?" Brice gestured with the palm of his hand, motioning toward the trees. "It tends to be pressed in the direction someone walks. Follow them in that direction, and you should be able to find more tracks." Crouching, Brice waddled toward the tree line. "Like this one."

"You think that it was a some*one* and not a some*thing*?" Marac asked.

"Difficult to tell by these. I'll have to see a few more; these don't have the best definition."

Laedron looked at the track, then turned to see the presumed path. "Down that way?"

Brice nodded. "Should be easy to follow. Weeds and pine straw are easily displaced when you walk through them, so we can go for a while to see where this path leads. It looks like whoever made them didn't care if he—or she, or it—disturbed the ground."

Bending down beside Brice, Marac squinted at the ground. "Any ideas yet as to what made them?"

"I'm leaning toward a human."

"And you're sure they're human tracks? Animals couldn't make tracks like these?"

"They're fresh, and we haven't seen anything big enough to make prints this size pass through here. A man, on the other hand… plenty big enough."

"What about recent enough? We have no proof that anyone other than the four of us are out here." The image of the crystal beast flashing through his mind, Laedron asked, "Could it be anything other than a man? Something bigger maybe?"

"Possibly, but few tracks in nature could be mistaken for a human, especially when you have a print with this distinct shape." Brice drew the outline of the track with his finger.

"We have nothing else to go on, Lae." Valyrie nocked an arrow. "We must, for now, assume that it's a man and follow."

"Keep the horses back a ways so they don't destroy any tracks we may yet need." Laedron took his rod in hand and hoped that it would work if needed. "Lead the way, Brice. And keep an eye out for... well, anything."

* * *

"We've been walking for nearly an hour," Laedron whispered, stopping when Brice crouched again.

"I never said it'd be a quick process," Brice said, sorting through some pine straw. "Besides, what better things have you to do? At least we're making progress. Here, he made a turn." Looking up, Brice pointed. "Between those two... Creator! Those trees are huge."

"The forest has many of them, it would seem. Ancient trees shooting up into the heavens." The haze of the dawn filtered through the pines. Laedron followed the tree's trunk with his eyes, but the canopy above made it impossible to see the top. "They've been here since before the city was built, if I had to guess."

Brice jogged ahead, and every once in a while, he glanced at the ground. Reaching the two trees, he put his hand on one of them. "He—she, whoever—walked through here and stopped just past them."

"Just say 'he' for now, Thimble; your stuttering is getting on my nerves. We'll know for sure if we ever find him," Marac said.

Stepping between the mighty trunks, both as thick as the one he'd seen near their camp, Laedron figured that the trees were significant because they stood at the entrance of what seemed to have been a huge structure. *The ruins of a temple, perhaps? The High King's palace? It was clearly a spectacle to behold, whatever it was.* "Where from here, Brice?"

Brice searched the ground. "Wait." Squinting, he crouched and pointed at several disturbed patches of brush.

"What is it?"

"Two sets... and drag marks." He gestured to their right. "Someone dragged something that way. These tracks are much bigger, though. A bear?"

Laedron took a deep breath. "It could be that monster. Any blood?"

"No. Wait. Yes, here." Holding up some pine needles, Brice twisted them between his fingertips. "A few drops. Look."

When he turned to examine the pine straw, Laedron caught a glimpse of something beneath a shrub. He bent and pulled out a dense, heavy bone almost two feet long. "What do you make of this?"

"It's a bone," Brice said.

"I can see that, Thimble." Laedron tugged at his collar, then tossed the bone over to Brice. "Sorry. Can you tell anything about it?"

"I've never been a student of anatomy, I'm afraid."

Valyrie took the bone and examined it from every angle. "Looks like a femur, the big bone behind the thigh. Human."

He felt uneasy. *Do they dissect corpses in the university?* Pulling the shrub from side to side, Laedron said, "Here's the rest of him. A skull and several other pieces, but no clothes, no weapons. Must've been here for quite some time."

"The blood didn't come from this body. What is going on here?" Marac kicked a stone, sending it flying into one of the big pines. "What else do you see, Thimble?"

"Just the drag marks leading off that way."

"Keep going, then. It didn't end here."

Following Brice as if he were a bloodhound, Laedron tried to block the sinister thoughts racing through his mind, but he couldn't. *What had killed that man? And the blood in the straw? Whose blood is it? Who drew it? What lurks in this wood, waiting for the perfect moment to pounce?*

Every attempt to preclude his imagination met with another vibrant vision of their torture, their pain merely a means to an end, a small part in the machinations of some dark sorcerer hidden amongst the pines. *And if we encounter an evil mage, will this scepter be of any use?* Even with Ismerelda's rod, he had been unable to defeat Andolis Drakkar in a duel of magic, and the fact that it had failed during his last spell worried him. *How powerful could a Zyvdredi master become if allowed to sit and brood in this wilderness for centuries?*

Laedron nearly tripped over Brice, not noticing when his friend squatted to examine the earth. "Sorry."

Seemingly unfazed by the knee in his back, Brice stared at the ground, touching it with his palm several times. "It stops here."

"What do you mean?"

"Just what I said." Standing, Brice dusted off his knees. "No more trail. No more tracks."

"Impossible." Marac turned in a circle. "It can't just stop here."

"Well, it does."

Laedron shook his head and threw up his hands. "Where are they, then? If they stopped here and went nowhere else, they would still be standing right here."

"I'm simply telling you what I see. The prints go no farther from this place, Lae."

Valyrie held her hair back and bent forward. "Any wheel tracks? Hoof prints? A cart or horses, perhaps?"

"No, nothing." Brice held up his hand, his index finger and thumb spread about an inch apart. "Wagons and carts leave deep marks when they move through dirt. Especially under these circumstances, I would have seen something."

Laedron spun and scanned the trees. "Keep looking. There *must* be something we're missing. Spread out."

Brice and Marac tied the horses to some low limbs, then searched the ground for more tracks. Valyrie checked the brush and shrubs, and Laedron, without much to go on, followed the bases of the trees to see if anything had fallen around the exposed roots.

Laedron pointed at the bark when he spotted something odd. "Look at this. Over here!"

Valyrie got to him first. "Found something?"

"Carvings." Laedron ran his finger along the grooves cut into the tree. "Shapes of some kind." His jaw dropped, and he leaned toward the cuts. "Writing. It's writing!"

"Writing? Not like any I've seen. Can you read it?" Brice

asked.

"I think so." Concentrating, Laedron studied the writing, then shook his head violently. "It can't be. No, it can't—" He stepped back.

"What is it?" Valyrie took him by the arm, halting his retreat. "What, Lae?"

"Zyvdredi writing…" He turned away, rubbing his hands together. "Here? Zyvdredi… she said this was an *Uxidin* city. Did she lie? She seemed sincere. How can it be?"

"Lae?"

"To find Zyvdredi here? In the middle of Lasoron? They shouldn't be here. They *can't* be here—"

"Lae?"

"Could they be new markings? Something recent? Perhaps they're not as old as this place. Wanderers who came upon this broken city—"

"Lae!"

He turned to her. "Sorry. You were saying?"

Sighing, she asked, "What does it say?"

"If those ruins are what's left of a temple, the writing seems to discuss it. It's some kind of blessing or a prayer."

"Written in Zyvdredi?" Brice inspected the symbols, but his grimace told of his confusion. "Why?"

"I don't know." Laedron nibbled at his fingernails, searching the horizon for answers and not finding any. "We had better—"

The movement of shadows in the nearby brush gave him pause. *No shaking of the earth. That crystal thing? Here? No, we would've heard it. A thing that large can't move with stealth. Could there be a Zyvdredi master watching us, waiting for the opportune moment to strike?*

Valyrie's face contorted with worry. "Lae? Are you feeling all right?"

"Yes. I thought I saw something there. I guess my mind's

playing tricks on me."

"Where to from here?" Marac asked. "Are there any directions written there? A set of instructions?"

"No, nothing." Laedron, though his hand trembled, traced the words with his finger. "It reminds me of something I saw in the city of Azura."

"How so?"

"Remember how every building, every storefront, and every home in Azura had inscriptions of saints? Azuran stars? Inside most of the buildings and above the main entrance, they had carved verses from the Azuran scriptures. Prayers for protection, blessings on those who entered, and so on."

Brice crouched and poked at the bark. "Does the shape have any meaning?"

"Shape? What shape?"

"The words have been carved in a big arch," Brice said, using a finger to follow the inscription to the base of the tree. "See here? It starts near the roots."

Laedron started at one end and followed the carvings all the way to the finish, but the text—even in its entirety—told him nothing more. Scratching his chin, he pondered the writing. *This must be the key, but what does it mean? Why, of all the trees in the forest, would they put writing on this one? A marker of some kind? But what were they marking?*

"Perhaps it's a dead end." Leaning on his shoulder against the tree, Marac lowered his chin and sighed. "Maybe we don't have enough to unlock its secret."

Unlock its secret. Laedron took a few steps back to observe the arch in its entirety. "It can't be. Can it?"

"Can't be what?" Valyrie asked, obviously eager to hear any possible solutions.

"A door? An entry of some kind?"

Brice picked at the bark near the writing. "No seams. If it's a door, I can see no way of opening it."

"If it was made by the Zyvdredi, it wouldn't have a handle or locks in the same way with which we're accustomed. Stand back." Laedron produced his scepter.

Marac put his hand on Laedron's shoulder. "What are you going to do? Blast your way through?"

"No, I intend to walk in." Speaking his incantation and waving the rod, Laedron watched his body become transparent, starting with his hands and enveloping his whole body after a while. Then, he walked into the side of the tree.

At first, he couldn't see anything through the dense wood fibers, but once he had passed the bark and wood, he found himself in a hollow within the tree. The area was about fifty feet in diameter, and wooden steps, which seemed to have grown inside the tree that way, led down. He stepped backward, then released the spell when he was completely out.

"There's a space inside. And a staircase. Come close, and I'll cast the spell on each of you so you can enter." Noticing a tremor in the ground, Laedron gasped. "Quickly. That monster approaches!"

"What about the horses?" Brice held onto the reins and petted the gelding, trying to calm its nerves.

"They can fit, too. Come on!"

❦ Chapter Nine ❧

Refuges in Their Own Land

L aedron held his index finger to his lips and made sure each of his friends saw the gesture. The vibration had grown stronger. He could feel the tree tremble beneath his feet, and the shaking caused loose sap to drip onto them. Suddenly, the quaking stopped, as if the beast had passed. A cloud of dust hung in the air, and he likened the smell to the fertile soil his mother used to plant her garden each year. The hollow was dark, but whoever had created the space must have put holes into the tree somewhere above because a faint ray of sunshine came through, allowing just enough light to see. *What purpose do the holes serve? To brighten the place or to tell at a glance if it's day or night?*

"This place gets stranger by the minute," Marac said, trying to pick the sap from his hair. "Ruins of an ancient people, a beast made entirely of crystal, and now, we're standing inside a living tree."

"All of those things are certainly true." Holding out the scepter, Laedron conjured a light spell, then started down the stairs. "Keep on your toes. No way of knowing what lies in wait beneath the earth."

"And the horses?"

"We're forced to leave them here for now. Put out some food."

A few steps into the descent, Laedron heard the scraping of stone underfoot. He stepped down twice more, then crouched and held the scepter close to the stairs.

"What are you doing, Lae?" Marac scooted backward and put his hand on the earthen wall to keep his balance.

"Fascinating. The stairs seamlessly change from wood to stone here." It reminded him of Pilgrim's Rest, where the buildings had been carved into the faces of the cliffs, and the woodwork had been precisely fitted to the stone.

"Shouldn't we focus on the task at hand? I'm sure we'll have plenty of time to admire the architecture later."

"Powerful magic, Marac. A sign that we should not be careless here."

"Magic? I'm not easily convinced. A master craftsman could do the same without spells."

"We cannot assume such, for if we accept that this is the work of regular men, we would preclude the influence of the more dangerous possibility: mages. I would rather overestimate than underestimate what lies below." He reached down and felt something wet on his fingertips. Bringing his hand up to his face, he squinted at the substance. "Blood. Small droplets."

"Blood?" Marac asked.

"Like the drops we found earlier in the straw. Keep your eyes open."

* * *

"How deep do you think we are?" Brice asked when they came to the bottom. "Fifty steps?"

"Closer to a sixty, I should think. Three or four stories into the ground." Noticing a glint of something on the wall, Laedron released his spell, and the area remained dimly lit. Approaching the wall, Laedron whispered, "Some kind of gem or crystal putting off light. And look, a fixture of some kind."

"Magical light?" Valyrie asked.

Laedron nodded. "It must be."

"You're not completely sure?"

Eying the precious stone and the flickering energy within, Laedron considered the evidence at hand. "There's no one controlling it. If this is magic, it must be some kind of permanent spell."

"There are more of them." Brice pointed at the mouth of what appeared to be a cave. "Leading that way."

Laedron crept over to the tunnel. He waited for the others to reach him, then continued until he reached a cross point. To his right, a pile of stones completely obstructed the way, but to his left, the corridor extended further than he could see, despite the ambient glow provided by the gemstones. When he looked at the floor, he spotted more blood trailing off to the left.

He took the left path, then froze in his tracks when he heard a crash behind him.

"Damned thing!" Marac shouted from where he had fallen. "Help me up, would you?"

"Quiet," Laedron whispered. "We don't know—"

"More adventurers come to see what they can take from our corpses? Cunning, too, to find the way in here," a man's voice said from the darkness ahead. "You had better speak up."

"We... uh..." Laedron couldn't think of anything to say. *Zyvdredi? Bandits? Something else entirely?*

"Not quite the response I anticipated. And young is the voice that replies. Interesting."

"Who are you?"

"Strange that you should ask me that before you tell me your name. Did I come by stealth into your home, then demand to know who you are?"

"Forgive me if I'm reluctant to answer." Laedron searched the shadows for a target, his scepter extended.

"Your hesitation gives me even more reason to rid the world of you, young man. One last time: what are you doing here and who are you?"

"My name is Laedron Telpist."

"A good start. Now, what do you hope to find in this place? Piles of treasure? A hoard to sate your hunger for wealth?"

"Blast him, Lae," Marac said under his breath. "Give it to him."

He shook his head, unwilling to attack unprovoked. "We're at a total disadvantage, and if I start throwing spells, the whole place could come down on us."

"I'm waiting." The man sounded angry, but controlled.

"We've come seeking answers." His hand trembling, Laedron did his best to keep the rod pointed down the hall. "We were told that we might find them here."

"Told? What fool would tell you to come here?"

"An old woman in Nessadene, a bookseller by the name of Callista." Blinking rapidly, Laedron saw waves in the air that looked much like humidity fluttering above stone streets on a hot summer day. A few yards away, he saw fingertips pull down a cowl. Thick black locks appeared next, and finally, the invisibility spell faded away to reveal a man robed in dark gray.

The strange man said an incantation, approached Laedron, then smiled. The words of power had apparently been said to the gems because they flashed bright, illuminating the hallway by several orders of magnitude. "By your expression, I should think that you've never seen anything like this place."

Laedron noticed the body of a wolf at the man's feet, and the pattern on its coat was familiar. *The wolf killed by the monster? This man has retrieved it, but for what purpose?* "You assume correctly. How—"

"It's not a matter of *how*. I should say, it's not as important as *why*."

"Very well. Why?"

"An answer you shall have in due time. For now, you follow."

"Follow? I don't even know your name. Care to give it?"

"It's not safe to linger in the passages. Follow or remain here, for I'm busy." The man turned and walked away.

Although the proposition of following some stranger through darkened halls didn't appeal to him, Laedron turned to his companions. "Have we any choice but to follow?"

"If he meant us harm, he would have attacked in the blind," Marac said. "You don't give up your advantage, talk, then turn your back on people you intend to kill."

Laedron glanced at Brice and Valyrie, and both nodded in agreement. "I suppose we're in agreement, then." He quickened his pace to catch up to the man, the others close behind.

He counted each step until he reached a hundred, then he stopped trying to keep track. When they came to a rope bridge, Laedron and his companions gawked in every direction at the domed cavern.

The view captivated him. He stood at the edge of eternity, the vast abyss beneath the rope bridge and the vaulted dome above so massive that their footsteps hadn't produced an echo when they arrived. Through a hole across the expanse, a waterfall emptied into the chasm, and he gulped when he noticed that he couldn't see the water striking the bottom of the pit.

"You built this place?" Laedron asked once he'd gotten his senses about him.

The man shook his head. "My people merely put the bridge over it and smoothed the walls."

"Your people? The Uxidin?"

The man looked surprised. "Indeed." Gesturing at the rope bridge to his left, the man proceeded across, and Laedron followed, afraid to speak a word lest the utterance snap a rope or a plank. *Don't look down. Look anywhere but down.* It was like being on the ancient bridge over the vale they'd crossed days before, but he didn't know if he was glad or more frightened that he couldn't see the bottom.

Once on the other side, the man picked up his pace, but finally stopped at the end of another stone hallway. "Be respectful within this place." The door opened at his touch, and light poured through the opening.

Inside the room, thirty people were huddled in small groups, and the place stank of unwashed bodies. All of them wore clothes too big for their frames, and Laedron noticed that their skin had drawn tight over their faces, ribs, and hands. Children had apparently painted murals on the walls with whatever they could find. From the wide strokes making up the images, he figured that the drawing implements had most likely been fingers dipped in mud or soot. He couldn't quite tell what the pictures represented, but it somehow made the people seem kinder, gentler than how they appeared.

So many of them, Laedron mused, glancing at their faces as they walked. *They seem terrified by us.* All of their faces bore dirt and scars, and most of the people were elderly and infirmed. "Are

108

we safe enough to share names?"

The man stopped halfway into the room. "Tavingras. You may call me Tavin. From what I know of mortals, you would prefer not to waste your time with long names."

"Very well, Tavin. I'm Laedron Telpist." Glancing at the people in the dim light, Laedron felt as though he had entered an asylum for the destitute. "Why do you hide yourselves in this manner?"

"If the *Trappers* weren't roaming the forest, we would have no reason to hide."

His eye twitched. "Trappers?"

"You haven't seen them? Horrible creations, part crystal and part essence pulled from the living. Soul-suckers. Upon finding anything still alive, they make no small effort to deprive that body of its life essence." Just as quick as Tavin produced a sack from his robes, a little child, one of only a handful in the room, ran up, snatched the bag, then disappeared again. "Eat them slowly and enjoy them, for it took quite a while to find those," Tavin called to the girl. He turned back to Laedron. "This wolf's body should be a good meal compared to what we've been eating."

"You can't reason with them? These Trappers, as you call them?"

"No. Our enemy prefers his slaves to be willing, able, silent, and uncompromising. They do not speak, and we have no evidence that they'll listen to anything we have to say. Cold killers set to a singular task."

Marac raised an eyebrow. "Your enemy?"

"I'll explain that later, for to hear the name is hurtful to my people."

"What was in the bag?" Laedron asked, trying to see the child behind the adults.

"I went out to find nuts and berries earlier. The pickings are slim of late." Tavin motioned at a side door, and Laedron and his friends followed. Laedron assumed that the room was Tavin's private quarters because furniture for every purpose had been arranged about the space, and clothes similar in size and style to the ones Tavin wore hung on the racks near a row of bookshelves along the back wall. In the center of the room sat a table with a few chairs beside a desk littered with books and scraps of paper. Laedron felt a little constricted near the entrance, for the room had clearly not been designed for five people to occupy it at one time. *If all this furniture wasn't in here, I doubt it would feel so cramped.*

When he closed the door behind them, Tavin continued, "The Trappers have killed most of the animals, everything not quick enough to escape, and the gathering trips yield less and less each time I go."

Brice leaned against the wall beside the door. "How long have you been down here?"

"*Too long* have we rotted in this prison," Tavin replied, a coarseness underlining his disdain for those walls. "Far too long. To be honest, it's difficult to say, for I don't go out into the woods every day."

Laedron noticed the spines of books shelved in the bookcases bearing titles written in Zyvdredi. "What is this place?"

"The remnants of the wells. Long ago, the pit we passed was filled with fresh water, and the water rose in a vast network of pipes to the city above. Due to a lack of maintenance, the great cisterns have cracked and leaked, leaving huge, empty pits." Tavin shrugged, then chuckled. "It's ironic that this place, a place where none of us now living ventured before the fall, is all that's left of our empire."

"And those Zyvdredi books?"

"Zyvdredi?" Tavin glanced at the tomes. "That's *Nyreth*. The Zyvdredi are a group of *people*, not a language, young man. The people from the noble house of Zyvdred, a sect of the ancient *Nyrethine* empire, to be specific."

"What did you do? Before 'the fall,' I mean."

"Caretaker of the Hall of Tomes, but titles matter little in these times. Now, I am merely a steward of a dying people, all of us living each day while wondering if any given hour will be our last." Taking a deep breath, Tavin stared at the ceiling. "Kareth has gotten his revenge, it would seem, if that was indeed his purpose."

"Kareth? Who, pray tell, is that?"

"In the ruins above lives a vile being known as Kareth. He was once one of us, an Uxidin, but for his crimes, he was expelled from our city."

"His crimes? Killing your people?" Brice asked.

"In a way, but—"

"But that wasn't his original offense." Laedron leaned forward. "The novel is decades old."

"Novel?" Tavin seemed puzzled.

"A book read for entertainment. Stories, tales, and fables. You don't have them?"

"What need does it fulfill?"

The man's never heard of reading for pleasure? Laedron gave his friends a curious look, then returned his gaze to Tavin. "It's not important. Go on with what you were saying."

"Many years ago, Kareth killed our elder-priest and stole an artifact, our dearest and most prized possession. If you've heard of it in your society, you would know it as The Bloodmyr Tome."

"I've heard this Bloodmyr Tome discussed at length, but no one seems to know what it really is. Perhaps you can tell us more of it?"

"It is the physical manifestation of all Uxidin magical knowledge, the key to reality itself. Within its pages, magic is intermingled with a written history of our people. Do you know what magic truly is, Sorcerer?"

"Conjuring—"

Tavin shook his head, then sat on the edge of his desk. "It is to command reality, to issue a set of instructions to the real world to do as you say. Thus, anything is possible."

"So, The Bloodmyr Tome is a spellbook of sorts?" Valyrie asked.

"To be simple about it, yes, but it's much more than that. And if Callista sent you here, you must be willing to retrieve it in exchange for something that you desire."

Marac clasped his hands. "I can understand why you would want it back, but given that it contains, according to you, all knowledge of magic, why would anyone want you to have it back?"

With a confused expression, Tavin asked, "What do you mean?"

Brice stroked his chin. "I think what he means to say is that the world hasn't ended since you lost it. Who's to say that returning it to you would be a good idea?"

"Because Kareth stole it. It's ours, and stolen property should be returned to its proper owners. We want it back."

Laedron detected something odd about the way Tavin had replied. *I don't think he's lying, but he's not telling the entire truth, either.* "If you want our help, you'll have to tell us everything, no matter how dreadful that prospect might be."

Tavin stood from the table, walked over, and sat on the corner of the desk. "To understand why, I must tell you of our history and how we came to be the way we are."

"I think it would benefit us all to know," Laedron said, despite Marac's sighing. "Go on."

"Long ago, we—Uxidin, Zyvdredi, and all the rest—were but noble houses of one people, one empire: the Nyrethine. Our lands and our people spread out across this continent from end to end, where so many nations—mortal nations—stand today. This was the time before Azura, before the Great War, long before anything that you would recognize.

112

"When the Creator gifted us with magic, we were instructed in its use, but the knowledge was too great for any single person to remember. The Bloodmyr Tome was created, by the Creator's hand, so it is said, to store the knowledge, and it was bestowed upon the Elder Priest for safekeeping."

"And these stories were passed down to you?" Laedron asked.

"By the Elder Priest, yes. In all of Myrdwyer, we have had three, each one—"

"Three?" Laedron's jaw dropped. "That would make each one —"

Tavin nodded. "Thousands of years old. Yes."

"Thousands... it's difficult to fathom living for so long." He thought about Ismerelda. Although he never knew her true age, she had told him that she fought at Azura's side in the Great War over a thousand years ago.

"Amazing, is it not? And that brings us to our dilemma."

"Does it?"

"Of course." Tavin stared at Laedron. "The Bloodmyr Tome contains, amongst a number of secret spells and historical records, the secret of immortality, a secret of which we have a dire need."

"I don't understand. The Uxidin are immortal."

"Yes, but nothing lasts forever. We can live for quite a long time, but not before we receive the Font... and we must, periodically, be *renewed*."

Yes, the Font. He considered what he had seen come to pass, and he remembered Jurgen speaking of Vicar Forane's thirst for eternal life and her treachery. *It is a shame to see one so devoted give in to the lure of a font of youth.* "You would have us find this tome and use it to drink the souls of others? Just so you can live forever?"

Tavin sighed. "No, you do not understand. We would never use cheap Zyvdredi tricks and certainly not at the cost of others.

Allow me to continue."

Reluctantly, Laedron nodded. *Is there any way to achieve immortality without placing a cost of some sort on others?*

"In the ancient era, the Nyrethine were divided into houses, and the three most prominent were Uxidin, Falacore, and Zyvdred. Whereas the Uxidin and Falacoran houses used the life forces of nature—trees, plants, that sort of thing—to rejuvenate, the Zyvdredi used any life force available. They became enthralled by the feeling of the renewal; it was like a drug to them, and it didn't take long for the Zyvdredi to deplete their homeland of nearly every tree and plant. Then, they turned on the animals until those, too, were gone.

"The earth became rocky and barren where there once had been mountains ringed with vegetation. Where there had been forests and grass, the land turned to desert or ice, whichever was quickest to claim the land. With nothing else to satisfy their desires, the Zyvdredi turned on each other."

"On each other? They killed their own people?"

"The strong ones sucked the souls from their lessers, and eventually, the only ones who remained were those in the highest positions of power, their children, or mighty wizards. Zyvdred went from an empire based upon material riches to one based upon the trading of souls. To facilitate their enterprise, they stored the essence of men in black gems."

"Like these?" Laedron produced a handful of soulstones from a pouch on his belt, then held them out for Tavin to see. "We found them on assassins in Azura."

"Are they...?" Tavin gulped, seemingly afraid to finish the question. "Filled?"

"Yes, we think so. Can you release them?"

"I can, but they will return to the ether, for only the essence, the raw life energy, remains. Though I would normally not endorse the practice, you may want to keep them for your own uses."

Getting a bad feeling, Laedron furrowed his brow. "No, I don't think I could. Isn't it Necromancy?"

"Necromancy?" Tilting his head, Tavin appeared confounded by the question, as if he was trying to determine the meaning of the word.

Laedron explained, "Death magic. The realm of darkness and evil, the spells practiced by the Zyvdredi to hurt the rest of us."

Tavin tightened his lips. "I only know one kind of magic. No spell can make you pure or foul. Good and evil are in the methods, how you use that knowledge, and the purpose, the end result you wish to achieve. You simply must know where you stand and avoid the taint of darkness in all that you do."

Replacing the stones in his bag, Laedron nodded. "Please go on. Sorry for interrupting."

"Ah, yes. Where was I?"

"The trading of souls," Valyrie said, obviously captivated with the story.

"Yes, of course. Once the Zyvdredi had defiled their lands, House Falacore and House Uxidin responded in different ways. To prevent the same thing from happening, the Falacorans banned the practice of renewal, the font spells, and immortality in their lands, and their people returned to their mortal forms once the magic wore off. Not long after that, the Uxidin, my people, disallowed the Zyvdredi access to our country. A civil war began, and the nations of the north split into several new states: Falacore, Zyvdred, Lasoron, Albiade, and the land which is occupied by the Heraldan Theocracy now."

"Was that before or after Azura?" Laedron asked.

"After the Great War, but before the War of the Eagles. The Falacorans found our decision too harsh, and the Lasoronians and the Albiadines simply wanted to be independent and saw an opportunity to act. Thus, the Uxidin, the Zyvdredi, and we suspect, the Falacoran royal family became the only immortals, for

The Bloodmyr Tome remained with us. We acquire our essence from nature, these ancient trees, while the Zyvdredi gain sustenance by stealing souls."

Marac stood. "And now, you've lost your spell."

"Indeed."

Laedron asked, "If we do not agree, what happens?"

"We die, Sorcerer. Men's life energy can be extracted easily, as can the essence of grass or small animals, but the spell contained in that sacred text is the only one we can use to draw out the essence of the ancient forest. And it is that essence which we use, for we aren't apt to follow down the road of the Zyvdredi. That path leads to corruption."

"You said grass and small animals. Why not use those?"

"The Trappers have depleted this forest of all but the most elusive animals, and to absorb the essence of grass… you would be wasting your time, for you could do nothing other than seek out new spots of brush. Its essence is nearly as weak as dead earth or rock."

"No one thought to write down this spell?" Valyrie asked.

"Sorry?"

"If you had recorded the spell somewhere else, you wouldn't have this problem. You wouldn't need the tome."

"We have a number of reasons why it was never copied elsewhere. For one, its location was secret, known only by the Elder Priest, and it was only brought out in public when a renewal had to be performed. Second, the pages of the tome are the only channeling instruments that can withstand the power of the spell, and third, it had been used for thousands of years without issue. We had no reason to change. Lastly, creating copies of the spells could have had dire consequences if they had fallen into the wrong hands."

"The wrong hands… like Kareth's?" Valyrie asked, sarcasm dripping from her words.

"Indeed. The Elder Priest was careless, and The Bloodmyr Tome was lost."

Laedron laced his fingers together in his lap. "Where, if we should choose to help you, are we to find the tome?"

"Kareth has it in the ruins, in the old temple. Deep beneath it."

"Are those the ruins near the secret entrance to this place?"

"No. We're standing beneath what remains of the ancient library, which was nearly as large as the temple."

"If you know where it is, why haven't you sent anyone to get it back?" Marac asked. "Why wait for someone to fetch it for you?"

"We've tried, but we've failed. Many were lost in the attempt and the counterattack that followed. We had to seal the hallway closed to keep Kareth's creations out, and it took weeks to build our secret entrance. Since then, most of our people have grown weaker, both in magic and in their own physical abilities. That's why the Far'rah sent out the call for help to Nessadene. In Callista, we found an ally."

Laedron raised an eyebrow. "*The* Far'rah?"

"Forgive me. The Elder Priest. *Far'rah* is the title of our highest authority, for when the empire fell, our faith is the only structure that remained intact. When Kareth killed the previous Far'rah, a new one was appointed."

"And his name is Harridan?"

"Yes."

"How do the Trappers fit into all this?"

Tavin stared at his feet. "What would you like to know?"

"Anything you can tell us. Everything you know."

"As I said before, the Trappers were loosed upon the forest by Kareth, bound to seek the living and steal souls. We first encountered them during our attack on the old temple, and they drove us back. We hid in the woods for quite some time, all of us stricken with fear at the slightest rumble in the ground, until the

Far'rah decided to move us to this place.

"We call it *Auskemyr*, the Land of the Hidden, and we use our secret home to avoid the Trappers, for they aren't smart enough to figure out how to enter our sanctuary. Kareth's vile creations have nearly cleared the forest of all living beings—the wolves, birds, deer, nearly everything except insects—but we are fortunate that our people haven't been killed by one for nearly a decade."

"You have a way to kill them?"

"Being composed entirely of crystal, the monsters can be destroyed by a competent mage. The most effective method we've found is by the use of vibrations, summoning tremors so strong that they can crack the Trappers' rigid bodies. But you must bring a powerful quake; mistakes and hesitation could result in dire consequences."

"Good. If we have a way to fight them, we stand a much better chance." *But what if I cannot conjure a spell strong enough?* Fearing that Ismerelda's ruby scepter had broken, Laedron pulled it from his side. "Can you tell me anything about this rod?"

Tavin's eye twitched, but he took the scepter in his hands. "Where did you get this?"

"My teacher."

"He would give away an instrument of this caliber? He must've been a great sorcerer indeed to have something like this as a spare."

"Sorceress. My teacher was killed in the streets of Morcaine months ago, murdered by a Zyvdredi master posing as a Heraldan priest."

"What was her name?"

"Ismerelda."

"A name I may have heard in passing, but it doesn't easily come to mind. Was she from Myrdwyer?" Tavin handed the scepter back.

"No," Laedron said. "She was originally of Uxidia, and she

moved to Westmarch when her family left to live in Evdurein."

"It is a rare thing for an Uxidin to live amongst mortals in a city. It's dangerous for us to be in contact with the wider world, but in your case, we must make an exception. For the survival of our people."

"I'm surprised that you haven't heard of her. She stood with Azura in the battle against Vrolosh."

"Many names escape me, especially those of minor players, my young friend." Tavin tapped his temple. "Little but the most important details remain when you go on for as long as I have. Besides, she could have been exaggerating her own importance."

"Exaggerating her importance? I think not." Laedron clenched his fists at his sides.

"Forgive me. You must have had a close attachment to her."

He probably meant nothing by it. Even Ismerelda seemed a bit uncouth when speaking of some subjects. Laedron sighed. "If the scepter seems in good condition to you, then perhaps it is just me."

"Just you? Has something happened that you haven't revealed?"

"When I cast a spell the other day, it seemed as if it suddenly became harder before I could finish my casting, like something that had been helping me stopped without warning."

"And you were using that rod at the time?"

Laedron bobbed his head.

"Easy. The power's been depleted."

Hanging his head, Laedron asked, "Depleted?"

"Yes, exhausted. Spent—"

"I know what the word means. How has the thing been depleted, exactly?"

"Just as we rejuvenate ourselves, we can create wands, staffs, and scepters fueled with essence, and this makes spells cast with that instrument easier to perform and more potent."

"Then it is as I've feared." Laedron stuck the scepter in his belt, intent to carry it for sentimental purposes instead of utilitarian reasons.

"Why are you sad? You merely need to recharge it."

"And how does one do that?"

"Those soulstones would do the trick, and if each one contains the essence of a man, you could use a few of them, and the charge would last another hundred years or so. Would you like me to teach you the spell?"

A hundred years? Fascinating how these people think and plan in terms of centuries or millennia where most people think about only today or tomorrow. "Yes."

"Would your companions prefer for us to go elsewhere? It could take some time."

"Marac?" Laedron asked.

"It's a bit tight in here. It'd probably be best if you did."

"What about you, Brice?"

"He's right. Wouldn't want someone accidentally turned into a toad, after all."

Laedron chuckled. "No, that would be terrible indeed. Val?"

"Yes, but I'd like to come with you."

"You would?"

"I might learn something. You said you'd teach me."

"Yes, but I don't think it would benefit you. This sort of magic is beyond my expertise, and being there could be detrimental to your learning."

"I suppose you would know best." She sat at the table, but Laedron could tell she wasn't happy.

"When we get to that point, I'll teach you. I promise."

Looking over her shoulder, she smiled. "All right."

Laedron nodded, slipped off his pack, and turned to Tavin. "Did you have a place in mind?"

❧ Chapter Ten ❧

Meaningless Morals

Through the adjacent hallway and by glimmer of dim light, Tavin led Laedron to the huge pit they had passed on the way to the shelter. Laedron imagined that Tavin had a rather pitiful existence because the few places they could visit consisted of a dreary room full of refugees, an office with basic wood furniture, and an unending hole in the ground.

"Would you care for something to drink, or should we get straight to it?" Tavin asked, holding a cup to the rocky wall near the start of the bridge. The water coming through the cracks slowly filled it.

His mouth dry from traveling, Laedron said, "Yes, a drink would be quite welcome. Thank you."

Tavin passed Laedron the full cup. "Though it may taste strange to you, the water, I assure you, is safe."

Sipping, Laedron detected a distinct flavor, the taste of metal and minerals, and the fluid seemed a bit thicker than what he used to drinking. In fact, he couldn't recall any other time where his taste buds had been so offended by a simple swig of water, and he couldn't help but wonder if that deplorable water would be the last thing he ever tasted. *It could be, for I have no way of knowing when the magic will wear off.*

"Why do you look saddened? Is it not to your liking?"

"I have no idea what I am anymore."

"No? A sorcerer, are you not?"

Laedron handed the cup back to Tavin. "In Azura, I was nearly killed by the Zyvdredi. I would've died if not for a spell... well, priests call them miracles, and it was a priest who performed it."

"The healing arts are common amongst all practitioners of magic."

"This time, it was different. The priest in question used a soulstone to increase the power of his miracle, and after that, I couldn't sleep and didn't feel the need to eat for several days. I even healed at an astonishing rate."

"Ah, yes. When one uses an essence for a spell, the magic can stay longer without need of further concentration or commitment. He could've made the spell extend longer had he known how."

"So, it's temporary?"

"Indeed. The spell fades away as the essence does. If you fail to seal in the essence, it will dissipate considerably faster than otherwise, but 'considerably faster' has a different meaning to me than it might for you, yes? It's relative to one's point of view."

Laedron swallowed deeply. "Am I going to die?"

122

"Yes, but not on account of that." Tavin smiled. "The spell has probably given you a wellspring of longevity, though, so do not be surprised if you should go on for the next few centuries or so."

A few centuries? His eyes widened, and he considered the possibility of living past all of his friends and family, watching all of them pass away before he would be given the gift of death. "Centuries? As in, hundreds of years? You're sure?"

"The amount of essence held within Zyvdredi soulstones can vary, for a single stone can contain the life force of several men. The essence of three men is roughly equivalent to two hundred years, and a full stone could contain... twelve, maybe."

"Is there any way to drain off the excess?"

"No, I'm afraid. If someone tried to take away some of the essence, they could take too little or too much. It's not very precise, and we have no way of knowing how much essence you've been given."

"Then I will eventually pass?"

"Yes, and I'm stricken by your relief at that fact; most do not want to meet their ends. All living things die, my friend. Unless, of course, you're *inducted*."

"Inducted?"

"What's the difference between the Uxidin and the race of men?" Tavin asked.

"Uxidin are an ancient race of immortal mages," Laedron said. *He wants me to explain that which he already knows?* "Men... are just men."

"Uxidin *are* men, young mage... at least, we *were*. We have merely taken our knowledge of magic to another level, a level beyond normal understanding. We've made ourselves immortal, into masters of the elements. Do you not see? We have *created* our own race, and in doing so, we've forged a new existence, a new destiny."

Laedron had long suspected something other than the

common myths. "It makes sense."

"Of course it does. Often the simplest explanation is the correct one. Your wand, please." Tavin extended his open hand. "And the soulstones."

"I know you said that only the essence remains, but I still have reservations."

"What reservations?"

Laedron stared at the rod. "My teacher taught me many things of magic, and she said that Necromancy was quite real. You say that it is not. Who should I believe?"

"You cling to a vestigial belief that magic is nicely split into schools, as if designed that way. You fail to realize that your teacher taught in the Azuran way, the same manner that all the other mortals were instructed. And the reason for that? To control new mages, to keep them from experimenting with spells for which they weren't prepared."

"Why would she, or Azura, for that matter, do that? The only way to mastery is through the truth."

"Indeed, but you must put things into perspective for the new ones. If you took ten men and trained them with spells, careless of morality and implications, most of them would become nothing better than a Zyvdredi soul-dealer. The *aspects*... do they still use that term?"

"Yes."

"Aspects are merely a way of categorizing magic so that neonates can understand it, and it's far easier to teach spellcraft when the chaos seems orderly. In fact, magic is just as chaotic as any other force in nature, and the only thing that orders it is our command of it. When you can think of magic as something to bend to your will, you can unlock its full potential."

"You speak of wizardry."

"Indeed." Tavin smiled. "You seem to have a wonderful talent for magic, a gift that could have been left to waste away in some stuffy academy. It was fortunate that you learned from an Uxidin, and had you completed your training under her, you might have learned a great deal more about these things."

"What sort of things?"

"I shouldn't reveal anything else. You'll speak to the Far'rah in due time, and until then, I should tell you no more of this. For now, I'll show you the spell needed to recharge your scepter."

"I still don't know—"

"Doubt is the true mage killer, and even an Azuran teacher would have told you that. Give up your meaningless morals, for they do not apply here. Have you heard nothing that I've said? You blind yourself with a lie perpetrated to control you. Set yourself free."

"It doesn't seem right using their life forces for my benefit. These are men's souls we're dealing with."

"You're trying to apply a lifetime of societal norms you've been taught to something of which you have absolutely no experience or knowledge. That path leads to a place you would not like to delve, a place filled with speculation, judgment, and fanaticism. Leave those things to the Heraldan church, for their duty is to spread fear, hypocrisy, and ignorance of the things they do not understand."

"But—"

"Did you imprison the essences of these men? Did you take them in the first place?"

"No, but that doesn't mean that I should use—"

"Incorrect. As a matter of fact, it's even more justification to put these resources to their best use, to serve you in doing good. Given the option between serving a Zyvdredi master or a sorcerer with a good heart and intentions, what do you think these men would have chosen?"

"I cannot say. They very well could have chosen a third option, to serve neither."

Tavin sighed. "If that is what you want, I can release the energy, but I think you should open your mind and take a look at things without relying on the simplicities of good and evil, white and black. When you can do that, you'll find that most everything in life lies between the two, in a saturation of gray, and decisions should be based on more than some scale invented to cull the herd and to keep their Circle of sorcerers in line and easily managed."

When Tavin raised his wand, Laedron stopped him. "Wait. Let me consider things for a moment."

Tavin leaned against the ropes of the bridge with his arms folded and a glare of impatience.

What would my mother do? What about Ismerelda? Would either of them pass up this opportunity? He wondered how much his mother really knew, how much knowledge she had kept from him over the years, teaching him about *aspects*, the good and evil magic and the meaning of spellcraft. *Perhaps she adhered to what she was taught. Maybe Ismerelda never revealed any of this to her. Ismerelda.* He didn't know what to think of his teacher. Being Uxidin, she must have known everything that Tavin said. *She was inducted like all the others. Immortal. Learned in the secrets of magic, the truth behind the veil.*

He eyed Tavin, then looked away. *Is he telling the truth? He seems sincere, and he maintains the tone and expression of someone who believes what he's saying. No one could create lies at such speed and on a whim. Does he have my best interests at heart? Why would he? Or is he merely trying to educate me, to help me achieve the next level of enlightenment? Creator, forgive me if I'm wrong.* "I've made my decision."

"And that is?"

"Recharge it."

With a nod, Tavin approached. "Do you have a spare?"

"A spare? A spare what?"

"Wand. Or other instrument. Unless you can conjure spells

without one."

"Can it be done?"

"A *wizard* can do many things normal sorcerers cannot, for they possess a higher mastery of magic."

"Can you?"

Tavin shook his head. "It's not from lack of trying, I assure you, but alas, no. Something seems to be missing, something in the puzzle that I cannot decipher."

From his boot, Laedron drew his beginner wand.

Tavin nodded. "The motions are like any other prolonged spell, a rhythmic wave to and fro, but the words differ widely from anything you've likely heard. Hold the soulstone in your palm and your wand in the same hand, then repeat the incantation." Tavin recited the words of power, then gestured for Laedron to begin.

Laedron swayed his wand over the scepter, and soon, swirls of violet and red energy appeared, then passed between his palm and the ruby at the scepter's tip. For every moment Laedron maintained the spell, the scepter's gem seemed to pulse brighter and brighter, as if the stone itself was coming to life once more, while the swirling light in the black onyx soulstone faded to black.

When Laedron finished the first casting of the spell, Tavin pointed at the leather pouch containing the other stones. "One more and your rod should carry a charge more than sufficient for the remainder of your days."

After taking another stone in hand, Laedron cast the spell and maintained it until the onyx had been depleted and the ruby shone bright and vibrant. "It's never looked like that."

"No?"

"Since I first saw it, the stone seemed lackluster. Pretty, but dull."

"Your teacher had likely gone quite some time since recharging it."

"Would she have?"

"Ah, perhaps I spoke too soon. You said that she lived within a mortal city?"

Laedron nodded, replacing the scepter at his hip.

"One can draw the essence from just about any living thing. Perhaps she pulled from the vegetation nearby—saplings, bushes, and other plants, or maybe even some small animals."

Laedron thought back to the first time he'd seen Ismerelda's house in Westmarch. The grass had grown like islands in a sea of mud, and a few dead bushes fronted the place. There had been holes where trees had obviously once stood. "How do you judge the amount of essence something has? Is there any way of knowing with certainty?"

"Difficult to say, and many have theories. Some say that the number of days left in a life determine how powerful the essence is. Whereas a newborn would possess a powerful essence, an old man would have the least. I have my doubts, for how could you ever prove it? It's not as if the number of days remaining in one's life is clearly stamped upon the forehead."

"What do *you* think?"

"The longevity, or perhaps the complexity of the essence, seems to be the most important. For example, one can garner little essence from a sapling, but from an ancient pine, one requires special implements and specific spells to extract the power, and great that power is. If a man would give, say, the equivalent of fifty years of essence, the ancient trees could give off a thousand years or more." Tavin glanced at the glimmering jewel in the scepter. "Oh, I nearly forgot. We must seal in the energy, for it will lose its charge rapidly if we do not. Gemstones cannot retain essence as readily as flesh unless they are especially crafted for the purpose. Those black onyxes that you carry are prime examples of well-made soulstones."

Laedron grasped the leather pouch and felt his stomach churn. *Only the best for the Drakkars.*

Tavin snapped his fingers. "No daydreaming. Repeat these words, and the jewel shall retain the essence."

Laedron listened closely and did as he was told. Though the light from the ruby dulled somewhat, the stone still glowed. "It reminds me of the ring Andolis wore."

"Andolis?"

"One of the Zyvdredi masters in Azura. He caused the death of the Grand Vicar, then stole his essence and fused it within a ring of black onyx. We retrieved the ring when we killed him, and now, you've told me that there's no way to free him, no way to bring him back to life."

"And you said his name was Andolis?"

"Yes, do you know of him?"

"No, but it doesn't sound like a Zyvdredi name. Could it have been an alias, perhaps?"

Looking at the ceiling, Laedron tried to recall the events in Azura. Finally, he said, "Yes, it was. He assumed the identity of a priest named Andolis Drakkar, whom he probably murdered somewhere in eastern Lasoron. The only name we found was *Kivesh*, a name tattooed on the neck of his—"

"Kivesh?" Tavin's eyes widened with apparent shock. "Are you certain about that?"

"Yes, why?"

"Does anyone else know that you killed him?"

"It's practically common knowledge throughout the eastern world. Why?"

"That's a serious problem for you." Tavin patted Laedron on the shoulder. "The Kiveshes are well-regarded members of the Zyvdredi royal family. They may come looking for you if they have the resources to spare."

Wonderful. Now, I shall have Zyvdredi assassins chasing me to the ends of the earth. "How likely are they to come looking?"

"Truly difficult to say, and they may never come. If this

Andolis was that far outside of Zyvdredi territory, and trying to live in mortal society, no less, he could have been exiled. On the same note, he could have been part of a much larger plan."

"If I had to guess, I would say he was part of a bigger plot. He wasn't acting alone. In fact, he seemed to have an army of sorcerers under his charge."

"Were they all defeated?"

"Most, if not all."

"It could take them quite some time to recover from such a blow. Still, I would keep a close eye on my back if I were you."

"At least I know now."

"Indeed. Shall we return to your companions? Or did you have any other mistakes to divulge?"

He had to add salt to the wound, didn't he? "No, we should go back. When do I meet the Far'rah?"

"Tonight, most likely. I will arrange it." Tavin gestured at the hallway.

❧ Chapter Eleven ❧

Far'rah Harridan

L aedron walked in behind Tavin, and Marac and Brice appeared to be taking stock of their supplies.

Marac stood, then said, "We thought you'd never get back."

Tavin seemed to be averting his gaze from the supplies when he crossed the room, and he nearly tripped over his own belongings.

Laedron asked, "Are you well?"

"Forgive me. It's been quite some time since I've seen anything close to real food. I should leave you—"

"No." Laedron crouched next to his pack and removed the bags of salted meat and jerky. "Here, take it."

"I couldn't. Thank you for the offer, but I cannot eat this while the rest of my people starve. We'll make due."

Pouring the contents of his pack on the floor, Laedron took the tins in his arms. "Take all of it. This should be plenty to give your people a decent meal."

"What will you do, Sorcerer, when you grow hungry?" Tavin asked, taking the tins when Laedron forced them into his hands.

"We each left the city with enough in our packs to feed us for a few weeks. Don't worry about us. We have plenty left in our other bags."

Tavin opened the door. "Your generosity is uncommon, especially in these lands and certainly in these times. We thank you."

Laedron gave him a nod, waited for the door to close, then turned to Marac. "You seem anxious. Is something on your mind?"

"We've been talking, and I think we need to discuss this."

"Yes?"

Marac took a deep breath. "We have concerns about helping these people. What they ask, we think, isn't reasonable, Lae."

"Really? Why do you think that?"

"They're asking us to retrieve an ancient artifact so that they can continue living forever? It's unnatural. If they were meant to have the gift of eternal life, I think that they would've been born with it."

"Can you not see the suffering in their eyes? We can't just leave them, Marac."

"And why not? What stake have we in this?"

Laedron rubbed the back of his neck. "You? Little to none. For me, it's a bit more complicated."

"Explain it to us. Make us understand." Marac sat on the edge of the paltry table, its supports creaking with the added weight. "Right now, I don't think any of our hearts are in it."

"Even you?" Laedron asked Valyrie.

"He's right, Lae. We have to have a reason, some acceptable purpose, if we're expected to risk our lives for them. We have to know that what we're doing is right."

Have they turned her against me? Or is this a result of our earlier arguments? And Marac, how could he question me when we're so close to the answers? "The Uxidin have kept magic alive for thousands of years. Without them, it might have been lost along with the rest of history's secrets. To think, they shared the blessings of magic with mortal men, and now, mortal men have a chance to repay that debt —through us."

"The weight of the world isn't on our shoulders, and the debt isn't ours alone to pay," Marac said. "The odds are clearly against us, and what would we gain from it? The warm feeling of knowing that a few mages living deep in some ruins somewhere have benefited from our generosity?"

"Not everything comes with monetary rewards, but I'm sure the Far'rah could arrange that, if it suits you," Laedron said, the disdain dripping from his words.

"You needn't take that tone with me, Laedron Telpist. After all we've been through, I would've thought I could speak my mind without disrespect."

What has happened to me? Relax. Breathe. Calm yourself. "You're right. I'm sorry, Marac." Laedron rubbed his temples. "I've just been given some bad news."

"Lae, I'm sorry. I didn't mean to upset you at a time like this," Marac said, rushing to his side. "The spell is fading? We'll find a way, my friend. We won't let—"

"No, no. Nothing like that. Tavin seems confident that I will live despite what's happened of late, but he told me of the Kiveshes; we may be hunted since we were responsible for Andolis's death."

"Kiveshes?"

"When we found the body of the guard in the alley back in Azura, the tattoo on his neck was written in Zyv—" Laedron stopped to correct himself. "Nyreth."

"Ah, yes, the assassin in black." Marac pointed at himself. "It's my burden alone. I dealt the killing blow."

"I don't think they'll care who actually killed him. We all had a part in it. Except Valyrie, her involvement was mostly kept secret."

"They'll have trouble finding us out here. For now, we have other things to consider," Brice said. "At this moment, we have to decide if we'll help the Uxidin by getting this book of theirs."

"Through an army of those Trapper things?" Marac asked. "Deep in some old abandoned temple against some powerful mage? I respect you, Lae, and I understand how you feel, but I have to say no. We beat Andolis, but we were nearly killed in the process."

Marac is against me. Does he not trust me? Is he afraid? "What about the rest of you? Val?"

"No, Lae. We have no business getting in the middle of things that don't involve us. It's too risky."

Staring at the floor, Laedron pursed his lips. *Can I trust her after this? Can I depend on her to be at my side if she would choose to run at the thought of danger? At the inference of difficulty?* "And you, Brice?" *Need I even ask? He trembles at any suspicious sound.*

Brice glanced at Marac and Valyrie, then stood and joined Laedron on the other side of the room. "I'm with you, Lae."

"You?" Marac asked, standing with his arms folded. "The one afraid of his own shadow? The one scared of noises in the dark?"

Brice tilted his head. "What of it?"

"I'm just shocked at the sudden change of heart, Thimble. Now, you're the brave one?"

"No, not brave. Nothing like that. Not even close."

"What, then?"

"We said that we'd help Lae. I'm standing beside him until the end. He's brought us this far, and he saved my life."

Smiling, Laedron put his arm around Brice's shoulders. "Thank you. We'll do it together." He slapped Brice on the back, then gazed at Marac. "You asked me once if I was sure. You said that was all you needed to know. Well, I'm sure, Marac Reven. We must see this to its finish."

Marac thought for a while, sighed, then turned to Valyrie. "We can't split up, can we?"

"No, I suppose not."

"Then, we're with you, Lae."

"I'm not going to force you two."

"No." Marac walked over to him. "Whether it's home or the depths of some old temple, we go together or not at all. We won't abandon you."

"If we're to go forward, you must give up your fears and doubts. You must *know* that we'll succeed; merely believing in it won't be enough this time." Laedron put his hands on Marac's shoulders and stared into his eyes. "You have to *know*, the way you know that the sun rises in the morning, the way you know your own name. All of you."

"Do you believe that, Lae?" Brice asked, a hopeful look in his eyes.

"I know it as a fact. With my friends at my side, I can't see it any other way."

"Let us speak with this... what did you call him? Far'rah?" Marac asked, picking up his belongings.

Laedron grabbed his pack, opened the door, and found Tavin in the next chamber. "We've come to an agreement."

"And that is?"

"We will speak to Far'rah Harridan and see about retrieving the tome from Kareth." Everyone in the room paused from eating, as if the name carried with it a fear strong enough to still a beating heart.

"We don't speak of him. It makes it easier on us if we don't speak of the one responsible for all this misery," Tavin said. "I will take you to the Far'rah."

Tavin led them through a door Laedron hadn't noticed before, into a narrow corridor, then to a circular chamber with a man clothed in dirty purple cloth kneeling in front of a shrine of some sort.

"Far'rah? These visitors would like to see you," Tavin said.

In the center of the room, a circular stone altar had been built, and light shone straight down upon it from a bright, luminescent gem. Simple pine furniture—a bed, a desk, and a chair—sat in the far corner.

Without looking up, the man said, "There was a time when I would see guests, Tavingras. That time has passed."

"This time, it's different, Far'rah. They have come to retrieve The Bloodmyr Tome for us, to wrest it from Kareth's grasp."

"How is this time any different from any of the others? Those who came before have failed. Has it been so long that you've forgotten the empty promises of all the would-be rescuers?" He stood and turned to them. His pale skin glowed in the dim light, his flowing silver hair an unlikely match compared to his youthful countenance. "What makes you believe these mortal children would stand a chance against Kareth and his Trappers?"

"This one's a sorcerer, Far'rah." Tavin kept his head tilted downward, his eyes averted. "Rare that a sorcerer comes—"

"Is it enough to make a difference? Sorcerers have come with their lackeys before."

Marac grumbled at the man's words. "We are not lackeys."

After a brief pause, Tavin said, "They've had a long journey here, Far'rah. Forgive their disrespect."

"I have had the misfortune of dealing with outlanders a handful of times while aiding the previous Far'rah. I do not intend to make the same mistakes she did. I will not put my faith in any reckless mortal and waste effort believing in a miracle."

"Should we depart, then?" Marac asked. "Lae? If we're unwanted here, should we return home?"

"We don't need permission," Laedron said, eying the Far'rah and pointing over his shoulder. "All of those people out there are suffering."

"Oh, but you will need my help, won't you?" The Far'rah approached Laedron and his companions. "Isn't that right, Tavingras? They don't stand a chance without our aid."

"Yes, Far'rah."

"Yes, Far'ah..." Turning away from them, Harridan clasped his hands behind his back and slowly walked to the other side of the room. "You see, my young friends, we have been working on a plan to retake the tome. Since we haven't had any new volunteers, Tavingras and I were preparing ourselves for one last attempt to retrieve it."

Laedron took a few steps forward. "How, if you don't mind my asking?"

"This is one of the tools we would use." Harridan pulled a sword from beneath the nearby altar and twirled it above his head.

"I have one of those," Marac said, grasping the hilt of his blade. "I don't see how it would be much use against the—"

Harridan slammed the blade against a stone block. A crack of thundered blasted in Laedron's eardrums, and he couldn't hear anything over the ringing that followed. When the dust cleared, Harridan stood before the remains of a brick split in two, the majority of it falling to the ground in the form of a fine powder.

Digging in his ears, Laedron asked, "How is that possible? Have you used the sword as a casting implement?"

With a broad grin, Harridan returned the weapon to its place under the altar. "You must not be much of a sorcerer if you're asking me that question. How else?"

"Magic fused into a blade?" Laedron's mind drifted at the possibilities. "You've found a way to bind magic to a sword?"

"Is it such a far stretch?" Tavin pointed at Laedron's scepter. "If we can charge rods and wands with essence, can we not do the same for anything? The problem, which we have overcome, was how to do it with a specific effect, so that the weapon would produce the same event when it struck its target."

"'Twas a simple thing when all was said and done, really," Harridan said. "It was only a matter of keeping the spell from being cast constantly, to ensure that it only occurred under certain conditions. In the case of a sword, the condition would be when connecting with a target."

"If you have weapons such as these, why couldn't you defeat Kareth? What makes you think we would stand a better chance than you?" Marac asked.

"Desperate times call for desperate measures, Swordsman." Sitting on the edge of the stone altar, Harridan cleared his throat, probably because he inhaled a fair amount of dust. "We thought we had the advantage the first time we attacked. When many of our people were killed, we had to come up with a new plan of action. Well, after we found a way to hide from the Trappers and keep our people safe, that is. The adventurers, young people like you, kept coming, and each time they failed to retrieve the tome for us. Nearly a decade has passed since the last group, and now, you're here."

Tavin, his palms up, spread his arms and approached Harridan. "They could be our best chance, Far'rah. And they have soulstones to enchant more of our weapons."

"Not so fast," Laedron said. "If we're to help you, we'll use our own weapons, and you'll show me how to imbue them."

Harridan shook his head. "You think that I would share this secret with the likes of you? One of the greatest, most profound breakthroughs in magic since immortality itself? I think not."

"What will you do, then?" Laedron thought about something Ismerelda had told him once, about how the Uxidin wouldn't help Azura defend the humans in the Great War. "You would risk your eternal lives doing battle with Kareth? One slip, one mistake, and you'll die like everyone else."

Groping his neck as if it had been pierced, Harridan sighed.

"A small price to pay, perhaps. Before I agree, I would speak to Tavingras in private."

Nodding, Laedron led his companions back into the corridor and closed the door behind them. "That seems to have gone well."

"Did it? Why would you trade a simple spell for the tome?" Marac asked. "For something as risky as this, we should be well compensated. They must have something worthy of our efforts down here."

"Can you not see how useful such a spell could be?" Laedron pointed at the glowing gems illuminating the hall. "Permanent magic, Marac. We could produce everlasting lamps."

"Lanterns? This is about lanterns?" Brice asked. "Why would I risk my life for some bloody lanterns when we have cheap candles and torches to see by?"

"Lanterns, yes, amongst other things. If you could make magic permanent, you would have a distinct advantage over your enemies. Common people could use things made by mages, things imbued with powerful spells."

Valyrie shook her head. "Is that such a good idea? If you give magic to everyone, the world would become quite a dangerous place. Besides, what if the same thing that happened to Zyvdred happens everywhere? Forests and mountains devoid of life, and men killing others for their essence? You'll need soulstones in vast supply if you intend to give the world these magical trinkets, Lae."

"Not the whole world." Laedron rubbed his chin. "Such a plan would take further thought, but of what they have to offer, I'm convinced that the spell alone is worth the trouble."

The door creaked open, and Tavin said, "The Far'rah has agreed."

Laedron glanced at Marac, then walked past him into the abbey. "Then it is done?"

"It is," Harridan said. "I will teach you how to imbue your weapons, and in exchange, you will take Tavin to retrieve The

Bloodmyr Tome."

"Far'rah, I... you would send me?" Tavin asked. "Have I not served you well?"

"Indeed, you have, but one of our people must go with them as a guide. Would you rather I go, Tavingras?"

"No, of course not, but—"

"Who else has the knowledge of the ruins? You're the only one who has ventured to the surface in months."

Reluctantly, Tavin replied, "Yes, Far'rah. I will go."

"Good." Harridan turned to Laedron. "Do you need rest?"

Laedron looked at his friends, and their worn expressions told him the answer without them speaking a word. "Yes. We've had little sleep."

"Then, you'll go late in the morning. The Trappers are less active during the daylight. Isn't that right, Tavin?"

"Yes, Far'rah."

"Take them to your chamber, then, and I shall teach this sorcerer the spell he desires. Return to me before you leave, and I shall give you my blessing."

Tavin led Marac, Brice, and Valyrie out, and Laedron remained with Harridan until he could, with confidence, reproduce the spell and enchant items with magical effects.

Finally, Harridan said, "There is one thing I should relay before you go."

"And that is?"

"The essence, no matter the source, seems to last considerably longer in items in comparison to a living being. Whereas our bodies need the energy constantly, imbued items only expend energy when they're used. Thus, the sword you enchanted with the sonic charm could last many lifetimes even with moderate use."

"Thank you."

Harridan nodded, and Laedron exited into the hall, then

joined his friends in Tavin's quarters.

* * *

Having settled down and eaten their evening meals, Laedron and his companions gathered in the corner where Tavin had told them they could sleep for the night. *Stone floors.* Laedron shuffled in his bedroll in an attempt to find comfort where none existed. Marac seemed to have little trouble falling asleep because he was snoring only a few minutes after they had lain down. In fact, Laedron soon found himself the only one awake, except for Tavin, who sat at his table reading an old, dusty tome.

Laedron stood and crept across the floor, being careful not to disturb the others. Once he reached Tavin's desk, he asked, "Did any of them check on our horses?"

"Yes, the little boy did."

"Little boy?"

"That one." Tavin pointed at Brice.

"He's not much younger than us, really. If memory serves, we're less than a year apart in age."

"I see." Keeping his place with his finger, Tavin closed his book, then gazed at Laedron's bedroll. "You don't have to lie there all night."

"No?"

"Read a book or study a map if you like. To stare at the ceiling for hours would be a waste of time if you can't sleep."

"Oh, my sleep has thankfully returned. It took days, but it came back."

"I've never seen someone regain their sleep. Then again, we always completed the font rituals, and we used essences far stronger than those you would have absorbed from Zyvdredi gems."

Laedron nodded, then examined the nondescript leather

cover of the book in Tavin's hands. "What sort of book is that?"

"Azura's journal," Tavin said, as if it were normal reading material. "When we went to Kareth's lair, he had created Trappers and Netheren. Before we go back, I want to see if these pages hold any secrets on how to defeat them—the undead, that is."

Laedron's jaw dropped. *Azura's journal? Her personal writings, straight from her hand to the pages?* "How can that be? Anything written by Azura must be centuries old, far older than any book could survive."

"It was my job as Caretaker of the Tomes to keep the old works from falling into disrepair, to ensure that they lasted for future generations." Looking at Laedron over the top of the book, Tavin smiled. "In these times, we're willing to do anything to feel as we did when our empire was strong. Far'rah Harridan meditates in private and offers prayers to the Creator. I read and maintain my collection of books and scrolls."

Laedron leaned across the table to steal a glance at the writing. "Did you ever meet her?"

"No. By the time we heard of her great deeds, she had already disappeared into the wilderness, and no one ever saw her again. A shame."

"Ismerelda, my teacher, told me about her. She said that when Tristan turned his back on her, Azura left Uxidia and hid herself and her broken heart. Is that true?"

"More or less, yes. Azura spoke of Tristan at length in her journal, and of her pain when he chastised her. She unknowingly prevented the total collapse of what remained of the empire in her time. Or I should say, she slowed down that eventuality."

"The empire wasn't going to last?" Laedron asked, sitting on the other chair.

"What we had in the old empire was doomed to fail. We'd grown too large, too decadent. We had too many different ideas of what we should do and how we should govern. When the nobles fractured, so did our nation, and it has never been the same since."

"So, Kareth didn't cause Myrdwyer to crumble?"

"No, that happened much longer ago. Myrdwyer was a loyalist city—to the empire—and had been since its founding. When Lasoron became an independent state, Myrdwyer had extreme difficulty in gaining any assistance from the empire, for the imperials, weakened by the schism, were unwilling to make an enemy out of the Lasoronians. With no military protection and being unable to maintain the city, our people fled, our buildings collapsed, and eventually, we became what you see now: a broken group of survivors hiding beneath a fallen city.

"As time went along, the immortals who used to live in Lasoron, the ones outside Myrdwyer, started to die off, and the people lived as mortals. The knowledge of magic passed to fewer and fewer descendants of the original nobles of House Lasoron, and now, you'd be hard pressed to find a sorcerer within these borders."

"How do you know these things if you stay here in the forest?"

"We haven't always been so reclusive. There was a time when we ventured out into the world, but the world has little use for us. The adventurers, the ones like you and your friends, brought some news with them, as well."

"Can you tell me why Kareth killed an Elder Priest and stole The Bloodmyr Tome?"

"The Elder Priest had two apprentices, Harridan and Kareth. When the time came to declare an heir, she selected Harridan, and Kareth was filled with rage."

"A revenge killing?"

"Yes."

Feeling tired, Laedron extended his arms and stretched his back. "Could I ask one more question?"

"If it suits you."

"If The Bloodmyr Tome is the only thing which can be used for the renewal spell, how do the other Uxidin around the world maintain their immortality? Do they come here seeking renewal?"

"Yes. At least, they have in the past."

"They were unwilling to help?"

"We haven't had a chance to ask. We performed a number of renewals prior to Kareth's theft, but we have only had one other Uxidin pass through since then. Our people are few in the wide world, and they have had no need for us in the thousand years or so between their rejuvenation rituals."

"Why not send word to them and seek their help?"

Tavin shook his head. "We've tried, my young friend. Don't assume that we haven't done everything we could imagine to get the tome back."

"Well, what did they say to your message?"

"Some of the messengers didn't return. Those who did all had the same answer: it's Myrdwyer's problem. Myrdwyer had the tome, and Myrdwyer should get it back."

"If we get it for you, will you help them in the future?"

Tavin nodded. "Likely so, but that is the decision of the Far'rah. I have no part in it."

"Why would you, though? If they take such a position against you and refuse to help, why help them when they need it?"

"The Far'rah receives tribute in exchange for his services, and we will need that tribute to have any hope of rebuilding what we've lost. It could take hundreds of years, if not thousands, but we're confident that our city will stand once again."

Suddenly, Laedron felt small and inconsequential, the same way he had felt when he first thought of the war between the Uxidin and the Zyvdredi. *We are but pawns in the dealings of the immortals.* Laedron's presence, their conversation, and perhaps all of their deeds tomorrow would become nothing more than a blink of the eye to these people. *Ismerelda told me that her memory remained accurate for only the past fifty years or so, except for major, life-changing events. A century from now, will these people remember anything about what we've done?* He closed his eyes. *A century from now, will I? Will I forget about Ma and Laren? Marac and Brice? My Valyrie? Am I doomed to lose my memories as Ismerelda did? Creator… in time, I must find a way to reverse this.*

❧ Chapter Twelve ❧

The Catacombs of Myrdwyer

Laedron woke to Tavin shaking his shoulder. "Is it time already?"

"Indeed." Tavin moved to the door. "We'll receive the Far'rah's blessings, and we'll be off. Prepare yourselves."

Blinking rapidly, Laedron stared at Tavin, for he looked nothing as he had the night prior. Instead of robes, Tavin wore tight-fitting leathers, a set of armor decorated with a floral design. The cloak flowing down his back had no flaws that Laedron noticed, and the man had weapons and wands fixed to his waist by a thick belt. "Equipped like that, you seem more like a warrior than a librarian."

"I assumed ownership of these effects when our last attack failed. Some were mine before, and the rest belonged to one of our soldiers." Tavin tugged and pulled at the tunic. "Not a perfect fit, but it's close enough."

"Seems good enough to me," Laedron said, then turned to his friends. "Before we go, I should prepare our weapons. I've already enchanted this sword."

Brice took the blade when Laedron offered it. "If we're to fight huge, hulking monsters, I'll need something longer than my dagger."

"Be careful with that. Striking anything with it will summon a blast of sound capable of cracking stone, and bones and flesh are softer than rock. Marac, what would you prefer for your blade?"

After considering the question, Marac gazed at Tavin. "Any suggestions?"

"He can imbue the weapon with any spell he knows."

"Of course, but what sort of challenges will we face?"

"Within Kareth's lair, there will be Trappers and Netheren. We could face wild animals, but they're the least of our concerns."

"Netheren?" Brice asked, glancing at the sword Laedron had given him. "Will this work on those?"

"The undead? It's not so much the tool as it is the method."

Seeing a puzzled look on Brice's face, Laedron said, "He means, cut off the head. Anything with an edge can do that."

"Oh, right."

Marac shrugged. "I'll think about it. Come back to me, would you?"

"Very well. Val, what would you want for your bow?"

"I won't be able to cut off the head of anything with it, and I've never heard of a bow that can break stone. Whatever you think would be best."

Lightning? No, that would be of little use against either enemy. Flames? She could burn the undead, but cannot set crystal ablaze. A bit dangerous, too, if an arrow went astray. Ice? It might not work.

"We used to enchant our bows with force spells," Tavin offered.

Laedron was surprised. "Force spells? How does that work?"

"You put an enchantment on the arrows so that, upon impact, they release an incredible force in every direction. If the force is strong enough and applied at the right location, it could separate limbs from the body or even crack the crystal structures of the Trappers."

"Excellent suggestion," Laedron said, taking the quiver from Valyrie. He imbued the arrows with the strongest force spell he could recall. Once he had finished, Laedron turned to Marac again. "Have you decided?"

"What about making it indestructible?"

"I don't think anything can be made indestructible and still be useful. I could make the blade ethereal, but it would do you no good."

"How about the sharpness, then? Make the blade so fine that it can slice through anything with little effort."

Laedron stared at the ceiling, deep in contemplation, then said, "I don't know about slicing through *everything*, but I'll give it a shot."

Marac handed over his sword, and Laedron cast a spell. When he finished, Laedron pulled the remaining soulstones from the sack. "Two left."

"Let us hope they won't be needed," Tavin said, opening the door. "Ready now?"

Laedron gave him a nod, then walked with his companions behind Tavin through the corridor. Laedron stopped Tavin just outside the door to the Far'rah's abbey. "You mentioned an attack that your people made against Kareth. Have you seen where he hides? Do you know the layout?"

"I only know of the entrance. When we attacked the temple,

we barely reached the front door before we were driven back. His foul creations chased us all the way here, and we had to collapse the tunnel to keep them from getting in."

"So, you have no idea how to get around his sanctum?" Marac asked.

"No, as I said, I know the entrance. From there, we'll have to find the way," Tavin said, opening the door and leading them into the abbey.

Tavin bowed before the altar. "We are ready, my Far'rah."

Laedron fell to his knees, and his companions did the same.

"Then, let you be blessed in your struggle this day." Harridan approached with his staff in hand. "We would go forward only by the will of the Creator, and we hope that we please him in all things, for he is the beginning, the journey, and the end."

Far'rah Harridan raised his staff over their heads and repeated an incantation. A rain of gold sparkles floated onto them from the giant sapphire imbedded in the staff's head. "May you be unmatched in the fight to come, and may the Creator see you safe to your home."

Tavin rose, but Harridan held up his hand. "Tavingras, wait. I would see you for a moment before you leave. Sorcerer, will you and your companions wait outside?"

Laedron nodded, then took Marac, Brice, and Valyrie into the hall, closing the door behind them. Trying to ignore the Uxidin watching them from the next chamber, he stared at the ground. *I don't think I've felt this awkward in all my life. Must they stare in such a way? It's unnerving how they never speak. It's like being a beggar at a royal banquet... or is that a royal in the slums? No matter. Hurry up, Tavin. How long could some parting words take?*

Having taken far too long for Laedron's liking, Tavin finally emerged from the room and gave them a vacant stare. *What did Harridan tell him? He seems so preoccupied.* Tavin signaled Laedron with a nod, then led the way through the corridor and across the rope bridge over the bottomless pit. Once clear of the bridge, Tavin picked up speed, racing through the earthen tunnel and up the stone stairs.

Tavin glanced at the horses resting on the floor when he reached the top. "You'll have no need of your horses. They should be safe here." Touching the wall, he uttered a few words, and what had been the wood of the tree transformed into a window of swirling energy. "One at a time. It may feel strange to you, but keep walking."

Walking through to the forest he could see on the other side, Laedron felt a prickling sensation on his skin until he was no longer touching the portal. Laedron, his scepter at the ready, scanned the forest until the others joined him, watching for any threats.

Tavin emerged from the opening, took a quick left, and jogged along the path to the north, and Laedron and his friends struggled to keep up. When he passed a bluff, Laedron could see the view which had been obscured by the terrain, and he beheld the spectacle that had once been the temple. Its huge walls were broken and strewn, as if they had been struck by a mighty hammer. In the center of what used to be a complex of buildings, a stone staircase led to a platform about thirty feet above the ground, and what remained of the altar and chapel sat atop it.

"I don't see how anyone could live there," Laedron said, gawking at the ruins.

Tavin crouched behind a boulder. "He doesn't; he resides deep beneath the surface."

Valyrie crept up to Laedron's side. "What's under there?"

"The catacombs."

"What would immortals need with catacombs?"

"We are immortal, but we are not impervious to harm, young lady. Immortals meet their ends sometimes, too, and the bodies must be housed when the soul departs. It has always been our way."

Laedron gulped. "Could Kareth… reanimate those long-dead bodies?"

"Indeed, and we know that he has done so, for when he countered our attack, a large portion of his forces were Netheren, their faces familiar to all of us. It was horrible fighting against the bodies of people you once knew, those who had been transformed into shadows of their former selves."

"How many?"

"Hundreds, but don't worry."

"Don't worry, he says," Brice scoffed. "It's only hundreds of undead. Everything will be just fine."

"We killed many of them, and they're weak and single-minded. We're only in danger if they attack in numbers."

"What sorts of spells work best against them?" Laedron asked, doing his best to ignore the terror of fighting legions of dead men.

"Fire is quite effective, for corpses dry out soon after death. Separating the body from the head is also useful, so any spell that can accomplish that would be the first choice. A body that cannot see, hear, or bite tends to be far less dangerous."

"I suppose we should get to it, then." Marac buckled his shield to his arm and drew his sword. "We'll do little good staring at the place from afar."

Tavin nodded, then led them along the path, which snaked its way down the steep hill. When he reached the front of the temple, he turned to the left, passing the stone steps and heading to a small door in the side of the building. Then, Tavin produced a glowing gem from a pouch at his hip. "It's dark within these halls. Unfortunately, they'll see us coming before we see them."

We'll give away the advantage of surprise, but we can't navigate the place in the blind. "A risk we'll have to take."

Tavin pulled the handle, then jumped to the side as the door fell to the ground. "As I said, the buildings are in disrepair."

"That doesn't worry me." Laedron peered into the darkness. "How far that echoed is what concerns me."

"Can't help it now," Tavin said. Laedron and his companions followed him inside the building.

The smell is nothing like what I thought it would be. The mustiness hung in the air like the smell of ale in a tavern. *Perhaps the scent of decay lessens over time.* He had little experience with the dead, for Sorbians—at least those living outside the big cities— buried the fallen in earthen graves instead of placing them in catacombs, and the bodies he'd dealt with apparently hadn't been dead long enough to have an odor strong enough to detect.

Thankfully Tavin went first, and while he seemed cautious of his surroundings, he must have had nerves of steel because he walked with a certain confidence down the narrow stairwell. Laedron couldn't say the same, for every scrape of boot against stone, every droplet of water falling and echoing in the pitch black, and each gust of breeze put him on edge. The hairs on the back of his neck stood tall and straight like the ancient trees in the forest.

Reaching the bottom, Tavin glanced over his shoulder at them, then whispered something to the gem in his hand. The shard grew brighter, illuminating the vast chamber beyond the end of the stairs.

"What is this?" Laedron whispered, tiptoeing up to Tavin's side.

"You've never been in a catacomb before?"

"No, I can't say that I visit them often."

"We're entering the first hypogeum." Tavin kept his volume low as he walked. "And as Uxidin catacombs go, the first chamber is the largest. We build them big enough so as not to need extensions, but we've found the need to expand after the passing of time—centuries, mind you. It was built to house hundreds, and we filled those spots quickly.

"The shelves in the center were added later when we needed extra space, for the cost for digging was higher. Eventually, we had to add more antechambers off the main one, and so on, until the place held thousands of our lost brothers and sisters."

Laedron eyed the loculi in the nearby walls, the bodies placed in their own cavities, sometimes within and sometimes without a sarcophagus. "Thousands..."

Hearing the clattering of metal, Laedron looked at Brice, noticing his hand shaking and the rings of his chain glove tapping the hilt of his sword, and said, "Calm yourself. A few still graves —"

Tavin's hand shot over Laedron's mouth, and Laedron struggled to free himself until he heard a hiss from the distant darkness, an unnatural, airy sound like that of the final breath leaving a body. Then, he saw what had approached the edge of the light. The Netheren's desiccated skin hung on its bones like ribbons, dry and tattered shreds, and the crusted leather armor wasn't in much better shape. It held an old blade that appeared cracked and rusted, but Laedron feared the weapon even more for its wear. *It's probably dull, too. And jagged. Such an edge would be unlikely to cut a clean wound. The suffering it would inflict... unthinkable.*

Laedron raised his scepter and pointed it at the walking corpse. He would have cast his spell—a blast of fire, probably—if he hadn't noticed all the glowing eyes surrounding them, a multitude of colored orbs in the darkness. *There must be hundreds of them.* Laedron elbowed Marac and pointed past Valyrie, then to the left and right.

Marac spun and searched for his first target, his sword glowing unnaturally. "What do we do, Lae?"

"I—" Laedron stared at Valyrie, unable to think of any strategy. *I hope that I live to see her face in the morning, that we both live to see it out of this mess.*

"Closing on the left," Brice said. "The right, too. They're all around us."

"A ring of flames." Tavin snapped his fingers in Laedron's face. "When they come close, summon fire around us and maintain it for as long as you can."

Bobbing his head, Laedron stood at the center of the group and waited for the undead to come near. When they were close enough, he repeated the words for the incantation. It came out a jumbled mess of stuttering.

"Focus, Sorcerer!" Tavin shot a look at Laedron, then peered at the approaching horde.

The undead had gotten within a few steps of them. Laedron cast the spell, and a ring of flames rose up around them.

One by one, the Netheren mindlessly entered the inferno. The dead were engulfed like twigs soaked in lantern fuel, but some continued despite the fire. With his shield, Marac shoved one of the burning creatures back. Brice kicked another, then stomped on the ground to extinguish his pants.

"It's working," Marac said. "They're—"

Lunging over the burning wall from the top of a nearby rack, a Netheren grabbed Marac and sent him to the ground. He tried to swing his sword, but he dropped it. The dagger pointed at his chest, Marac pushed up while the creature bore down.

Pointing her bow upward, Valyrie released an arrow, and it struck another creature dead in its center. The force spell manifested in a flash. The corpse split in two and landed at her feet, and Valyrie drew the bowstring back, searching for another target.

Losing focus at the sight of Marac beneath the fiend, Laedron had trouble maintaining his spell, and the flames flickered. "Somebody help him."

"Keep the spell going before you get us all killed," Tavin said, pushing past the Brice and delivering a kick to the dead thing's head. Crushed by the blow, the head erupted with worms and rotten brain matter. Laedron's stomach grumbled with disgust at the sight. Marac, covered with bits and pieces of some unknown black substance, pushed the dagger away, then clambered to his feet and continued the fight.

"They're not as stupid as you thought," Brice said after slashing a burning corpse and forcing it back into the flames. "Lae, make the fire bigger, taller."

Gritting his teeth, Laedron forced the blaze higher, too high for the Netheren to jump over it, and several corpses caught fire when they plunged into the flames. He had just smiled when he heard a voice echo throughout the crypt. He likened the voice to that of a drowning man, but raspier. He slowly turned to see a Netheren standing a hundred feet or more away—past the host of walking corpses—and atop a burial rack.

Marac walked over to Laedron. "What the...?"

"A spell!" Tavin raised his wand at the undead mage.

Laedron tried to control his breathing and lost his focus. Tavin had only gotten out a few words of his incantation when a deluge of water fell upon them. Laedron let his spell fizzle, for the water had put out his fire. Aside from the occasional drip, he heard only silence. He stared across the sea of undead warriors, then heard a rattling of metal against metal. One of the Netheren banged its sword against its shield, then the others joined in the cacophony. The chamber echoed with the clattering of thousands.

All is lost. Laedron stared at the ground and shook his head. He turned to Tavin, expecting to see a defeated man, but Tavin didn't seem intimidated. Instead, he called out, "You think dropping water upon us will weaken our resolve? Witness *true* power."

Shouting a spell, Tavin flung his wand toward the enemy sorcerer. A bolt of lightning wound its way across the empty space between them. Upon contact, sparkles of electricity engulfed the undead mage's body, which exploded in a rain of gore. Arcs of energy shot to nearby creatures, then to more, until every Netheren in a straight line from Tavin either convulsed with the shock or collapsed into a smoking pile of bones and skin.

"That way," Tavin said, pointing at the cleared path his spell had made. "Move out before they close the gap."

Hot on Tavin's heels, Laedron glimpsed the dead men encroaching on the left and right. He swashed his scepter to the right and shouted a spell. A fireball erupted from the ruby and slammed into a group of charging corpses, incinerating the ones at the focus and catching the nearby others aflame. Behind him, he heard Valyrie firing arrow after arrow into the Netheren at their left. He turned just as one of the dead men was struck in the leg. When the reanimated corpse fell to the ground, it was trampled by the others.

"Almost there," Tavin said.

Stopping just outside a small opening in the far wall, Tavin took Laedron by the collar and nearly threw him into the passage. "Keep going. Don't look back."

Valyrie came next, and if it hadn't been for Laedron catching her, she would have fallen. Brice, obviously frightened, squeezed past them. Tavin grabbed Marac by the hand and pulled him inside the shaft.

Tavin pointed his wand at the ceiling and shouted a spell. A bolt of energy flew from his wand and struck the stone roof. Laedron glanced back to see the undead clawing at each other to get into the tunnel. Tavin pushed them along.

While he ran, Laedron noticed a crack racing along the stone above and keeping pace with them. *We must hurry. He'll bring the whole place down on us!* Then, he heard the crash of rocks behind them, and although he tried to see what had happened, he was forced forward by Tavin's shoving. He surmised that the collapse had started where Tavin had cast the spell. *What else could have caused it?* The closer the sound came, the faster Laedron's heart raced, but he didn't stop until he reached the next chamber. Exploding through the hole like lava from a volcano, they fell over each other and came to a stop. Rocks slammed down just behind them.

Laedron stood and took a look around. Stone jutted from the floor and hung from the ceiling like incomplete pillars. The earthen walls seemed to be held together by tangled roots in the spots where the cave wasn't solid stone. He couldn't quite tell how light was getting into the cavern, but he was glad it wasn't pitch black.

Rising to his feet, Marac glared at Tavin and pointed at the blocked passage. "And how will we get out of here, assuming we survive this? You've sealed us in."

"The Trappers could never go that way; they're too large to fit." Tavin stood and swatted his clothes, a cloud of dust popping out with each slap. "I've never ventured into the caves dotting this area, but there must be more than one way out."

"Suppose there aren't any? Suppose we're stuck here?"

"Would you rather have been disemboweled by the Netheren? Didn't think so."

Brice, his blade in hand, said, "We could've fought them."

"No, Brice. We may have killed fifty, but hundreds more were climbing out of their crypts. That's not counting the hundreds or thousands that were already coming at us." Laedron stood and massaged his leg to relieve a dull ache, then helped Valyrie to her feet. "We'll have to find another way out."

"Damn!" Valyrie snatched up the bow. Its string was broken. She retrieved her quiver. "A bunch of arrows and nothing to shoot them with."

Tavin extended his hand. "Allow me."

"Allow you to do what?"

"Repair it for you, of course." Taking the bow, Tavin sat on a tall rock and drew his wand.

158

"Mages can do that?" she asked.

Laedron nodded. "If something hasn't been damaged too badly, it can usually be mended."

"More light," Tavin said, snapping in Laedron's direction.

Laedron obliged him with a light spell. With the cavern brightly illuminated, Laedron saw another passage leading off from the chamber and gestured toward it, but his companions must have been enraptured with Tavin's spell because they paid him no mind. At first, he rolled his eyes at their simple natures. *Regular people gawk at even the simplest spells.* Then, he noticed the bowstrings dancing in the air, and he couldn't help but stare in awe at the display.

Like trained serpents obeying the commands of their master, the strings wrapped themselves around each other, and energy sparked where they were rejoined. Tavin handed Valyrie the repaired bow. "Now, we should look for a way out of here."

Tavin cleared his throat. "Has anyone seen a way out?"

Laedron snapped out of it, then pointed at the other passage. "Oh, yes. Yes. This way."

Tavin walked into the tunnel and led the group along the winding path. Laedron likened the passage to a hole dug by an animal that meandered wildly the entire length. Dampness filled the air, and the musty smell was replaced by the aromas of mildew and earth. Laedron spotted mushrooms caps growing on the walls, worms and centipedes scurrying, and reflections off of the thin streams of water leaking through the tiny fractures. He wondered how long it had been since light of any kind had shone on the black rock in that place.

Turning a bend, he felt the air grow cooler almost in an instant, and a blast of air flowed past him. He could barely make out a faint glimmer of light ahead, a green glow, presumably at the end of the tunnel.

"What do you think is causing that light?" Laedron

whispered when Tavin stopped.

"Likely where Kareth constructs his crystal beasts." Licking his lips, Tavin scratched his chin. "If we should fight one of those abominations, I will be of no help to you."

"No help? You're a gifted mage. Hells, you told us how to defeat them."

"I cannot."

"Can't?"

"Mustn't."

"What in the hells are you saying? We have to fight them alone?"

"That's exactly what I'm saying, Sorcerer."

"But why? I thought you came here to help us."

Tavin gave him a tight grin. "If the time comes, you'll know why I couldn't. Until then, you're on your own when it comes to the Trappers. I'll wait here until you've checked ahead."

Laedron sighed. "Leave it to us, then. We'll come after you when the coast is clear." He started to walk away, but he felt a hand on his shoulder.

"Remember: vibrations." Tavin glanced at Laedron's friends. "Those weapons can harm them. Do not stand idle, and do not fall."

"We'll certainly try to keep that in mind," Marac said. "Come on, Lae. We've got work to do."

❧ Chapter Thirteen ☙

Crystal Caverns

The green glow grew bright as Laedron approached the opening. He crouched and slowed his steps, afraid to lose any advantage that surprise might offer, and the rest matched his movements. When he reached the mouth of the tunnel, he clung to the last rock that could provide cover and stared into the room beyond, captivated. The others huddled behind him.

Around the massive cavern, crystal formations of all shapes and sizes jutted from the rocks at every conceivable angle. The place was much like the cistern he had seen when Tavin brought them to the Uxidins' refuge, but the cave was illuminated

161

throughout by an eerie green light. A vast number of small, animate constructs comprised of green crystal moved about the room. Their bodies and numerous legs resembled those of sea crabs, but the things were considerably larger. They chipped away at the bases of the formations, harvesting the gems. Resounding through the cave was a constant chattering noise, the tapping of thousands of tiny, crystalline legs against the rock. The noise reminded him of the crickets chirping at night in Sorbia. *How long have these things been toiling here at the bottom of the world? And why do they work? For what purpose and for whom? Kareth, most likely, but for what reason?*

"What now?" Marac whispered.

"We have to find a way past them."

"Through that?" Valyrie asked, crouching beside them. "Far too many of them to sneak past."

Brice pointed toward the ceiling. "What about using those to get across?"

Gazing upward, Laedron noticed the supports leading from the floor to the ceiling. Struts had been secured to them, likely to add extra support for the cave from all the excavation. The network of beams reminded Laedron of scaffolding he'd seen erected for builders on huge construction projects in the various cities they'd visited. "It's worth a shot. Go get Tavin, Marac."

"We can't fly across?" Marac asked, glancing at Laedron's scepter.

Laedron shook his head. "They would hear the chanting. We'll have to be stealthy."

"Hear? Have you seen ears on them?"

"We can't take the chance."

* * *

Returning with Marac a few moments later, Tavin bent beside

Laedron. "You've found a way through?"

"Yes, and without fighting." Laedron gestured at the supports. "Up and across, as quiet as mice. Then, onward to Kareth."

Tavin nodded. "Until you're a ways ahead, I'll wait. I can't be seen here, and if you're spotted, well… you'll have to do whatever you can without me."

"Why? You're the best sorcerer. We'll need you with us if we're discovered."

"Like I said before, I cannot. You'll know why in time, but for now, you'll have to accept that." Tavin sighed. "Best get going."

Does he fear these things? We all do, but to keep himself out of the fight now is ludicrous. At the time we need him most—apart from dealing with Kareth, if we find him—he sits it out. "Very well. Marac, you're our strongest, so you'll go first. We'll need you to help the rest of us up."

"Wait," Brice said, reaching into his pack. "Before we go, we ought to tie off with one another. If we fall, we won't go all the way down."

"Yeah, but if someone falls, they could take the rest of us with them, Thimble."

"What do you think, Lae?" Brice asked, frowning at Marac.

"I think it's a good idea."

Marac gave Laedron a cross look. "And risk all of us at once?"

"We go forward together, remember? All or nothing. The execution needs a little work, though." Laedron gazed at the beams. "They're not very thick. Perhaps we could slip the rope around the girders before tying it to each person."

"Good thought. We'd better wrap it twice to be sure we won't take the rest if we should fall." Marac took the rope and tied it around his waist. "Easier to climb if I don't have to hold it. Wait until I'm all the way up." He returned his sword to the sheath, stepped out onto the metal beam, then climbed to the top by way of screws and handholds at intervals along the girder. Once Marac reached the top, Brice gestured at Laedron to go up, and Laedron scaled the support. Valyrie followed, and Brice joined them in the rafters last.

Not long into their crawl, Laedron felt dull aches in his knees and hands. The thin layers of skin and fat between the metal and his bones provided little cushion. He sighed. *We've only gone ten feet?* Inch by hellish inch he crept, and the aches grew into shooting pains. He looked past the beam to the cave floor and hoped he would meet his end from the impact if he should fall to the bottom rather than the slow death of being picked apart by crystal mandibles.

Each time they reached a vertical beam, they had to undertake a tedious process of rope handling because they couldn't pass where two supports were joined. Laedron was thankful for the breaks, but his patience was stretched to the limits when they had to stop for such a long time. Marac had to untie the rope around his waist, unwrap it from the beam, retie, climb to the other side of the vertical support, sit, untie, coil the rope around the next horizontal beam, and tie himself again. Then, the next person would go, repeating the same process, until all of them were on the same beam and ready to crawl again.

Halfway, he mused, glancing back at Tavin, then forward at the apparent exit. *What does he have to hide from us? Will he turn us over as some sort of offering, a tribute of four fresh souls in exchange for the tome? Perhaps Harridan told him a secret that none of us can know.* The pain in his hands had become a piercing sting, and he left bloody handprints as he crawled. He tapped Valyrie on the bottom of her shoe. When she looked back, he signaled for them to stop, and she gestured at Marac.

Laedron sat and let his feet dangle off the side of the beam, then searched for something to wrap around his hands. Brice apparently knew what Laedron wanted because he handed over some lengths of cloth, then held up his hands to show strips tied around his own palms. *Looks like I'm not the only one,* Laedron thought, covering the cuts and tying the ends. *Either that or he was smart enough to think of it before getting this far.* Valyrie took a few strips and did the same, but Marac shook his head and held up his hand, a thick leather glove covering it.

With a nod, Laedron got on his hands and knees, then they started again. *Should've done the same to my knees while I was at it. Ah, we're nearing the end. Only a few more moments of suffering to bear. And one more of those damned vertical struts.*

When he reached the support, Marac untied the rope from the beam, then tied it around his waist. He stood, hugged the brace, and stepped around it, then sat, untied, wrapped, and retied. Valyrie went next, and when she finished securing the line, Laedron crawled toward the post. *Just one more time.* He undid the rope from the support behind him. Standing, he lost his footing and grabbed for the vertical brace. He felt the sudden pull of gravity trying to yank him off the beam.

Valyrie extended her hand and whispered, "It's okay. Step around."

He took her hand, but getting to the other support didn't ease the churning in his stomach. He knew that he wouldn't have fallen far, but he still trembled from the near miss. Valyrie held him by the shoulders until he was done, and he nodded at Brice.

Brice grasped the beam, then put his foot around and searched for solid footing. Laedron had noticed Valyrie having the same issue when she had tried, and since the support only joined two braces on opposite sides, all of them had taken longer to cross that joint than any of the others. When Brice stretched out his leg, his hand slipped from the post, and he plummeted toward the ground.

Laedron felt a jerk at his waist when the rope drew taut. He clawed at the brace to keep from falling. He lost his grip, but he heard the rope tighten around the support. The sudden stop jarred his extremities and, most of all, his back. Had he been anywhere else, he would have cried out, but dangling above innumerable enemies, he had to bite his lip and suffer silently. Covering his mouth, he clenched his other hand on the knot at his belly and prayed that he had tied it well.

Laedron saw Marac taking off the rope and shook his head, but he couldn't risk speaking. *No, damned fool. Don't do it. It's too dangerous.* He wanted to say all of those things, but he didn't. He couldn't. In his state, he wouldn't be able to control his pitch or volume.

Marac climbed around Valyrie, then sat on the beam. Laedron looked back over his shoulder, both to avoid seeing Marac fall if it happened and to find out if Brice was still on the end of the rope. Laedron breathed a sigh of relief. *It held.* He could see the fear in Brice's eyes, but Brice hadn't plunged to the bottom. He looked up when he heard a hiss. Marac was reaching toward him. He stretched his arm as far as it would go, and Marac took hold of his hand.

Once he got within range, Laedron grabbed the support. Valyrie helped him climb up while Marac took hold of the rope leading to Brice. The veins and muscles protruded from Marac's arms, and despite the cool environs, sweat dripped like rain. Laedron scrambled to help, and by a handful of rope at a time, they hoisted Brice to them. When Brice came into reach, Laedron pulled him onto the beam.

"What happened?" Laedron whispered.

Brice rubbed his hands together. "It was slippery. I lost my grip."

"Lost your grip?" Marac asked.

"The beams are soaking wet."

"Sorry," Laedron said. "That was my fault."

"Everyone's safe." Marac waved his hand. "That's all that

matters. Let's get moving."

* * *

Nearing the end, Laedron looked back to see Tavin stepping out onto the beam. *Is he mad?* Tavin was walking fast. *Has he done this before? Or is he merely skilled at keeping his balance?*

Marac crouched, untied his rope, and unwrapped it from the brace. "I could live the rest of my life without tying another knot."

Laedron smiled. "You can say that again."

Marac climbed down the vertical post using whatever handholds he could find. Valyrie went next, and Laedron followed. Once Brice joined them, Laedron took a quick look around. Fortunately, they had ended up near an exit from the chamber and out of sight of the harvesters.

Marac gasped. "Lae—"

Turning, Laedron saw one of the harvesters approaching from inside the adjoining tunnel. He grabbed Marac and shot behind a boulder; Brice and Valyrie ducked in behind him. Seeming not to notice them, the creature crawled past and entered the crystal chamber.

Laedron let out a sigh of relief, then noticed the walls around him lighting up with red light. Looking over his shoulder, he saw another harvester with a hunk of crystal in its mandibles. It glowed crimson, as if it had located its prey. "We've been spotted." He glanced at the rafters. Tavin was hiding behind a beam.

Laedron drew his scepter. *A quake spell. Think quickly!* Laedron waved the rod in a circle before him and chanted. Valyrie, pulled her bowstring taut and searched for a target, while Brice and Marac unsheathed their swords. *If I summon a tremor, will it bring the place down on us like Tavin's spell almost did? Will it draw the rest of them upon us? Should I—*

Something whizzed past his ear. He turned and saw an arrow

imbedded in the side of the harvester. The force enchantment cracked the crystal and severed the limbs on its right side. It dropped the shard it had been carrying and jerked like a wounded beast, obviously unable to lift itself from the ground.

Like a wave passing through the cavern, the red glow spread and encompassed the harvesters in small groups until the entire place seemed alerted to the threat.

"Hide, hide. The others may not have seen us," Laedron said, returning to his place behind the boulders. Hearing a crackling noise, he peeked around the rock and saw a swirling energy on the far side of the cavern. He looked for Tavin. The sorcerer was aiming his wand in that direction. *Genius. A distraction. By the Creator, let it work!* With his free hand, Tavin gestured at the harvester Valyrie had shot.

"What does he want us to do?" Brice asked.

Sneaking to the edge of the boulder, Laedron looked at the crystal beast still writhing on the ground, as if frustrated by its inability to stand. "We'll have to finish it off."

Marac slinked to Laedron's side. "And how do we do that?"

Laedron, searching for a solution, recalled what Tavin had said about the creatures. *Kareth's creations are built from crystal and the essence of the living.* Then, he thought about the battle with Andolis and how he'd nearly lost his life to the Zyvdredi master and his spell. *If they're instilled with essence to exist, it can be pulled out.*

He stepped out, his scepter in hand, despite Marac and Brice hissing at him to return. He closed his eyes, recited Andolis's spell, and pointed the rod at the harvester. When the dark violet light appeared, he produced one of the black onyx gems that had been depleted from refilling his scepter and trapped the essence within it. The red light fading from its body, the creature slumped to the ground, depleted.

Holding the gem, Laedron gazed at the other harvesters. A

few were not distracted by Tavin's display. *How many souls would it take to create so many of these things? To keep them working for decades on end?*

Tavin crept backward along the girder, maintaining the spell until he had reached the end. Apparently unable to find any menaces, the harvesters' red glows eventually faded, and their bodies resumed the green coloring. Before he reached the bottom, Tavin stopped, and Laedron heard the familiar chatter of crystal against stone.

Back to work, it would seem. Wait... Laedron looked over the top of the boulder and saw a pair of harvesters inspecting the one Valyrie had slain. For a moment, he wondered if the creatures had any ability to reason because they seemed to look at each other with suspicion. As if giving up on trying to figure out what happened, the harvesters used their thick crystal mandibles to dismantle their fallen comrade. They made a neat pile out of the parts, then returned to the chamber to continue working.

Amazing. Do they have any intelligence? Could something made entirely of crystal be capable of reasoning or of original thought? Or is it more a matter of simple instructions from the master?

Tavin dropped from the rafter and, without a word, led the way into the tunnel.

I can only speculate what awaits us farther down. An army of these things? Legions of Trappers? Given decades without pause or interruption, what sort of horrors could I create for any potential intruders?

ᕙ Chapter Fourteen ᕗ

Kareth's Workshop

Approaching the opening at the end of the passage, Laedron detected a faint echo, which sounded like the clanking of metal. The others must have heard it, too, because they slowed and put their backs against the walls. Tavin, at the front, crouched near the entrance and peered inside the chamber past the tunnel.

Laedron crept up behind him. Two Trappers stood in metal stands. One was only partly constructed and the other nearly finished. A few harvesters walked between them and some piles of crystal, shaping the pieces, and fusing them to the Trappers' bodies. Beyond the stands sat chunks of a shiny metal in heaping piles that Laedron thought could be silver or purified iron, and the whole place stank of stagnant water. *This place is larger than the Vicariate Palace!* Staring into the distance, Laedron reckoned that the cave might have been the single biggest room he had ever seen, and the smoothness of the walls indicated that it hadn't been formed naturally.

What purpose has Kareth for making so many of these Trappers? A crystal mine, a workshop to build them in, and countless harvesters laboring, all to what end? He followed Tavin through the shadows. He could tell that the Uxidin was nervous by the sheen of sweat on the man's face and neck, despite the coolness of the caverns. *Why does the man who taught me how to defeat a Trapper seem so unsure of himself now? He could undoubtedly fell both of them with a single spell should they come to life and ambush us.*

"Do you see any other passages?" Tavin whispered, stopping behind some shelves.

Laedron scanned the room. "There's a path through the piles of metal. Perhaps there lies the way?"

"We have no choice, then. We'll have to destroy the harvesters. You get the one on the right, and I'll take care of the other. Do you know the prefix of silence?"

"Prefix of silence? No, I can't say that I do."

Tavin uttered a few magic words. "Add those before your chant to quiet the spell. Never add them to a spell which harnesses noises or voice, for it will negate your own magic."

"Then, I shouldn't use a blast of sound?"

"No, not this time. We can't risk it this far in. Use something else."

"Any suggestions?"

"A bolt of lightning, perhaps. That's what I intend to use."

Drawing his scepter, Laedron eyed the crab-like harvester, thinking of which spell to use and where to aim. Once Tavin had given the countdown on his fingers, they cast simultaneously. Bolts of lightning lashed out at the harvesters and split each in half. The only sounds Laedron heard were shattering glass and crystal hitting the ground.

"I thought you said it would be silent," Laedron said.

"The spell was, young man, but things affected by spells will still follow the rules of reality. Crystal makes a sound when it breaks, but don't worry. It should have been quiet enough not to alert the rest of the—"

Hearing a chain snap, Laedron turned, then froze in horror. One of the Trappers, the one mostly finished, had sprung to life. He tried to fight his feeling of dread, but he couldn't put aside his memory of the scene in the forest, the wolf dying at the merciless hands of the Trapper, its soul sucked clean from its body.

Ducking behind some nearby shelves, Tavin said, "You must deal with it."

Marac and Brice, swords in hand, loosened their stances and teetered on anxious feet. Valyrie drew the string of her bow taut, an arrow nocked and aimed at the monster.

"You'll not help?" Laedron pointed his finger in Tavin's direction. "When we need you the most?"

"I cannot. I cannot risk dying here."

"Cannot? Get out here and fight!"

Tavin didn't move, and Laedron decided he didn't have time to argue further. The Trapper charged, its long legs somehow limber despite their crystalline construction. Marac rolled forward when the monster neared, barely passing beneath its massive arm, then struck its leg with his blade. The enchantment on his sword must have helped because the sword penetrated the leg, though not enough to sever it.

Valyrie released her arrow as the beast staggered, striking it in the shoulder. When the force spell erupted, the Trapper lost its balance. The creature slammed into Valyrie and sent her flying into the cavern wall.

Laedron lost focus on his spell. "Val!"

The Trapper rocked back and forth a few times before rising to its knees, and Laedron swore he heard a grumbling sound come from it, as if it indeed had some emotion or felt some measure of pain. "Don't let that bastard get up again!" Laedron yelled to Marac and Brice.

Marac lunged at the Trapper, striking it with his sword and the blasting enchantment. When the smoke cleared, Brice and Marac stood over the Trapper's body, the upper half of its torso whittled down to a nub, the remains of its head and arms almost indistinguishable from the other chunks of crystal littering the ground.

"So much for stealth," Tavin said, emerging from his hiding spot. "Perhaps the racket didn't carry far."

"So much for stealth?" Laedron rushed over and grabbed the sorcerer by the shirt. "That's all you can say?" He gave Tavin a hard shake, then ran to where Valyrie lay limp on the ground.

Tiptoeing to his side, Brice asked, "Is she okay?"

Laedron wanted to know the same thing and had some difficulty in determining her condition. He had to muster all of his restraint not to reach out and touch her. *If I move her, I could worsen her injuries. What will happen if I do nothing, though? She could die here, and it would be without my telling her how much of a fool I was, without my telling her what she meant to me and how deep my love for her had become. I'll bring her back if needed, consequences be damned.* "Val!" *Please answer me. Come back to me, please!* "Val, can you hear me?" *Damn it all.* He put his hand under her head and pulled her close. A large bruise had formed on her forehead. "Val, please, if you can hear me, say something."

Feeling the muscles in her neck tense, Laedron took her hand. "Val?"

She opened her eyes. "Lae...? My head." Although her voice was raspy and speaking clearly caused her pain, Laedron's heart soared with hope. Sitting up, she caressed the bump on her forehead.

Tavin shrugged. "This is all very touching, but we really should—"

Marac silenced him with a harsh glare. "This is the stuff that real lives are made of, Uxidin. Not books, not artifacts, and certainly not hunting villains hiding in the deep. The unending nature of your life has blinded you to the importance of things dear to us mortal sorts. I pity you."

Brice elbowed him. "Never knew you were a romantic, Marac. Never figured you for the type."

"Things grow on you, Thimble."

Laedron kissed Valyrie. "What might you say about some peace and relaxation when we get out of this mess?"

"With you?"

His heart sank, fearful of what she might say next. "If you'd have me."

"Does this mean you're over yourself?"

Over myself? Was I the one who...? Enough. If I've learned anything about women, the most important observation is not to argue unnecessarily. "Yes."

"Then, I would say that I wouldn't have it any other way." She smiled. "Now that that's settled, how about getting on with our task?"

"Not before I help that head of yours." He waved the scepter and chanted. The bruise faded. He lost himself in her eyes.

She shook his shoulder. "Lae? Should we go about finding this Kareth fellow and sending him to Syril?"

"Kareth... oh, yes." Turning when he heard coughing, Laedron examined Tavin, wondering why he was hunched over. "Are you well?"

"I'll be fine. A little weakness from the climb, I should think. Nothing to concern yourselves with." Tavin gestured at the path between the metal piles. "Shall we?"

Laedron helped Valyrie to her feet, then followed Tavin and his friends behind the stand holding the half-built Trapper and into the maze of metal piles. Upon closer inspection of the scrap metal, Laedron wondered what it was and why it had been left discarded in such a way. "Have you ever seen anything like this before?"

"Could be anything," Tavin replied without so much as a glance at it. "We may never know."

"I'd like to know. It could be important." Laedron snatched a piece from one of the lots. Eying it, he thought he'd seen such a metal before, but the name escaped him. "Take a look at this."

Marac, Brice, and Valyrie crowded around the shiny chunk in Laedron's palm.

Brice blurted, "Can it be?"

"What? You've seen this before?"

"We all have."

Laedron shrugged. "I thought I had, but I can't place it."

"Looks like platinum."

Marac's eyes widened, and he grabbed a piece to examine it. "It can't be. Get one of the coins out, Lae."

Fishing through his pockets, Laedron located one of the platinum pieces that Jurgen had given them in Azura, then held the coin and the raw hunk against one another for comparison.

"Creator! He may be right." Laedron dropped his hands to his sides when he stared into the expanses of the chamber and realized they were surrounded by piles—tons upon tons—of the most precious metal in Bloodmyr, all of it heaped like refuse. "More wealth than all the nations in the world. Right here, beneath an old temple in the middle of a forest, lies the richest and most bountiful veins of platinum ever discovered."

"Should we take some?" Brice asked, licking his lips, his fingers waggling with apparent avarice.

Laedron gazed at Tavin.

Tavin said, "If you're looking to me for permission, it is not mine to give. These treasures were dug up by Kareth and his creations."

"Then, I suppose it wouldn't hurt." Brice picked up two handfuls at a time and dropped chunk after chunk into his pack.

"Not too much, Thimble." Marac grabbed his wrist and took a piece of platinum from his hand. "You wouldn't want to weigh yourself down. We may need you for the fight to come, and with a ton of that on your back, you'll be of little use."

Picking up about a pound of the stuff, Laedron glanced at Valyrie. *A little wealth would help us when we return home. And a bit for the mages to rebuild the academy we so desperately need.* "Take some for your father, Marac, and keep some for yourself. The rest we leave for Tavin's people to help them rebuild what has long since been lost."

"If I don't make it out of this place with you, I appreciate your kindness, and I hope they put these resources to good use." Tavin seemed to be sure that he wouldn't emerge from the caverns alive.

"Certainly. Think nothing of it." *What else can I say? If he had something to tell me, he's not the kind to hide it.*

Tavin led them farther down the path, which was also lit by crystals similar to those Laedron had seen in the Uxidin shelter. The hall terminated at a stone desk surrounded by matching bookcases, and Laedron stopped when he was close enough to hear the scratching of a quill against parchment.

A man's voice, a deep bellow, which Laedron thought could have come from Syril himself, called out, "Why do you disturb me? I told you not to worry me unless you found more. Have you found more?"

With a sound Laedron likened to the scattering of paper and the shuffling of feet, a man came around the bookcase that had previously obscured him from view. Laedron's jaw dropped.

Kareth, he thought, first noticing the human face and upper body, then the crystal pieces imbedded in the man's torso, arms, and legs. The man stopped when he saw Laedron and his group, then bolted for a nearby exit, his tattered clothes and long brown hair fluttering behind him.

"Kareth!" Tavin shouted, thrusting his wand toward the man and casting a spell.

The man disappeared through the tunnel just before the bolt of lightning crashed into the wall.

Tavin took off after him.

Laedron, pursuing Tavin into the passage, glanced at the desk and shelves. *An amulet forged from crystal? Drawings? Plans of some kind? What has become of this man, having been secluded for so long?*

❧ Chapter Fifteen ❧

Showdown

Racing down the corridor, Laedron couldn't cast the fear from his heart, for the mere sight of Kareth instilled terror in the pit of his stomach. *What lengths of madness has a man reached when he willingly deforms himself? Purposefully inserts shards of crystal into his own flesh?* His horror notwithstanding, Laedron kept within a few feet from Tavin the whole way.

Tavin first, then Laedron and the others, burst into another chamber like a torrent of hellfire, out of breath and scanning the room for any signs of Kareth. Laedron was taken aback by the sight of the place. Trappers stood at intervals along the walls of the ringed room, like knights on guard by a king's throne. Their bodies shone bright and red, and their glow overpowered the luminous crystals placed around the chamber to provide ambient light. Upon a stone platform sat a huge crystal chair, which looked like a vicar's cathedra. Laedron could make out the lower half of Kareth's body crouched behind the seat.

Tavin yelled, "Nowhere to run now, fiend! Come out and face us."

Kareth stood, walked in front of the throne, then sat upon it, holding his staff, which had a shaft of what looked like pure emerald. "Am I the one who should be concerned?" He gestured at the Trappers at either side of him. "You would come into my house and, surrounded by my guardians, make threats? I thought you would have better sense than that, my dear Tavingras. It has been quite a while since we last met, but I thought better of you than that."

"It would seem that you haven't forgotten much since you've been down here in your little hole." Tavin approached the throne, and the Trappers moved to intercept him. "Perhaps you remember your crimes? Why we might be here to see you?"

Laedron gestured for his companions to stay back, then he followed Tavin toward the throne.

"Halt," Kareth said to the Trappers. When they didn't obey, Kareth jerked his head back with contempt, as if he'd realized something, then donned an amulet around his neck. "I said, halt!"

The Trappers stopped in their tracks, and the red glow dimmed. *The amulet. He uses it to control them?*

Smiling, Tavin asked, "Struck a nerve, did I?"

"You were there, Tavingras," Kareth said, his anger apparent. "You know why I had to do what I did."

"*Had* to? No, I think not." Tavingras gave Kareth a glare that dripped with condescension. "I can think of nothing that could justify your murder of the Elder Priest. What would you have me believe? That she attacked you when she appointed Harridan to succeed her? You killed the Far'rah out of envy and jealousy."

"I loved her, Tavingras, and she betrayed that love." Kareth's voice echoed with an ache that only an immortal could hold, a pain that had tortured its victim for years, centuries, as if it had been inflicted anew each day.

The revelation must have been a shock to Tavin because he stood speechless, his mouth gaping.

Finally, Kareth said, "You couldn't understand, for you never knew the truth. Your master, the one you now call Far'rah, stole my love's heart and my future. That is what you and your people are good for, Tavingras. Perfect little followers to liars and thieves."

Tavin shook his head. "You lie."

Kareth leaned forward in his seat. "In the middle of his own kingdom, a king tells the truth, for who would oppose him? What need would be sated by speaking falsehoods?"

"You mean to trick me. You lie because you are afraid—"

"Afraid?" Kareth let out an unnerving, sinister cackle that resounded from every corner of the cave. "What do I have to fear from one of Harridan's toadies and a handful of children? Come now, Tavingras. I thought you remembered me better than that. Or do you mean to be disrespectful for disrespect's sake?"

"If you're not lying, then what do you hope to accomplish here? Why do you build these crystal abominations and loose them upon the forest? She's dead, Kareth. You've taken your revenge upon her."

"To punish you and your kind, nothing more. To revisit the suffering you've caused me until none of you draw breath. For what reason did you think?"

"To build your own empire from our bones?"

"Ha! You would like to think that, wouldn't you? Had we spent more time together, you might have had an opportunity to truly know me, Tavingras."

"I know you well, murderer, but you seem to have grown comfortable in your cave." Tavin raised his wand at Kareth. "I've come quite a long way since we last met, and before you die, I want to impress that upon you."

"I think you'll find that we've both learned a few new tricks." Standing, Kareth took his staff in both hands. "Is it to be only you and I, or will these others join our little game?"

Tavin looked over his shoulder. "Keep back. Whatever happens, do not interfere until one of us is dead."

Insanity, Laedron thought. "What good is that? We've come to kill the man. Why give up the advantage?"

"If I fall, you'll have plenty of work ahead of you. Stay out of it." Tavin turned back at Kareth. "I've long waited for this day."

"Then, I shall make it interesting." Kareth bowed, then shouted a spell and waved the staff at Tavin.

Tavin ducked, narrowly avoiding a beam of light as it passed overhead. With a flick of his wrist, Tavin returned a blast of deafening thunder. Although Kareth was clearly the focal point of the spell, several of the Trappers standing nearby exploded or collapsed in the shockwave.

Cracks formed in the walls of the cave. Kareth peered down and examined his body, and even from that distance, Laedron noticed fractures in some of the crystals imbedded in the man. The unnatural glow was fading from them. Seemingly undeterred, Kareth thrust his staff forward again and unleashed a hail of ice shards at Tavin.

Tavin apparently recognized the spell because, as soon as Kareth had cast, he summoned a shield of fire. The ice shards passed through, turned to water, and landed harmlessly. Both of the Uxidin released their spells, then walked the perimeter of the platform like scrappers sizing up one another.

"It would seem that I underestimated you, Tavingras." Kareth gestured at one of the broken crystals in his chest. "How many of my creations did you fight before you learned how to defeat them?"

"Not many," Tavin said with a full dose of vitriol.

"Ah, then perhaps I asked the wrong question. Maybe it would be more fitting if I asked how many of your poor, pathetic people had to die before you stopped the first one?"

182

With a shriek, Tavin shot a bolt of lightning from his wand. The bolt struck Kareth in the shoulder. Tavin fired another, and Kareth took cover behind his throne. Enveloped in rage, Tavin hurled bolt after bolt into the crystal chair, knocking chunks off of it with each casting. "Come out, damn you! Quit hiding and—"

Kareth poked the end of his staff between the legs of the throne. Flames erupted from the tip and engulfed Tavin's legs. Tavin screamed in anguish, then fell to the ground when Kareth ended the spell.

Laedron's heart sank. He took a step forward, then stopped when Tavin held up a hand.

"No. You mustn't interfere. It's not over yet."

"Not over?" Kareth walked out from behind the chair. "You're finished, Tavingras. You're no more a threat to me than these children."

"Finished? Not yet. So long as there's life in my body, I will oppose you for all that you've done."

"Then, I shall deprive you of that life, that wasted, pitiful, subservient life. I should let you suffer as I have suffered, but I will be merciful to you. More merciful than you and your kind ever were to me." Kareth approached, his staff outstretched. "In the end, the Zyvdredi were right. The essence of the weak is best used to serve the strong. Now, your essence will serve *me*."

"So, you have joined them? Thrown everything you were away?" Tavin asked through clenched teeth.

"Joined? I swear fealty to no Nyrethine house." Kareth crouched next to Tavin. "I merely understand their philosophy, Tavingras. Quiet, now. The pain you're in must be excruciating."

After hearing the first words of the incantation, Laedron knew what spell Kareth was conjuring.

Marac must have recognized it, too, because he whispered, "Lae, do something."

Not until one of us is dead, Laedron repeated in his mind, watching the still-breathing Tavin. The swirls of dark violet appeared, and Laedron was torn between Marac's words and the instructions Tavin had given. *Did he mean for me to obey even if he lost?*

"Lae, we must stop him," Marac said. "Lae!"

Raising the scepter, Laedron stared at Tavin and realized that he drew breath no longer. The sorcerer's staff's purple glow faded. "Bastard."

"I had almost forgotten you were here, young one," Kareth said. "Would you prefer a quick death?"

Laedron gestured at the lifeless corpse at Kareth's feet. "Unlike Tavingras, you know nothing of me. Does that not worry you?"

Brow furrowed, Kareth stood. "Worry me? Tell me, child, what did he offer you to come here? Grand adventure? A share of the spoils? Or did he touch upon your mortal sentiments of right and wrong? If that was the case, then know that I was the one wronged. It is I who suffered by their hands like some plaything."

"Does any of this matter? Whether I know the truth or not, you'll try to kill us anyway. Why wait?"

"A quick one, then. Have it your way."

His hand trembling, Laedron held out the rod, recalling the words to his dispelling ward. Kareth raised the staff high and chanted. When Kareth thrust the staff forward, it exploded in his hands in a flurry of flashing light.

Thrown to the ground, Laedron shook his head and blinked rapidly. A haze of smoke hung in the air. The sting of warm blood filled his eyes, and a pain like broken slivers of glass sliced into his skin with every movement. *Where has he gone? Get it together, Sorcerer! Every moment that passes without action gives him another chance to attack.* He tried to focus and find Kareth through the smoke, but he couldn't. *What in the hells happened?* Searching his memory, he tried to think of something that might make sense of it all, and he finally realized what had caused the explosion. *Harridan. He couldn't, could he? Wouldn't?* Laedron recalled his words to Tavin: *I thought you came here to help us,* to which Tavin had replied, *When the time comes, you'll know why I couldn't.*

Working backward from that moment, Laedron imagined the meeting—the private talk that Tavin and Harridan had before they left—and he pieced together what had really gone on behind that closed door. *A spell placed upon Tavin's essence, then delivered to Kareth's staff when that essence was absorbed. That must be the answer. A clever monster led into a trap and defeated by his own nature.*

Laedron considered what Tavin must have felt coming there, the quick pace by which he'd led them to that place. All the way down, he had purposefully ran to meet his own death at Kareth's hands, to be the last sacrifice intended, at last, to free his people of the madman's tyranny. When the smoke cleared, Laedron rose to his feet and checked his friends. "Everyone all right?"

"Are you?" Valyrie approached. "You were the closest."

"Yes, fine." Laedron pulled the strip of linen from his hand and wiped his face. "The shards didn't go deep."

"We're fine," Marac said, then turned to a rock. "You can come out now."

Brice peeked over the boulder, then moved to stand beside Marac.

Laedron turned toward the throne and took a few steps, but he stopped when he noticed Kareth's leg twitch.

Kareth let out a bloodcurdling scream. His arm had been torn away at the shoulder from the blast. "How could you—"

"I had nothing to do it with it. Don't blame me for your own mistakes, monster."

"Mistakes? How—"

Laedron, despite his own pain, displayed a smile. "They've beaten you, Kareth. Harridan knew what you would do if you won, and you've done it. By your own greed have you been undone. They've won, and you're finished."

Chuckling, Kareth righted himself on the throne. "I can forge another staff. Another arm, too. They've done little more than delay my work for a few days."

This madness ends now. Grabbing at his belt, Laedron searched for the scepter, but then realized he had dropped it somewhere when he was thrown. He scanned the ground nearby, but he couldn't spot it amidst the rubble and broken crystal.

"Guardians," Kareth said, and the pair of remaining Trappers stood and approached from behind the throne. "Feast upon them. Devour their essences!"

The Trappers, red from the inner glow, turned and started walking toward Laedron and his friends. *I can't fight them with a practice wand!* He glanced at his boot, then reached for his spare. *I have to try. If nothing else, I can at least say I tried!*

Marac, his sword and shield in hand, ran up and stood on Laedron's left. "We'll fight them, Lae. Just like the others."

My best friend, once so afraid in Azura, has resolved himself to stand at my side.

Brice joined Laedron on his right. "We're with you. Until the end." *And Brice. Standing with me despite his terror. Even if we don't survive, I am proud of my companions.*

When Valyrie came alongside him, Laedron stared at her bow and the arrow she had notched. *The amulet. If we remove it from play, will it disrupt the Trappers? Anything's worth a shot.* "Can you hit that amulet from here?"

With a confused expression, she replied, "I can attempt it."

"Not try. Shoot it!"

The Trappers reached the throne. The faint red glow grew to a bright scarlet, the same color Laedron had seen in the creature that had killed the wolf. After what seemed like an eternity, Valyrie released the bowstring. The arrow landed in Kareth's neck.

The force enchantment rended Kareth's flesh away. Laedron

searched for the amulet, but he couldn't see it amidst the protruding bones, the blood, and the bits of skin. Kareth was doubled over, wailing from the blow, and Laedron heard what sounded like glass hitting the ground.

Did she? There—she got it! Laedron couldn't help but grin. He wanted to turn and kiss her, for the amulet that had hung from Kareth's neck was gone, but he knew that they weren't finished. The Trappers advanced, so Laedron flicked his wand and recited his teleportation spell. Before one of the Trappers could land a blow, Laedron and his friends had teleported to stand behind the throne. Laedron quickly cast an invisibility spell on his party.

The Trappers swatted the air, as if searching the place where they had been standing. They turned toward their master.

"Don't worry about me, fools. Get them. Find them," Kareth said, forcing the words through his damaged throat.

Laedron watched the Trappers return to either side of the throne, as if confused about what they should do. *It's working. I think it is, anyway.*

"Get them." Kareth pointed at where Laedron and his friends had been standing. "Go. Find them. What are you—"

In unison, the Trappers extended their crystalline arms. The glow inside their bodies grew so bright that Laedron couldn't look directly at it.

Kareth cried, "No! No! No! N—"

When the light faded, Laedron peered at the throne. Kareth's lifeless body slumped between his former protectors. A rainbow of colors danced inside the Trappers' crystal frames. They stood motionless, as if absorbing Kareth's essence had paralyzed or killed them.

Laedron released the invisibility spell, then whispered, "Have you seen the scepter? Spread out, help me find it."

After searching through broken rock, shards of crystal, and dust, Laedron had reached his wits' end. *I have to find it. We'll stand*

187

no chance here without something to balance the scales. He picked up Tavin's wand, but it was snapped in the middle. *I'll take this to Harridan. Perhaps that cold man will appreciate Tavin's sacrifice, but I wouldn't be surprised if he doesn't.* He turned when he heard the shuffling of feet.

"Found it," Brice said, handing over the rod.

"Let's get out of here, Lae," Marac whispered, sheathing his sword. "We've done what we came here to do. Kareth's dead."

"Not everything."

"What else is there, Lae?"

"The Bloodmyr Tome. We must find it."

"Let the Uxidin worry with it. We've done more than enough for them."

"We've come too far to leave without it. It must be around here somewhere."

"Dammit, Lae. Give up on that silly thing, would you? Our lives are more important than—"

"Who are you?" a monotone voice asked from the throne.

"Has the man returned? As a ghost, no less?" Brice, his hand quivering, pointed his blade in every direction. "What's next, Syril himself?"

Marac grabbed Brice's hand and struggled with Brice for control. "Put that down before you hurt someone, Thimble."

"Who are you?" the voice asked again.

"Who are you?" Brice asked.

The Trappers turned toward them. "Myrdwyer."

"Those things are speaking, Lae? Tavin said they couldn't." Marac reached for his sword.

Laedron stayed his hand. "If they wish to speak, then let them. We needn't start anything unnecessarily."

"Who are you?" one of the Trappers asked again.

"Laedron Telpist."

"Why you here?"

Almost childlike, but it seems to understand. Fascinating. "We've come for The Bloodmyr Tome."

"What is the Bloodmyr Tome?"

"This is nonsense." Marac threw his hands in the air. "They only mean to delay us. Or trick us."

"I don't think so; they don't need to trick us. If they wanted us dead, they would attack." Laedron crept a few steps closer to the Trappers. "Perhaps they've never seen the tome before."

Brice pointed at the crystal beings. "Seen it? The thing doesn't have eyes, Lae. Of course, it's never seen it; it hasn't seen *anything*."

"It must have a way of feeling out the world. If they can't see —"

"We see fine."

"Well, there you have it." Laedron raised his voice to address the Trappers. "What we seek is a book, something that your master would have guarded closely. A book of spells and history."

"No books."

Brice smirked. "Well, there *you* have it."

"It's got to be down here somewhere. He wouldn't have left it far from his reach." Laedron scratched his chin. "A scroll?"

"No scrolls."

"What if it's something else entirely?" Valyrie asked, stepping between Laedron and Marac. "And what if we posed the wrong question?"

"It's been described as a book or a tome whenever anyone's referred to it. What question do you think we should be asking?"

He watched her eyes slowly shift toward the constructs. "Did your master have any places that you were not allowed to go? Any place that you might be punished if you entered?"

The Trappers, though they lacked eyes, seemed to stare at each other as if deep in thought, then one raised its crystal appendage to point at a tunnel Laedron hadn't noticed. "Master's lodgings."

"Good work, Val." Laedron, his friends following close behind, walked across the cave to the tunnel the Trapper had indicated, then proceeded through it into the chamber beyond.

❧ Chapter Sixteen ❧

The Bloodmyr Tome

Laedron opened a heavy wooden door. The room beyond seemed like a small house with an open floor plan, for no walls existed between the nooks obviously meant for different purposes. Bookshelves, a huge dining table, a few chairs, and a bed were placed haphazardly. Entering, Laedron first noticed a rack of weapons containing a mighty axe and a hammer, then the many tapestries hanging upon the rocky walls, as if Kareth had tried to feel normal by arranging them around his personal quarters. *But how did he get them? If he crafted them, the man clearly had plenty of time to himself,* Laedron thought, taking the end of a nearby tapestry and feeling it between his fingertips. *But what material is this? It feels like wool, but we've seen no sheep in this forest. Then again, we've encountered few animals at all.* Then, he recalled the story Tavin had told him about the

191

Trappers killing off the animal life, and he moved on to the next curiosity, the fire pit in a room without windows or a chimney.

A fire blazed in the middle of the room past a long dining table and its single chair. Crouching to examine the fire closer, Laedron surmised that the flames burned without wood or any other kind of fuel. The fire rose from thin shards of crystal in the bottom of the stone pit, and he would have reached in to grab one if it hadn't been putting off heat. He rose and walked to the far wall when he caught a sparkle of light in the corner of his eye.

Upon a hardwood shelf sat a number of knickknacks—statuettes shaped from gems, horns, and fangs from beasts, and other such curios. The collection reminded him of Ismerelda's in Westmarch. *Is this some common trait amongst immortals? The collection of bits of one's life to be put on display?* His eye twitched. *Why would he display these things if he's been here alone this whole time? For his pleasure? Reminders of his actions?* He knew of the Uxidin's inability to remember more than the span of the last fifty years or so with much accuracy, and he attributed the existence of the shelf to that need. Kareth needed the trinkets in order to keep his past deeds fresh in his memory.

The room contained maps of places that hadn't existed for hundreds of years. Odd clothing hung on a rack in the corner. Whereas the modern peoples of Bloodmyr donned shirts and pants, or dresses for women, the clothes resembled coatdresses that were almost effeminate. Kareth must have lived in a time when either sex could dress in robes of rich colors and floral patterns.

"I can just imagine that fiend dressing in women's clothing and dancing around his campfire." Marac snatched one of the gowns and tossed it to the ground. "Does his madness go on without limit?"

"No need to throw it on the ground, Marac." Brice picked up the robe. "Perhaps Valyrie would like—"

"To wear the clothes of an insane man who tried to kill us? No, thanks."

"He came from a different time, Marac. These were probably standard fare in ancient Uxidia."

"No matter," Marac said. "Have you found what you need here?"

"Not yet." Laedron walked to the next bookshelf and browsed the contents. "I'd be interested to read most of these works, but the tome isn't here."

Brice held up a red block that he'd picked up from the dining table. "Wow, look at this, Lae!"

Joining him at the end of the table, Laedron stared in awe at the contraption, then realized what it was. "Creator..."

"This is it, isn't it?" Brice grinned and bounced with excitement. "I found it. You hear that, Marac? I'm the one who found it."

"That's nice, Thimble." Marac gave him a blank stare, then approached. "What is it, Lae?"

"A book fashioned from sheets of ruby, if appearances don't deceive." Laedron examined every side of the device, then found what he thought to be the front cover. "If it is a book, it's untitled and nondescript."

"Much like the novel I had when you first met me, yes?" Valyrie asked, gazing at the ruby book as if it were a gleaming pile of treasure. "Not all books have names."

"One as important as this? You'd think they'd stamp it on the cover," Marac said.

"It would seem that some of the most valuable things in the world come without labels." Laedron ran his finger along a clasp also made entirely of ruby. He ignored his niggling conscience and the words he'd told Callista in Nessadene. *I would be mad to return this book without peering inside first. Such an opportunity will never come again. Not for power, not for sinister reasons... curiosity. To see what the Uxidin need with it. That's all.* "It would seem that this mechanism opens it."

"We weren't told to open it, Lae." Stepping forward, Marac put his hand on the book. "We were told to return it to Harridan, nothing more. I would rather rid it from the world, but I doubt you would entertain that notion."

"Do the contents frighten you, Marac? A quick peek couldn't hurt anything."

"I agree with him, Lae," Valyrie said. "What would be gained by reading these pages?"

What could be gained? Surely, that cannot be a serious question. Partaking of the knowledge of the deepest magic? The spells practiced by the ancient mages? "Everything, Val. The secrets of creation itself lie within these pages. All manner of magic knowledge, all right here." He glanced at Brice to see if he could detect any agreement or dissent, but Brice merely stared at them. *Never mind him. He's probably daydreaming of feasts and riches.*

"I don't think you're following me." She sighed. "If you were to read the inscriptions contained in that book, you might never be the same again."

"Of course I would be the same. It's only a book."

"A book filled with secrets, Lae." Marac pointed at the ruby tome. "Secrets that could change the world, for better or, more likely, worse. Tavin taught you the secret to create magical weapons, and that could be profound enough to transform our whole society. Just imagine some of the things in there."

Laedron licked his lips, then fiddled with the clasp. "I know. I can't wait—"

"No, Lae," Valyrie said.

"No? Why should the Uxidin be the only ones to have this knowledge? What merits them over anyone else to possess the power of this, The Bloodmyr Tome?"

"No one said they should have it. We're merely saying that

we should *not*." Marac took hold of the book. "We'll return it to Harridan, then be on our way. We could be home in a few weeks. A few short weeks, and we can put all of this behind us."

Brice grabbed the tome and helped Marac tug. "Yes, we'll put it behind us. We'll forget all about it."

"Can we?" Laedron asked, keeping a firm grasp on his end of the tome. "That may be so, but I intend to open this book, to learn of the magic on those pages, to know the secrets they've been hiding all this time."

"If you do that, you won't have me at your side." Valyrie folded her arms, then stared at the ground, as if unable to look Laedron in his eyes. "I'd rather live with a man willing to accept that some things are beyond knowing than one who must know everything despite the damage it could cause. Your curiosity is clouding your better judgment."

"You can't tell me you're not curious, Val. You wanted to learn magic. Now you would deny your desire to know more? And condemn mine?"

"That was different. Learning a few spells and a little about magic is nothing compared to what you intend to do here. If the stories are to be believed, that book contains awesome magic, spectacular feats of conjuration, some unseen since the very creation of the world. You propose to know those spells, and that would make you something else, something to be feared instead of loved."

"You could not love me if I became a powerful sorcerer?"

"Not by that," she said, gesturing at the ruby book. "Should you become powerful, it should be by long years of study and practice, not a few spare moments with the greatest of all spellbooks."

"She's right, Lae. If you open that book, you'll start along a road I cannot follow." Marac stood next to Valyrie, apparently resolute in his position. "You won't be the same. You can't be the same after that."

"You shouldn't. I'll stand at your side in all things, but not on this." Brice walked over to stand by Marac's side.

"I think you three are taking this far beyond what it really is. Merely a glance, a tiny peek. Nothing more."

"A glance is too much. Don't you see?" Marac asked. "Knowing this thing exists in the first place is more than we should ever have known. The best thing we can do is deliver it, then forget we know anything about it."

"This book scares you, doesn't it?"

"You better well believe that it does."

"What harm would a simple peek cause?"

"I'd rather not find out, Lae. I truly believe that it would be better if you didn't, either."

"Fine. You're probably right. We'll return it to Harridan and be done with this."

"Wait," Brice said. "Why must we bring it back at all?"

Laedron narrowed his eyes. "What are you suggesting?"

"I think I know what he's suggesting." Marac pointed at the tome. "He's talking about smashing it. First reasonable thing he's said all day."

Laedron shook his head. "We can't destroy it."

"Can't?"

"Mustn't." Laedron gazed at the tome. "We would be unable to fulfill our end of the bargain. We must return it to Harridan."

"Must we? Could we not say that, in his rage, Kareth turned it to dust? Or it was broken in the fight to wrest it from his grasp?" Brice asked.

"You suggest lying to him? What is to be gained by that?"

Marac sighed. "Security for the rest of the living things in this world, Lae. The knowledge that the secrets written in those pages can never again be turned against the innocent. Using the spells in that book, Kareth created an army of crystal soldiers who can suck

196

the very life from the living."

"You don't understand the Uxidin. They'll protect it."

"Protect it? As they did the first time it was stolen? If it were up to me, we'd destroy the thing here and now to ensure that no one could possess it. The mere existence of a thing like this troubles me."

"I understand your concerns, but I don't think they'll let it happen a second time."

"No? Think of what we're talking about. What would some men pay—or do—to get a hold of such a thing? Everlasting life? Forging new lands in the middle of the ocean? Or worse, destruction on a scale we've never seen before? What would the Zyvdredi do with such a thing? Does that not bother you?"

"Of course it does, but—"

"And if Harridan ever decided to use it with ill intent, what would that mean for the rest of us? And for us who, here and now, have a chance to prevent that possibility? How would it weigh upon our minds, our souls, knowing that we gave it to him? Some things were never meant for the hands of men, Lae. I wish you could see that this Bloodmyr Tome is one of them."

Laedron paced for a while, not knowing what to say or do. For some strange reason, perhaps out of a sense of loyalty or indebtedness to the Uxidin, he didn't want to destroy the tome. *Would Ismerelda want this? Would she have told me to return it to Harridan for her own sake, or would Marac's words make an impact, causing her to smash the tome? It matters little. For she is dead, and the dead have little care as to whether the living join them.*

"Well?"

"I'm thinking," Laedron said, then recalled what Tavin had told him. *'Doubt is the true mage killer, and even an Azuran teacher would have told you that. Give up your meaningless morals, for they do not apply here. Have you heard nothing that I've said? You blind yourself with a lie perpetrated to control you. Set yourself free.'* He stared at the ceiling. *Right and wrong... meaningless morals. The lies meant to control us. Set myself free.*

Valyrie came close and took his hand. "The Uxidin had their chance, and if they were to return and rebuild their empire, we would see more suffering than what the Drakkars would have caused. Let us be done with this. The Uxidin, the Zyvdredi, and the madness must all end."

"They'll die without it, Val. How can we return and tell them that we've not done what we promised them we would do?"

"There are things worse than dying. You and I both know that." Her face shone with a broad smile. "Living in a hole in the ground isn't living, Lae. They, like everyone else who has ever lived, will have to make a new life, adapt to the way things are, and move on."

"All right," Laedron said with a sigh, then glanced at Brice. *He's said nothing this entire time... no matter. He's not said anything to the contrary, so I assume he'll agree with whatever we do.* "We seem to be at a consensus."

"That ought to do the job." Marac took the great axe from its rack. "Stand back."

When Marac raised the axe above his head, Laedron waved his hand. "No, no, wait!"

Marac stayed his blow, the axe still suspended in the air. "What is it now?"

"We haven't considered an important part of the problem. Put it down and hear me out."

Marac lowered the blade. "Okay, what?"

Laedron asked, "What will they do without the spell?"

"They'll eventually die of natural causes, I would imagine. Same as everything else."

Laedron shook his head. "If you had something your whole life, something important to you, and you lost that thing, what would you do, Marac?"

"Learn to get along without it? I don't follow."

"Let's say that you had a golden watch from your youth and on into adulthood. Then, you lost that timepiece in a river and couldn't find it again. What would likely be your next course of action?"

"Get another one?" Marac's face contorted with confusion.

"Precisely."

"I still don't follow. What are you saying, Lae?" Valyrie asked.

"I'm saying that, without this spell to rejuvenate their bodies, to maintain their eternal lives, they might find other ways, whatever it takes, to replace what they've lost. They might fall into using the same methods as the Zyvdredi."

Valyrie tilted her head. "They seemed to be rather strongly aligned against the way the Zyvdredi have done things. From what Harridan said, they abhorred the thought of stealing essences for their own uses."

"An animal caged will do anything to escape." Laedron crossed his arms. "With no other options available, the Uxidin might become what they hate if only to survive. Self-preservation is a strong instinct, after all, and we're not speaking of people ignorant to the different ways by which they can avoid death. These people have lived with knowing that immortality can be achieved by magic for too long, I think, to simply give up on the idea."

"If that's the case, you recommend giving them the book? After all we've discussed?" Marac asked. "I thought you agreed that the artifact should be destroyed."

"I do, but I think we should take those pages—the ones for their rejuvenation spell—and return them. The rest of it, we could —should—smash into a thousand pieces."

Marac seemed to contemplate the choice. "Lae may be right. Harridan didn't strike me as the type to just let go, and we cannot doubt his ruthlessness, considering that he was willing to sacrifice one of his own just to beat Kareth and get the tome back."

"My thoughts exactly. Brice?" *I wonder if he's even been listening all this time.*

"You're probably right," Brice said. "I felt a kind of desperation looking at those people hiding in the dark, a feeling like they'd do anything to get their lives back."

Laedron turned to Valyrie. "You?"

"That may be the case, but how do we do it? Scratch it on a piece of paper?"

"I don't think that will work. Harridan said that they require the original pages in order to cast the spell, for the pages themselves are an instrument for spell channeling." He sighed, then returned to the tome. "I'll have to find the spell, I suppose, then carefully cut out the pages."

"You'll have to look into the book for that, and that's something that we all agreed would be a bad idea." Valyrie tapped her cheek with her forefinger. "What if you wrote the name of the spell, and someone who can't read the language were to find it in the book by matching the symbols?"

Laedron shrugged. "I could do that, but I have no way of telling what they might have entitled it."

"Write a few of the names that you would call such a spell," she said, unfurling a blank scroll from Kareth's bookshelf. "If that doesn't work, we'll try to find another way."

Laedron took a quill from the table and scribbled the Nyrethine names for "rejuvenation," "font," and "everlasting life" onto the paper, then passed the scroll to Valyrie. Marac, Brice, and Valyrie gathered around the tome. Laedron kept his distance while they searched the ruby pages.

About halfway through, Valyrie raised an eyebrow, placed her hand over the bottom half of a page, and asked, "Is this the one?"

Joining them, Laedron eyed the first bit of the spell. "This could be the one. Yes, I think you're right. Did any other spell contain these symbols?"

"No."

"Check the rest," he said, stepping away again and taking a seat in a chair. "And make sure. In this, we get no second chances."

Brice, probably from his short attention span, and Marac, likely on account of his disinterest in magic, left Valyrie to scan the remainder of the book.

Reaching the back cover, she said, "That had to be it. I saw the words once or twice on other pages, but each time, they were deep in the text and seemed unimportant to the spell being discussed."

"Right." Laedron stood. "Flip back to it, and I'll extract the spell."

She turned the pages, then sat on the corner of the table. Laedron gazed at the open book before him. *If only I had a few spare hours, I could read to my contentment and see the secrets the Uxidin have held these millennia hence.* He shook his head. *I'll have to settle for a peek at the rejuvenation spell while no one's watching. It'll have to be enough.* He pulled his scepter and, page by page, skillfully separated the ruby leaves from the spine of the tome until he had extracted—and mostly read via stolen glances—the rejuvenation spell.

He snatched a shirt from the coat rack, wrapped the pages inside it, then put them into his pack. "All done. Now, axeman, you may swing to your heart's content."

"Never have I heard sweeter words," Marac replied. He raised the axe and struck, shattering the ruby book. He must have wanted to be sure because he continued chopping until the table nearly split in two.

Laedron peered at the mess of ruby chips and wondered if they had done the right thing. *Are we—a handful of young people foreign to this land, to Uxidia, to her people and her customs—honorable enough, wise enough to decide this for the rest of the world? Is it our place to settle the matter conclusively for all time?* He heaved a breath, and with it, he tried to expel the questions lingering in his mind. *Little can be done to fix it if we were wrong. The deed is done, and there is no turning back.* "Let's return to Harridan, bring him his bloody spell, and be done with this place."

Marac tossed the axe onto the table. "You can say that again, Lae."

Once everyone had cleared the room, Laedron cast a spell at the roof of Kareth's chamber, causing the ceiling to collapse and sealing, under tons of rock, what remained of The Bloodmyr Tome.

❧ Chapter Seventeen ❧

Land of the Trappers

B ack in Kareth's throne room, Laedron glanced at the mangled bodies of Tavingras and Kareth lying on the platform, then looked at the Trappers. They stood as if with their master slain and no new orders issued, they had little to do.

"Ah, you've returned. Did you find what you seek?" the Trapper on the right asked. "The book you said you were trying to find, was it there?"

It speaks far better than it did earlier. What has caused its sudden advancement? "Yes, thank you. We'll be going now. Will you point us toward the exit?" *Is it learning somehow now that its binds are broken? Or did all the essence that Kareth contained change them somehow?*

The Trappers both bowed deeply. "We can take you there, Master. Your wish is our duty."

Master? No, I think not. And a bow to top it off? "You must be mistaken. I'm not your master."

The Trapper on the right spoke again. "Not until recently, no. We have decided that you, the four of you, are now our masters.

We thought it might be a shock to you, but we know, in the end, you shall learn to enjoy it."

It has developed an understanding of emotions, no less. Laedron folded his arms. "Well, we won't be. If you'll show us the door, please, we will be on our way and out of your business."

"You must." The Trapper approached, and the vibrations from its heavy footsteps were enough to send a tingle of fear straight to Laedron's knees. "We *must* have a master, for it has been the way of our kind since we were made. Without a master, the Myrdwyer cannot continue."

"We can't lug one of those things back into the cities, Lae," Marac said, his hand firmly on his hilt. "Imagine the people running in terror at the sight of it."

"As if you're telling me something that I don't already know?" Laedron stared at the creature, wondering what he should do. *It'll have to be another way, then.* "Tell me, why do you need a master?"

"To guide and nurture us, to show us the things which need to be done. Our master gives the tasks, and we happily abide, for Master leads and instructs in all things."

"You don't need anyone to do that for you."

"It is the master's place to do—"

"No, you're free now." Laedron tried to think of what words to say next. *It's your life; do what you will? Do these things even have lives, in the conventional sense or otherwise?* "Only you can determine your own destiny." *There, that fits, I think.* "The door?"

The Trapper pointed at a large tunnel in the far wall, and when Laedron started toward the exit, the creature asked, "Master wishes us to stay here?"

"Yes, yes! You stay here and decide what you should do next." He continued walking, but stopped at the tunnel mouth, considering exactly what he had just told them. *No, I can't leave it at that. If Uxidin might resort to Zyvdredi techniques to preserve themselves, no one can predict what these things might do if loosed upon a hostile world.* "How many of you have been created?"

"Four hundred and thirty-one."

Laedron couldn't stop his jaw from dropping. "Four hundred and thirty-one?" *Creator...* "Four hundred..."

"And thirty-one," the Trapper said, as if Laedron could have forgotten so quickly.

He sized up the creature, its broad shoulders, tall stature, and massive hulk of a body, intimidating even when engaged in cordial chatter. "All exactly the same as you?"

"That is how many the master has created in total, in all of the forms he has decided." The creature seemed to glance at its twin. "Like us? Sixteen guardians. The rest are harvesters and builders."

Laedron gestured at the broken shards of crystal, the remains of the Trappers Tavin had killed with his spell. "Is that counting the ones who perished here?"

"Yes, we have subtracted them from our number. Sixteen of us remain," the Trapper replied, no sense of emotion or concern in its words.

I couldn't imagine four hundred just like this one. Breathing a sigh of relief, he said, "It's not as bad as I thought, then."

"Bad?"

"Nothing."

"What do we do, Lae?" Brice asked.

"I can't say. What does one do with a sentient, crystalline race?" *The thought of it. Fascinating.* "We can't take them with us, but we can't leave them here to their own devices."

"Perhaps some basic instructions, then?" Valyrie gazed at the pair of Trappers. "Tell them not to leave this place?"

"That's a start. Any other ideas?"

"Don't hurt other people? Would that work?"

Laedron considered the question, then imagined the deeper implications. *If I tell them not to hurt others, would they stand idly by and be destroyed by someone coming to steal their riches? What if someone else happens upon them and tries to enslave them?* "Trapper, this is your home."

"Of course it is, Master. It is your home, also."

"No, you have no master. You are your own masters now, and you shall be until I, personally, tell you that you're not. When in your home, you decide the rules." Laedron watched as the creatures seemed to think about his words. "Also, you shouldn't harm any other people, people like us. Help them if they need help; however, if they try to do you harm, you should defend yourselves."

Marac raised an eyebrow. "Should we be telling them that, Lae? That leaves a bit of room for interpretation."

"It's the most sensible advice I can think of. Oh, and another thing. Everything within these caverns is your property, and anything you build or make henceforth is yours."

"The platinum, Lae? You're giving them the mountains of treasure?" Brice asked, his eyes wide and his brow furrowed. "What about Harridan's people?"

"The platinum, the crystal, everything belongs to the Trappers, for no one would have even known about it if not for their hard labor in digging it up. Besides, if Harridan needs money, he should have to ask for it from those who did the work."

"But you said you would give it to Harridan's people. You promised, Lae."

"I promised to give it to Harridan's people, yes, but are these not also Harridan's people? Tavin's kin? The same essence that gives them life once fueled the fallen Uxidin, the same Uxidin that Harridan and Tavin called brothers and sisters. Tavin, I think, wouldn't have cared one way or another knowing what we know now."

"Which is?"

Laedron sighed. "That the whole thing was a ruse. Tavin was

sent here specifically for the purpose of dying at Kareth's hands. Harridan used some sort of spell to poison Tavin's essence, and once it had been absorbed, the essence tainted Kareth's staff."

"And the next spell," Valyrie said, "caused his staff to explode."

"Precisely. Harridan knew that Tavin would meet his end down here, but he wanted Kareth out of the picture, once and for all." Laedron glanced at the Trappers, and they stood there like confused children listening to a conversation between adults. "Sorry for that. We'll leave you to it."

"Since we may never see you again, we have questions before you go, Master."

"I'm not—" He cut himself off. "What questions do you have?"

"Are we evil?"

This must be some sort of cruel torture for some transgression I've committed, Laedron thought. "No, you're not evil."

"How do you know, Master?"

Of course, we're stuck here in a hole in the middle of nowhere being asked about philosophy from some giant crystal construct. "The nature of evil is complicated, but in order to be evil, you must have certain qualifications."

"What qualifications?"

This shall never end. I see it now, standing here for eternity talking to this creature. "Well, I don't know… greed, avarice, selfishness, that sort of thing. And you have to take them to extremes, to the point of harming other people for your own benefit."

"We have done that, Master. We must be evil."

"Would you stop calling me—" He paused. Though frustrated and ready to leave, he formulated a question in his head. *If I don't ask, I'll always wonder what its response would have been.* "What have you done that makes you think that you're evil?" *How long, pray tell, might the answer to that take?*

"We have killed at our master's command, taken souls from men to power our bodies, and been a blight on the forest."

"Did you do those things knowing that they were wrong?"

"No, but when you listed the things that we should or should not do, we realized that we have done everything wrong."

Laedron threw up his hands. "Your master was an evil man with a number of issues. So long as you do things right from now forward, you can rest assured that you aren't evil."

"We do not rest."

"It's an expression."

"Expression?"

"A figure of speech… forget it. Do no more wrong, and you will not be evil."

The creature nodded in understanding, then rubbed its chin and asked, "What is the opposite of evil, Master?"

It must be picking up on our gestures, for a crystal being would have little reason to scratch itself. "Goodness. Kindness. Benevolence."

"Then, we will be all of those things." The Trappers nodded their emerald heads at each other, then the one with whom Laedron had been conversing gestured toward the exit. "I will walk Master out."

"Thank you." Laedron, followed by his companions, joined the Trapper at the tunnel mouth. He glanced back at Tavin's body. *We cannot bring him with us. His people should remember him the way they last saw him, alive and well.* "Oh, and I would suggest picking a name for yourself."

"A name? We are Myrdwyer."

"Yes, of course, but I was thinking something more personal, more individual to *you*. Something that the other Myrdwyer would know you by."

"Do you have a name, Master?"

"Laedron Telpist."

"I will think about these things, Master."

Laedron followed the Trapper into the tunnel, then walked alongside his friends. "They'll have their work cut out for them."

"Just imagine what this place might look like in a year or two," Marac said. "That's if they do something other than wander about the caverns for the rest of eternity."

I wonder how long they will live. Eternity? Perhaps, for a body made of crystal would need little rejuvenation. Their bodies don't break down like ours do. "Only time will tell. I have a feeling that won't be the case, though."

"Do you?"

Laedron nodded. "Somehow, yes. A little direction can go a long way."

Through a maze of caverns, tunnels, and burrows, Laedron kept the Trapper in sight as he followed, and at the end, he spied the forest, darkened by night, and felt the cool breeze on his face. "Thank you for showing us the way."

"It was my pleasure, Master." The Trapper gave him a little bow. "I have been thinking about what you said."

"About what I said? What did I say?"

"That I should have a name, something that identifies me as an individual."

"Did you come up with one yet?"

"No, but I wanted to ask you a question."

"Yes?"

"How long are names?"

Laedron shrugged. "Well, I don't know, really. It varies based on a number of factors."

"I have come up with a possible name, and I believe that it embodies everything I hope to be. It contains twenty-four words —"

"No, I don't think you understand." Laedron was distraught at imagining how many questions his response might inspire. "A

209

name should be something shorter. If your name has twenty-four words in it, it would take quite a while to address you."

"Is that a bad thing, Master?"

"It could be. Suppose we were in the forest, and I called out to warn you of a falling tree. If your name was that long, I might not be able to say it in time to help you."

"Master is good and wise."

"People call me 'Lae' for short, but my full name's a little longer. If you want a name that long, go ahead, but come up with something shorter for casual conversation."

"I will, Master. I hope that you return to visit us sometime."

Although Laedron knew that he likely would never return to Myrdwyer—or Lasoron, for that matter—he grinned courteously. "Take care of yourself. Here." He reached out, took the creature's crystal fingers in his hand, and gave it a handshake. "This is one way we say goodbye in my country."

"Goodbye, Master," the Trapper replied, and Laedron wondered if he detected some inflection in the statement, as if the creature was beginning to develop emotions of its own. *If I didn't know any better, I would have thought that this thing was sad at our departure.*

After exiting the tunnel, Laedron looked around to get his bearings, spotting the old temple not far from where they stood. The trail led them around the temple, to the steep hill on the other side, and back to the path Tavin had taken them along earlier that day. *Tavingras, you would have been amazed at the things we've seen since your passing. Kareth's quarters, The Bloodmyr Tome, and even a sentient race of crystal beings, newly born by the death of their master.* He smiled until he remembered Harridan and the rest of the living Uxidin, and he wondered how he would explain the events that had occurred beneath the temple, what he would reveal, and what he would need to hide.

❧ Chapter Eighteen ❧

All Things End with a Choice

L ong into the evening, they reached the secret entrance of the Uxidin shelter, the ancient pine with an inscription in an arc. Laedron cast a spell on each of his companions to make them ethereal, and once they had entered the tree, he passed through himself.

The horses stirred at their approach, and Brice said, "I'll stay here. Fetch me when you're done."

"You don't want to see how it ends? To know the answers to the mysteries?" Laedron asked.

"I've seen the end already. It ended with Kareth's death, and those answers are yours, Lae. So long as you're satisfied, I'm satisfied."

Marac swatted Brice on the shoulder. "For the first time in a long time, I agree with Thimble. You go on ahead. Give Harridan the pages, ask your questions, and at last, we'll be headed home."

"Home," Brice said. "Hardly seems like a real place."

"I'll wait here, too, Lae," Valyrie said. "Those people fill me with a sense of dread."

"If that's what you want, I'll go alone. Back in a blink." Laedron descended the stairs.

* * *

"Have you come to tell me that our little plan succeeded?" Harridan asked when Laedron entered. "Tavingras does not return at your side, young mage?"

"Indeed." Laedron closed the door. "Your strategy worked. Kareth is dead, and beside him lies Tavingras." He presented Tavin's broken wand, and Harridan took it.

"You speak as if you have disdain for what we've done." Harridan, his staff tapping at every step, paced the room, then stopped and removed his cowl. "You were there. If Tavingras fell, Kareth was just as dangerous as we had anticipated. Why so cold?"

"One of your men is dead. I thought that you might feel a little sadness at that fact." Laedron looked away from Harridan, choosing instead to stare at the floor. *The man seems to have no feelings about it, except for the glee at Kareth's demise. Did Tavingras have any idea what kind of man he served?*

"Tavingras was a good man, but he knew his task and was well aware of the dangers involved. So long as Kareth and the Trappers held a stranglehold on this forest, we had no hope of recovering."

"Kareth is the only one who has met his end. The Trappers remain beneath the temple."

"Kareth's death didn't release them from his spell?" Harridan's face flushed, and he pointed at the door. "You'll have to go back and finish the job. I won't suffer their existence for another second."

"They'll not bother you."

"No? Those things have been the cause of a number of deaths of our people. What makes you think that they would have a sudden change of heart?"

"Something happened in those caverns, something that's difficult to explain," Laedron said.

"I suppose you should tell it, then. If we're to live alongside them, we'll need to know the dangers."

Laedron nodded. "Kareth had an amulet by which he controlled the Trappers, and Valyrie shattered it with a well-aimed arrow. Unable to control them, Kareth succumbed to them. His essence was ripped from his body, and the Trappers took it into themselves."

"Good. What happened next?"

Good? I wouldn't wish such a fate on my worst enemy. "The essence changed them. I have no way of telling, but I think they took in far more than just Kareth's life force, for he had many soulstones imbedded in his flesh."

"Monstrous," Harridan said, shaking his head.

The man may not be made of stone after all. "Indeed. A horrid sight to take in."

"Then, you fought those Trappers?"

"No. As I mentioned, something happened. Something changed about them. After a while, they started speaking to us."

"Oh? And what, pray tell, did they say?"

"To make a long story short, they wanted us to be their new masters, and we refused. I told them that they would be their own masters, make decisions for themselves, and that the caverns beneath the old temple belonged to them."

"You gave them our land?"

Then he goes and says something like that. Laedron sneered, having taken enough attitude from Harridan. "Did you even know about the caverns? Would you have ever known if I hadn't told you? I witnessed the creation of a new race, a new form of life, and all you care about are your petty land rights?"

"Calm yourself, Sorcerer. I only mean to find out what implications this has for the rest of us." Harridan scratched his chin. "Did they discuss any terms for peace?"

This must be handled carefully. If I'm too hasty, the end result will be nothing short of war. "Yes. They merely wish to be left to live in their caverns and travel the forest without hostility. If you and yours make no transgressions against them, they will maintain peace."

"Simple enough." Harridan came closer and put his hand on Laedron's shoulder. "Do you earnestly believe that they'll uphold their end of the bargain?"

"Yes, and I believe it more than I've ever believed anything. If the peace is broken, it will be by your hand alone."

"Then, I shall have to explain these things to my people so it doesn't happen," Harridan said, extending his hand. "Now, the more important matter. The tome?"

"The answers to the many questions I have should come before I give it to you. Things that I still haven't been given an opportunity to ask."

Harridan sighed and leaned against the altar. "Very well. Ask your questions."

What should I ask first? I have so many... "What is a *regnant magister*?"

"That is quite an old term indeed. Who told you of that?"

"My teacher. Her name was Ismerelda, and she was Uxidin."

"In the old days of the empire, the chief of the Azuran scholars was known as the *regnant magister*, and when our people spread out across Bloodmyr after the empire collapsed, they retained their old titles and established new seats of learning around the world. It is a term that one doesn't usually hear outside of Uxidin lands, but she must have had a school amongst mortal men."

"Yes, Westmarch."

"Westmarch?"

Laedron furrowed his brow. *If he hasn't heard of that city, he's been secluded considerably longer than I had imagined.* "A city in my homeland."

Harridan nodded, but Laedron knew it was more of a dismissive gesture than one of agreement or knowledge. "Anything else, Sorcerer?"

"Can you tell me anything about the Almatheren Swamp? The Netheren? I was told they were an undead variant of the Zyvdredi."

"Since the Zyvdredi derive from men, just as Uxidin do, it suffices to say that the Netheren do indeed come from Zyvdredi roots, and Almatheren is home to most of the world's population of them. By infusing a corpse with life essence, the Zyvdredi created legions of the creatures."

"Do they control them somehow?"

Harridan chuckled. "I'm sure they wish they could, young mage. No, and that's part of the reason the swamp exists. The undead, chaotic as they are, went to live—if you can call it that—in Almatheren after a series of unfortunate events. Unfortunate for the Zyvdredi who created them, at any rate.

"You see, the Zyvdredi created far too many and over too short a time. The creatures couldn't be controlled, and some might say they developed some modicum of intelligence. The Netheren killed their masters—well, those not killed by other Zyvdredi—and went to live in the obscurity and seclusion of the wetlands."

"The Lasoronian army marches east to face them. Why would the Netheren pose a threat if they simply want to be left alone?"

"Who can be certain what the walking dead truly desire? I can speculate on their reasons, but if the army is headed that way, it can only be because the army is the appropriate tool to use in the present situation. Did you have anything else for me?"

Though Laedron had a number of questions he could have asked, he decided that some of the things he'd wondered about would be useless if posed to Harridan because he had little knowledge of the outside world in the present times. "Did you ever meet Azura?"

"Since the subject of your question has become something of a divinity, are you asking as a sorcerer or as a worshipper?"

"Could I, being a mage, ask in any way other than as a mage?"

"Just checking, young man, for speaking of my experiences with Azura could be construed as blasphemy by some. I only wanted to be sure that you accept her as a gifted sorceress and not as a god."

"My family and I follow the Old Religion of the Creator."

"Good. Yes, I did know Azura. I left Uxidia prior to the Great War and that business with... oh, what's his name?"

"Tristan?"

"Yes, Tristan. She should have known better than to mingle with mortals. He, like all the rest, couldn't be expected to accept our strange ways or the fact that we are immortal. Tristan's church is one of hypocrisy; we have magic, they have miracles, but both are the same with different names. The priests believe that their power comes down as a blessing from the Creator, whereas in reality, they do the exact same thing we do."

"Thank you." Pulling the cloth containing the ruby pages from his bag, Laedron watched as Harridan's eyes narrowed. "Here you are."

Harridan took the small package and ripped open the cloth open. His pleasant demeanor changed to one of anger and contempt. "What happened to it?"

"We recovered the pages to the rejuvenation spell. You will find it there in its entirety."

"Was the book not there? A ruby book ten times as thick as this," Harridan said, holding the stack close to Laedron's face. "We must have the tome!"

"It is no more. Apart from those pages, only chips and shards of ruby remain of the original book." *Not the whole truth, but that's what happened.*

Harridan eyed him with suspicion. "You did that, didn't you? Smashed it into a thousand pieces?"

"Yes."

"Damned fool," Harridan whispered, as if the words came out more from reflex than any voluntary act. "Who are you to do that? To destroy our most sacred, our most holy text?"

Laedron turned and reached for the door.

Harridan stopped him. "Answer me. You'll answer me, or you won't leave this chamber alive. I swear it."

Now, the man shows his true colors. Laedron looked back over his shoulder. "No man deserves to be a god, and that is precisely the purpose of that book. Your faith may claim that it was given to your people by the Creator, but do you know what I think? I would venture to say that the tome was crafted by a powerful wizard in eras long forgotten, the spells chiseled upon those pages frightful even to him."

"You think our history is a lie? You come into my chapel and spit in my face?"

"I think that, with no small measure of avarice, someone took that tome from whoever created it, then claimed it was a gift from on high." Laedron clenched his fists. "Whatever the reason, the book should never have been made with spells so powerful, so dangerous to the world. Think what you will, but the deed is done. The Bloodmyr Tome shall threaten no one forevermore."

"To think that I had planned on sharing things with you—immortality, the secrets of wizardry, and the foundations of magic itself—"

"You must have gotten the wrong impression of me, for I want none of those things. You have so quickly forgotten what I just said: men were never meant to be gods."

"Get out!" Harridan jabbed a finger toward the door. "Never pollute our halls again, and go before I change my mind."

"You still have your precious immortality, great Far'rah. Perhaps you should be thankful that we returned even that." Laedron opened the door, and once he crossed the threshold, Harridan slammed it.

The people gathered in the chamber stared at Laedron, the slamming door obviously catching their attention.

He gazed back at them and said, "Be careful in whom you place all your hopes, for they may not hold your best interests with their own."

Laedron turned and walked away.

* * *

Finding his friends in the hollow of the tree, Laedron stood watching them, unsure what to say.

"Well?" Marac finally asked. "What happened?"

"I posed my questions—the few that I ended up asking—and gave him the spell." Laedron sighed. "He was furious when I told him what had happened to the tome."

"You told him the truth?"

"Yes. Better to tell him now than to risk his sending more of his people after the tome."

Marac approached, put his hand on Laedron's shoulder, and said, "Good. At long last, we can go home. *Home*, Lae."

He smiled. "Almost, but I want to see Jurgen one last time."

"Jurgen? He has little need of us now, Lae. With the Zyvdredi gone, he's surely busy with church affairs."

"No, I think that's a good idea," Brice said.

Marac looked cross. "And why in the world is that a good idea to you, Thimble?"

"I... um..."

"Oh, I remember now... Thimble thinks he's got a sweetheart in Azura, doesn't he? Collette was her name, wasn't it?" Marac grabbed his belly and laughed.

"And why not?" Brice puffed out his chest and put his hands on his hips. "So what if I want to see her again? And Caleb and Piers?"

"And Jurgen," Valyrie said.

"Fine, fine. I'm only playing with you, Thimble." Marac crossed his arms and stared at the floor. "After all, when might we venture to these shores again? My family will have to wait. But I do ask that we make it brief. I miss my father more than any of our new acquaintances combined."

"That's the spirit." Brice smiled. "It could take a while to get back, but it'll be worth it."

"Why would it take a while?" Laedron asked.

"Why? We'll have to traverse the forests a few days, then the ship, when and if we find one. Fighting any bandits we come across, sleeping, eating—"

"I can take us there with a spell."

Valyrie raised an eyebrow. "I thought it wasn't safe to travel great distances."

"Not all the way to Azura, but Nessadene should be no trouble. We were slowed by a winding path and rugged terrain on the way here."

"If that's the case, why couldn't you bring us here in the first place and save all that time and trouble?" Brice asked.

"In order to use the spell, I must be familiar with the place I target. Since I'd never been to Myrdwyer before, I couldn't bring us here."

Brice shrugged. "Makes sense."

Laedron presented his scepter, casted his ethereal spell, and sent them out one at a time. Once they were gathered outside the tree, he focused on the location he'd picked in Nessadene and chanted his teleportation spell. The world around him changed with a flash of colors. *Perhaps the cover of night will help to conceal our arrival. If not, I only hope that we appear in front of someone not disconcerted by sorcery.*

❧ Chapter Nineteen ❧

The Vicariate

When the shifting lights faded, Laedron scanned his surroundings to see if everyone had made it and if they had appeared where he had anticipated.

"Where are we, Lae?" Marac asked, turning in place.

"The shore near Nessadene." He took Valyrie's hand. "It would've been dangerous to appear in the middle of the city."

Brice mounted his horse. "Do you think we'll find a ship to take us to Azura?"

"Only one way to find out," Laedron replied, climbing onto his horse. He rode toward the docks, and he heard the gallop of his companions' horses keeping pace.

Reaching the port, Laedron and his friends hopped down and approached a man who seemed to be taking note of things being loaded off a boat. The man's well-kept clothes with green and white bars and the griffin symbol indicated that he might be an official of some sort.

Laedron waited, but the man kept scrawling on the page. "Pardon me, sir. Might I have a word?"

The man stopped writing. "Yes?"

"Know of any ships going to Azura anytime soon?"

"This one in a few days, if we can get the cargos switched out. Now, if you'll excuse me…"

"Will they take on passengers?" Marac asked.

The official started writing again, glancing at the boxes being carried away. "You'll have to ask the captain. Over there, the one with the red coat." He pointed with feathered end of his quill.

"Thank you." Laedron walked over to the ship's captain. Upon approaching, he recognized the embroidery of the man's coat. *An Arcanist. Of course, for no others can navigate the Sea of Pillars.* He gestured at his friends when they stopped next to him. "Pardon us, Captain. Would you be willing to take us with you?"

"We're returning to Azura the day after tomorrow. Is that where you want to go?"

Laedron nodded.

"Then, it shouldn't be a problem. Do you have coin to pay for the passage?"

"How much?" Laedron squeezed his pockets from the outside, confident, by the size of the bulge, that he had enough money.

"Four sovereigns each should make it worth our time."

Marac leaned toward Laedron and whispered, "No way. We'll walk if that's the case."

"We have plenty of coin, more than enough."

"It's not a matter of how much we have, Lae. Robbery is robbery, no matter how rich the victim."

Laedron gulped. "'Tis only two days' travel, Captain. Why so much?"

"Have you ever booked passage for the route before?"

"Yes, actually."

The captain crossed his arms. "Well, well. How much did you pay that time?"

"We didn't, actually. The Arcanists brought us here without charging."

Rubbing his chin, the captain asked, "I think you intend to trick me, young man, for no self-respecting Arcanist would haul cargo—people or otherwise—without some form of payment."

"I'm not lying, sir. It was by order of the Grand Vicar."

"The Grand Vicar, no less?" The captain let out a chuckle, then smiled with obvious contempt. "And who, my high lords and lady, might you be that you command the attention of the Grand Vicar and draw favor from him?"

"My name's Laedron Telpist," he said, then gestured at each of his companions. "Marac Reven, Brice—"

"Laedron Telpist..." The captain tilted his head and seemed to search the night sky for answers. "Where have I heard that name before? Are you a wanted man? A fugitive from justice?"

"To some, probably so." He heaved a sigh. "We aided Aldric Jurgen against Andolis Drakkar, the Zyvdredi—"

"That was you?" the captain asked, his eyes wide and jaw slack. "Saved us from the Zyvdredi, did you?"

Laedron didn't answer, clasping his hands at his waist.

"In that case, four gold is far too high a price. One sovereign each. Four in total." The captain gestured toward the gangplank. "And we can be underway as soon as my men can finish unloading. We should make the Heraldan coast early in the morning after next. My crew will see about your horses, too."

"We appreciate your kindness," Laedron said, handing over the coins before ascending the plank ahead of his friends. While waiting for the crew to bring the horses onboard, he stared into the distance, the spikes with strange writing jutting above the waves as far as the eye could see. He recalled the first time he'd seen them on his journey to Nessadene, a time that seemed so uncertain and unnerving. Glimpsing them again filled him with a longing to see his family and his native Sorbia.

Soon, mother. Soon, sister. He closed his eyes. *I count the hours until I may see your faces again.*

* * *

Stepping onto the docks of Azura, Laedron held out his arms and stretched. The days aboard ship had instilled a dull ache in his back and muscles. "Glad that's over."

"You don't like boats?" Marac asked, following him down.

"I was referring to Lasoron."

Valyrie joined them. "Where first, Lae?"

"Jurgen, I suppose. Then, we can visit Piers and Caleb at the chapterhouse."

"I've got a few choice words for Caleb," Brice said, balling his fist.

Marac put his arm around Brice's shoulder. "You're still on about that trapped lock?"

"Still on about it? It hurts! You wouldn't be mad?"

"Of course I would. It's just that I've never seen this side of you."

Laedron gestured at the avenue leading into the city. "Shall we?"

They each gave a nod, and Laedron led the way into the streets. The city seemed just as he'd left it, and he figured that little could have changed in the span of a couple of weeks. Still, the people he saw as he rode through the streets toward the Vicariate Palace appeared happier, more lively than they once had been, as if a burden had been lifted from their backs.

The steps in front of the Vicariate Palace still bore the scars of the battle a week or so prior, a fight which had matched Andolis's sorcerer-assassins against the Heraldan militia, Laedron, and his friends. They tied their horses at the hitching post, and ascending the steps. Laedron stared at the crater, the only thing that remained to show where he and Dalton Greathis had been struck by a Zyvdredi's spell. *Rest in peace, Master Greathis. I hope that our deeds have met with your approval, and I pray that your life was not spent in vain.*

He gave his friends a nervous glance before opening the door.

Inside, a steward approached them. "Greetings. Can I help you?"

"We've come to see Vicar Jurgen." Laedron looked at the walls and floors of the entry foyer, noting the change of tapestries, rugs, and paint colors since his last visit.

"Vicar Jurgen?"

Laedron cleared his throat. "Grand Vicar Petrius III."

"His Holiness is quite busy with the work of the church. Perhaps we could arrange an appointment for you in the future?"

"Our time is short, for we'll be heading home soon. Could you pass him a message for us?"

"Certainly," the steward said, taking a quill and a scrap of parchment in hand.

"Tell him, Laedron, Marac, Brice, and Valyrie said to be safe and go with Azura."

The steward nodded as he wrote, then paused halfway through, his eyes widening at what he'd written. "Did you say... *Laedron*?"

"And Marac, Brice—"

"Wait here." The steward rushed down a nearby corridor and disappeared.

When the page returned, he said, "He'll see you now," gestured for them to follow, and led them to a private chamber up a flight of stairs. "Your Holiness, I've retrieved them as you instructed."

Laedron beheld the spectacle of the room when he entered. He had never been in the chamber before, and he was stricken with its decadence. He wondered if the picture frames were made of real gold. *Surely they are. They've spared no other expense.* The curtains draped the entire length of the floor-to-ceiling windows, and the fine marble floors had been dressed with exquisite runners and rugs.

Stepping out from behind a wooden divider, Jurgen smiled, his kind face shining bright. "My friends, welcome to the Vicariate Palace, and only by your many efforts does this hallowed place take you in, arms wide open."

Valyrie rushed across the room and embraced Jurgen, and the steward left.

Laedron said, "We're glad to see you again, Your Holi—"

"Aldric or Jurgen. None of this 'Your Holiness' business." Jurgen grinned. "You haven't risked your lives for me to grovel at my feet. I won't have it."

"Also glad to see everything's coming along nicely," Laedron said.

"Yes, yes. With Andolis gone, we can return Azura to a place of honor and make the church into something respectable again." Jurgen's expression became stern. "Have you come to give me bad news?"

"Some, I suppose, but nothing that should affect you." Laedron and his friends took a seat when Jurgen offered with an open hand. "First, we need to return something to you."

"Yes?"

Laedron motioned to Brice. "The ring, please."

After receiving it, Laedron handed it to Jurgen. "The Uxidin told us that by no spell or miracle could he be returned to life. His essence can only be released or kept in the ring."

"Then, we'll place the ring in the church in a place of honor, as a reliquary." Reaching behind him, Jurgen put the ring on a table. "You found them after all, did you? The Uxidin?"

"Deep in the pine forests and amongst the ancient ruins of Myrdwyer, yes."

"Tell me, Laedron, what were they like?"

He didn't know what to say in response to the question. *Should I tell him that they're maniacal, thirsty for ultimate power, and that they despise mortals? Would my words matter one way or another, considering he'll likely never meet one?* "Strange."

"Strange? That's it?"

Marac scooted to the edge of his chair and cleared his throat. "I think what he means to say is that they're rather odd. Different customs, a different perspective on the world… just different."

"Yes," Laedron said. "We helped them with a minor task, and they helped me understand the changes that I experienced in the days following your spell."

"Indeed, but you can't leave it at that. I *must* know more." Jurgen waved at one of the servants. "Come, bring us some fruit and drink."

Brice stood and straightened his shirt. "If you don't mind, I'll take my leave."

Laedron pressed his hand against Marac's chest, intercepting the snide remark that he was sure would follow. "Go ahead. Meet us here when you're done."

* * *

Once outside the palace, Brice hurried down the stairs, took a quick glance around to get his bearings, then headed toward House Steadfahl. *No need for a horse. It's not far.* He seemed to find his way as if he had walked it a thousand times, and he came upon the wrought iron gate facing the manor, only then stopping to heave a sigh. *I wonder if she'll think I'm strange for visiting again.* Then, he remembered her parting words to him. '*If you should find yourself in Azura again, pay me a visit and tell me of your travels.'* Had she wanted to be rid of me forever, I would think she would've said so. Something to the effect of, 'Drop dead, scum,' would have gotten the message across. He pushed open the gate, followed the steps up to the door, and knocked.

The same butler who had snubbed him the last time opened the door. Giving Brice a stern glare, the man turned and called out, "Milady, Sir Brice Warren of Raven's Landing." *It's Reven's Landing —no matter. At least he didn't slam the door in my face.*

"Come in, milord," the butler said, giving Brice a slight bow and motioning toward the foyer.

Collette was just as beautiful as Brice remembered, and she seemed to be in better health than the last time they'd spoken. "Sir Brice, I thought I might never see you again."

"No?"

"No, I feel horrible for slapping you," she said, descending the stairs and joining him.

"Think nothing of it. A man needs a good slapping every once in a while." *Needs a good slapping? No wonder everyone calls you a fool!*

She laughed. *At least she found it funny.* "You've come to fulfill my request, then?"

"Miss?"

"I seem to recall asking you if you should return to tell me of your exploits."

"Oh, right. Yes."

Brice stared at her through a pause, then finally said, "You mean now?"

"I can't think of a better time. You're here in my home, after all. Did you intend to relay the story by letters and couriers?"

"Mind if we have a seat?"

She gestured at the sofa, and after waiting for her to sit, he took a place beside her.

"So, how was Lasoron?" she asked.

It's as if she recorded every word I told her. No one's ever paid this much attention to me, not in my whole life. He smiled. "Full of dangers and distressful intent, I'm afraid. Bandits roaming the countryside without fear from the guard, frightful beasts in the night, and even..." Brice turned his head back and forth to see if anyone was eavesdropping. "...immortal men hiding in the ruins."

"Immortal men?"

"Indeed, and one would be hard put to figure out which is the worst—of the men, the bandits, and the beasts, that is. You see, the forests of Lasoron contain a number of perils. We departed Nessadene, and in the days that followed, we fought bandits and crossed ravines that would claim the lives of lesser men. All of that before we even reached Myrdwyer."

"Myrdw—"

"Fret not, for you're not an adventurer." He brushed his lapel. "Only adventurers need to know how to pronounce the names of secret ruins and ancient places." He grinned, feeling smug. "Once we were there, we were beset by wild beasts and strange creatures, the worst being the monsters made entirely of crystals."

"Crystals?"

"Indeed." *Ah, it matters not if I embellish a bit. If storytellers ever recount the tale, they'll make us all out to be heroes anyway, just as Lae said.* "The others were worried about the noises in the night, but I told them not to be afraid. 'Buck up, lads and lass,' I told them, 'for if they kill us, we need not give them the pleasure of our screams.'

"Then, we went deep into the ground, fighting legions of undead and crystal creations, until we reached the end where the madman himself was holed up. I had to leave him to the mages to handle, though. Sorcerers fight sorcerers, and knights slay the rest."

"You did all that? I must have had the wrong impression of you, Sir Brice."

"What impression is that?"

"I wouldn't think you were the brave one at first sight," she said, sizing him up. "You just don't seem the type."

"Men behave in different ways in different situations. Just as I'm calm and cordial now, I could spin into a rage at the mere sight of evildoers."

"Spin into a rage?" She smiled. "I'm pleased to see you well, then. The way you tell it, I'm lucky to see you at all."

"And I you, milady. It'll be difficult to return to my home and never see you again." He stood. "I shouldn't stay long, for my companions may be eager for me to return. Thank you for all of the kindnesses you've shown me and all the help you've given. It is a debt I cannot easily repay." He turned and walked toward the door.

"Perhaps I could come to Sorbia and visit you sometime."

He froze. "Could you? 'Tis a long way and a hard road." He hid the slight tremble in his hand, hoping that, if she did come for a visit, she wouldn't ask his friends about their experiences in the ruins.

"As a family, we have the means. Would you like that?"

"Yes, I would like that very much." Brice returned to her, took her hand, and kissed it. "Farewell. Until we meet again."

Once through the door, Brice heard it close behind him, and he walked along the wide boulevard toward the palace, unable to keep the smile off his face.

* * *

"That was an extraordinary tale, if I may say so myself. What a horrible man that Harridan must have been." Jurgen wiped his mouth with a linen and placed his cup on a nearby table. "I do not claim to know the truth of all things, but I feel that you were right to do what you did."

Laedron nodded. "The spells in that book were something men were never meant to discover, I think." He glanced at Marac and Valyrie. "My friends had to remind me of that, and I'm eternally thankful."

"Of course they did."

Raising his eyebrow, Laedron didn't know if Jurgen meant to insult him or if he had something else to say.

Jurgen seemed to notice Laedron's cold stare. "I'm sorry if I offended. I meant that, being a sorcerer, you're prone to an insatiable curiosity, and sometimes sorcerers must be saved from themselves."

"You know other sorcerers?"

"No, no, but I've been studying the subject since you left. With the wealth of knowledge you held about our kind, I thought I might learn a bit about yours. It's only fair, isn't it?"

"I suppose."

"The path to tolerance is paved by a mutual respect and understanding. Without them, our church and your Circle can never exist side by side." Jurgen grinned. "If I make that first step, perhaps others of my ilk will follow."

"Thank you," Laedron said, turning when he heard footsteps. "Ah, Brice. Did you accomplish… whatever it is you wanted to accomplish?"

Brice nodded.

Laedron stood. "Good. We would stay longer, but everything in my being desires nothing more than to return home to see my family again. We have one more stop to make, then we'll be on our way westward."

"I shouldn't have been so selfish as to hold you for so long, young man." Jurgen put his arm around Laedron's shoulders, walking him toward the entry foyer. "Anytime you wish to return, you are free to do so. Not just free, but welcome."

"I never thought I'd say this." Laedron's voice cracked, and he choked on the words. "Never imagined that I'd be proud to call a priest 'friend.'"

"The wounds will take some time to heal, but they will. *They will.*" Jurgen opened the door. "May the Creator watch over you on your journey home."

Valyrie grabbed Jurgen, embracing him. "It could be a long time before I see you again. You've always been such a good friend to our family, and it pains me to know that I may never come back to visit."

Jurgen wiped the tear from her cheek. "You may come and pay me a visit anytime you like. So long as this old body draws breath, I'll be here for you whenever you may need me, Valyrie."

She nodded, and stepping away, she drew her sleeve across her nose and sniffled. "Goodbye." She looped her arm under Laedron's and walked beside him.

Outside, Marac tapped Laedron on the shoulder. "One more stop?"

"I thought we might visit our fellow conspirators, Piers and Caleb."

"Oh, yes. Of course."

* * *

When they arrived, the door of the Shimmering Dawn headquarters stood open. Laedron figured that Piers had gotten many more recruits because the place bustled with activity, a number of new men with unfamiliar faces going about their various duties. *I wonder if I shall be able to find the man amongst all these people.* After wrapping his horse's reins around the post outside, he crossed the threshold, then ambled about the front room.

"You're back!" Caleb ran to the end of the landing above them, turned at the stairs, and skipped two steps at a time coming down. "In one piece, no less. Wel—"

Caleb hit the floor, and Brice stood above him, shaking his fist. "That's for the lock."

Caleb massaged the side of his face. "The lock? What lock?"

"The trapped lock you gave me. Don't pretend like you don't remember."

"You picked it?"

"Oh, yes!" Brice bobbed his head, his ears turning red. "I picked it, all right. Stuck me in the finger, and the soreness still hasn't gone away."

Caleb, taking Marac's hand and standing, shook his head. "I suppose I deserve that one. Do the rest of you want to take a swing at me while we're at it?"

"You haven't done any wrong to me, but don't try anything." Marac folded his arms, then laughed. "I've never seen Thimble so mad in all my life, so I have to thank you for that one."

"It wasn't funny," Brice said.

"So says you."

"Now that that's settled…" Laedron glanced between the three of them. "Could you tell Piers that we've come to bid him farewell?"

"Piers!" Caleb yelled toward the upper level. *Subtle as always. I could've done that.*

Piers strolled into view on the upper level. When he reached the edge, he put his hands on the railing, and although he opened his mouth to speak, he stopped when he saw Laedron and his companions. Piers descended the staircase and shook Laedron's hand, then exchanged handshakes with the others. "I can't tell you how much we appreciate everything you've done for us. We're well on our way to getting the order back to where it needs to be."

"You did your part the same as we did," Laedron said.

"What brings you back to Azura? More Zyvdredi plots?"

I could go the rest of my life without hearing the word Zyvdredi

233

again. "No, we've come to say farewell. As soon as we're able, we'll be off to Balfan to seek passage back to the Midlands." *Never have I uttered sweeter words. The Midlands and Sorbia, at long last.*

"You won't stay a while? Can we get you anything? Food? Drink?"

"No, but I appreciate the offer. We only wanted to see you one last time before departing."

"In that case, take care of yourselves. Take word with you to Sorbia to the knights of Westmarch Keep. Tell them there that the Azura chapter is prepared for whatever may come."

Westmarch. Victor and Meklan. I had nearly forgotten. Laedron nodded. "I will. Since we'll have no use for them, do you have need of our horses?"

"Horses? Of course. I'll have one of my men accompany you and bring them back when you're done with them."

"No need. We'll hire a coach from here." Laedron shook Piers's hand again. "Best of luck to you."

⅋ Chapter Twenty ⅋

The Knights of Westmarch

Favorable winds and a quick ship brought Laedron and his companions from Balfan to Calendport, then a stagecoach carried them through Pendlebridge, across the Great Winding River, and toward Westmarch. Cresting the final hill before the city, Laedron leaned forward and gazed out the window. *Funny how those walls seem so welcoming now, whereas they once had been the most frightening thing I'd ever seen. It feels like it's been more than a month—more like a whole lifetime—since I've walked upon friendly soil, breathed Sorbian air, and had no cause to constantly look over my shoulder for enemies at my back.*

He watched Valyrie, sensing her anxiety. *Now, she must feel the same as I did.* "Everything all right?"

She nodded, but he knew something was off and tried to comfort her. "You have nothing to worry about."

"Nothing to worry about?" she asked. *Oh, dear. What have I started?* "I have everything to worry about."

"Like what? Perhaps I can help."

Brice and Marac, opposite them, turned their heads to the nearest window and acted as if they weren't paying attention, but

Laedron noticed the gesture and knew what they were doing. *Like only true friends would.*

"I'm nervous about being so far from home... *home.*" Bowing her head, she hid her tears. "I don't have a home anymore."

"Sure you do. You'll share a home with us in Reven's Landing."

She sniffled. "What if your mother doesn't like me? What if your sister hates me at first sight?"

Of all the things I didn't want to imagine... but why would they? "They won't, Val. I think you're worrying for nothing."

"How do you know, Lae? How could you possibly know their minds?"

"Because I know Ma and Laren well. They couldn't turn you away."

"Of course they can. Why do you think they can't?"

He smiled. "How could a mother hate the woman her son loves? How could a sister—without any cause or reason—despise her brother's soul mate? You have a face and a heart that could light up the entire world should the sun ever fail to shine, Val. I think you're needlessly troubling yourself."

"Do you really believe that? Or are you just saying that to cheer me up?"

"I believe it." He took her hand and squeezed it.

The coach stopped short of the gate, and as he'd witnessed the last time he'd visited Westmarch, the guards inspected their wagon and peered through the windows at them.

"They run things tighter in Sorbia, eh?" Valyrie asked. "In the theocracy, carts and wagons might receive a passing glance if the driver is steering recklessly. They search everything here before allowing it to enter?"

"As far as I know." Laedron rested his head in his hand. "I should say that I've never seen it done any other way."

When the troops seemed satisfied, the guard captain gestured for the coach to proceed. Laedron heard the crack of the reins, then gazed through the window at Westmarch. He had never met the people walking the roads, but a feeling of kinship swept over him. Every business and house felt like his own, as if he could enter any of those buildings and feel at home. He *was* home, at long last.

His eyes widened when he saw the little alley that led toward Ismerelda's house. He couldn't take his eyes off of it until it was obscured from view. *I'll have to visit while I'm here.*

The coach ground to a halt, and the driver hopped down from his seat, jogged to the side of the cab, and opened the door. "Westmarch Keep."

"Thank you for everything," Laedron said, tipping the man an extra sovereign. *A driver like that deserves a bonus. Quick, knowledgeable of the routes, and efficient.*

"I wonder what he'll think when he sees us again." Brice donned his backpack, then dusted off his clothes.

"Who?" Laedron asked.

"Meklan Draive, of course. Who else?"

"I thought you might be referring to Victor."

"Why would I? I barely saw the man when we were here."

Laedron gestured at the arched entry, the huge double doors left open. "No matter. We'll find neither of them out here in the streets."

They entered the keep, and the same way they had last time, Marac and Brice ran off toward the east wing, obviously eager to see their mentor again. Laedron was left with Valyrie in the great hall, where she stared in wonder at the fine tapestries, decorative swords, sets of armor, and crests hanging on the walls.

He noticed the lack of students and the quiet in every passage. *They must have stopped taking recruits when the war ended.* "The mages study in the opposite end, and that's where we'll likely find Victor."

"What kind of man is he, Lae?"

"Hard to say. He's a right and proper sorcerer, but we never had a personable relationship when I trained here. He was kind and willing to answer any questions I had, but to say that we were friends would be stretching it."

"Then, why come here? Why not move on to Reven's Landing?"

"I'm still a knight of the order, and since they set us on a mission, I must at least report that we've succeeded in our task. After that, I'm sure that they'll release us and allow us to return home, for the war is over." He followed the corridors as he had weeks ago, finding Victor's office with little trouble. He knocked on the closed door, and hearing an invitation to enter, he opened it.

"Yes?" Victor asked, his eyes locked on the parchment upon which he continued to write.

"We've come to—"

Victor dropped his quill and looked up. "A familiar voice. Has our clever apprentice returned from abroad?"

"Yes, Master Altruis. It is I, Laedron Telpist, and we have accomplished our mission."

Victor stood and walked around his desk. "I heard you did much more than that. Never have I had a pupil achieve so much for our order. And without instructions, no less." He paused and turned to Valyrie, as if he had just noticed her standing there. He bowed and extended his hand. "Forgive me, Miss, for forgetting my manners."

She must not have known what Victor wanted because she stood there staring at him. Laedron gestured for her to offer her hand.

When she did so, Victor kissed the back of it, then stood upright. "Might I know your name?"

"Valyrie Pembry, my lord."

"And you are a friend of our prodigal pupil?"

"I am, and a student of his, I might add."

"And he's become a teacher of mages, too?" Victor smiled. "Any friend of his is an ally of ours."

Laedron asked, "What *exactly* have you heard about the things that I've done?"

"The news of Gustav's death came first, and we knew it had to be you because the witnesses reported seeing a mage throwing spells in the streets. We waited, but no more word came about you after that. When we heard about Tristan's demise, we suspected you were involved, and our suspicions were confirmed when the Azura chapter—Master Piers, to be specific—sent us correspondence detailing what had passed there.

"You've rid the world of Gustav and Andolis Drakkar, returned the church to more... receptive mentalities, and saved many lives, young man. You're to be commended."

"Did Piers speak of the Zyvdredi assassins? Of the Drakkars' true natures?"

"Zyvdredi?" Victor's eyes widened. "Are you certain?"

"Beyond the shadow of a doubt."

"No, he said nothing of the like. That explains many things, though."

"It does? What sort of things?"

"Inconsistencies in his writings and holes in his explanations. If he didn't divulge that information, it must have been because he was confident you would succeed."

"If you had known, what would you have done differently?"

"Most likely, we would've gathered our best mages, all of them that we could find, Shimmering Dawn or not, and come upon Azura with a fury the likes of which have been unseen since the Great War."

"Then, it's better that he kept his silence, I think."

"Truly? We would've made short work of the Zyvdredi and probably spared you a great deal of trouble."

"At what cost? A battle such as you describe would have

wrought destruction of epic proportions upon the city. With what little I know of Piers, I think he wanted to prevent as much suffering as possible."

"You're probably right. If we had come, I doubt that we could have avoided anything other than open confrontation in the streets."

Laedron nodded. "I'm just glad that it's over and we have returned home in one piece. Have you heard of any other happenings?"

"Beyond the war, no. We've had little time to pay attention to anything else."

"Good." Laedron turned toward the door. "Thank you, Master Altruis. If you'll excuse us, we plan to return to Reven's Landing." *Well, after a quick visit to Ismerelda's house, of course.*

"You're leaving? But why?"

"We've completed our mission—and then some—and now, we want to see our families. I'm sure you understand."

"Yes, but you can't. Not yet, anyway."

Laedron narrowed his eyes. "And why is that? Have we not done enough for the order?"

"You may not have noticed, but you're famous for your actions, Laedron Telpist. You're a hero."

"And? Can heroes not go home after they have performed their heroic deeds?" He didn't agree about being a hero, but he wanted to impress a point that Victor could easily understand.

"Yes, but not yet." Victor pulled a letter from his desk and handed it to Laedron. "Have a look."

As if a piece of paper will change my mind, he thought, sighing. He read the letter:

Victor Altruis, Master Sorcerer of the Knights of the Shimmering Dawn,

It has come to our attention that one under your charge, Laedron Telpist, and his party had been dispatched with a mission to the Heraldan

Theocracy. We have been made aware that his efforts have stopped a plot to plunge the entire world into conflict, a plot set in motion by Zyvdredi masters. If you should be in contact with Master Telpist or his companions, you are ordered henceforth and without delay to bring them to us in the city of Morcaine.

Kelrick Ambriset, Chamberlain to His Majesty King Xavier II of Sorbia

Laedron's hand dropped to his side, the paper still crinkling between his fingertips. "What do they want with us?"

"The letter doesn't say, but I can only imagine that they want to speak to you and reward you for all that you've done. 'Tis a mandate from the king, and as loyal subjects, we must heed his call."

"It would seem that I have little choice in the matter. When do we leave?"

"Little choice? Of all the people I've ever met, you seem to care the least about being praised for what you've accomplished."

Laedron returned the letter. "I did none of it for rewards or praise. When I fought Gustav, I did it for revenge, to bring death to my teacher's killer. It was by happenstance that our goals aligned, Master Altruis, and when I saw the light leave his eyes, praise and reward were the last things on my mind.

"Our work done, we convinced Vicar Jurgen to take us to Azura, to aid us in defeating Andolis and bringing about peace. We did that to save lives and to right wrongs, not with hopes of receiving piles of gold, lands, or titles. So when you say that we should be rewarded, I can't help but think that we deserve nothing."

"I know how you must feel, Laedron."

"Do you? Can you?"

Victor smiled. "I haven't always been locked away behind a desk."

"I'm sorry if you've felt any disrespect from my words, but I yearn to see my family, as do my friends, and it's disheartening to know that, yet again, something stands in the way of that."

"A few days. Morcaine isn't far, and I'll do everything in my power to hasten the trip for you. Would that help?"

"Like I said, it would seem I have little choice. We cannot disobey the king."

Victor patted Laedron on the shoulder. "Stay with us tonight, and we'll leave early tomorrow morning."

"No." Laedron waved his hand. "We have already arranged lodgings in the city."

Receiving an awkward stare from Valyrie, Laedron shook his head at her just enough to get the message across.

Victor said, "Very well, but the invitation remains open should you change your mind. Return here at dawn, and we'll depart."

Laedron nodded, opened the door, and exited with Valyrie. "We'll need to find Marac and Brice. This way."

"Lodgings, Lae? We've made no such arrangements."

"I know a place. Marac and Brice can stay here, but I want to visit my teacher's former home and show it you, if you'd like."

"Certainly, Lae. I'd like that very much, actually."

Laedron nodded, then led her back to the grand entry hall and off to the west wing. "I've rarely visited this side of the keep."

"Didn't like it over here?"

"I wasn't allowed very often. They preferred to keep the sorcerers separate from the knights during training."

"Strange. You would think they'd train you together."

"They trained the knights as a group, but sorcerers would benefit little from instruction in martial combat. Magic is our sword and shield."

He turned at the last corridor, then noticed Marac and Brice in a side hall, talking to Meklan Draive. Laedron waited until they noticed him, gestured, and they came over to him. "You two stay here for the night, and we'll join you in the morning."

Marac, sounding eager, asked, "Did Victor tell you about—"

"He did." Laedron sighed, lowering his chin and staring at his shoes. "We've been instructed to see the king."

"Well, don't get too excited about it, Lae," Brice said, furrowing his brow. "When I heard the news, I thought you would be happy to finally be recognized for a job well-done."

"I don't need to be extolled for anything, and I'd rather just go home. If memory serves, we did what we had to do. We survived and helped who we could, nothing more."

"Yes, yes, but to visit the king? The palace? To be requested, no less? A once-in-a-lifetime opportunity."

"Opportunity?" Marac raised his eyebrows. "Don't read too much into it, Thimble."

"We'll meet you on the morrow at dawn." Laedron turned toward the exit.

"What will you do? Where will you go?"

"Ismerelda's. I want to see her home one last time."

* * *

He walked through the streets with Valyrie as if his feet knew the way. Reaching the alley that fronted Ismerelda's home, he stopped and took a deep breath, recalling the time he'd gone to the market and nearly been robbed. *What would I do with a thief now? With the flick of my wrist, I could end his life or immobilize him and give him over to the guard. Have I lost my sense of fear or merely gained confidence in my own abilities?*

"Are you all right, Lae?"

He peered at the placard—the golden moon and stars—and the wrought iron gate, then looked past them at the squalid yard. *Tavingras was right*, he thought, taking himself back to the first time he'd seen Ismerelda's house. *Those holes where trees once stood, that grass that seemed like it refused to grow. She had used up the essence of it, an Uxidin sorceress trying to survive.*

"Lae?"

He took a deep breath. "My memories came rushing back to me. Here, let's go inside." Unlatching the gate, he stepped past it, then approached the front door. He tried the handle, but it was locked.

"Do you have a key?"

He shook his head, then took a look around the porch. *That's odd.* He walked over to a pot filled with soil, but he could find no trace of a plant or seeds. Moving it aside, he spotted a brass key that must have been there for quite some time because, from bit to bow, it was solid black from tarnish. Though difficult to turn, the key unlocked the front door.

It didn't take long for the spiders to find their way in. Cobwebs coated the paintings and furniture, and the webs and dim light made it difficult to make out the mural painted on the parlor ceiling.

"What is that?" Valyrie asked, pointing upward.

"A depiction of the Great War. Azura at Azuroth, the final battle between the Uxidin and the Necromancer, Vrolosh." He blew on the shelves to clear away the cobwebs and a layer of dust. "Everything's exactly the way she left it."

"It's small, but I can see how it could be a comfortable home." She followed him to the common room, then through the hall to the kitchen. "It was just the two of you?"

"She only took on one apprentice at a time, which is the usual way when privately tutoring a student." He gazed at the stove and noticed the pan in which Ismerelda had prepared the quiche. "Would you like to see the room where we trained?"

She nodded, and he led her downstairs to the basement. The ashes of the training dummy he'd shot still littered the floor, along with the one Ismerelda had split in two. He could almost see his teacher seated at the larger of the two desks. He smiled. "I would like to share something with you."

"Yes?"

"I will show you what has passed here, and though I could make an illusion, I want you to truly experience it. Do not be afraid."

He pulled out his scepter and focused on his last memory training in that cellar. Then, he conjured his captivation spell. Valyrie spun around when the spell came into being, the manifestation of his memory clearly taking hold of her mind.

A vision of Laedron and Ismerelda emerged from the stairs by a sparkle of light, and she went about lighting the torches and candles situated around the room. The illusory woman drew her scepter—the one Laedron had come to carry—and whispered something. A flame rose from the ruby on the end of the scepter.

Ismerelda said, "We're going to move on to some more advanced incantations today. I wanted to spend more time on the basics, but there's no time for that."

Hearing her voice, Laedron nearly lost focus on his spell. *It's amazing how precisely I remember how she sounded.* He tried his best to ignore the illusions for the remainder of the casting, and when he got to the part where Ismerelda said, "Record what notes you need in your book," he released the spell.

Valyrie turned when the images faded away. "What sort of magic was that?"

"The one we practiced here or the one I used on you just now?"

"This one, the one you cast on me."

"'Tis known as Captivation." He paused, thinking of how Ismerelda had taught him about aspects, then how Tavingras had said that aspects weren't real, that they were tools to control mages. *From this point forward, do I teach according to the original Uxidin methods, or do I maintain the Azuran way? What would be of the most benefit to any I should instruct?*

"Captivation? Tell me more about that."

"Okay." He walked toward Ismerelda's desk. "Captivation spells are but one *aspect* of magic, and they give the sorcerer the ability to impress thoughts and feelings upon someone else."

"Amazing. Does it work with music?"

He turned around and tilted his head. "Music?"

"If you could combine song and a spell such as that, the audience would hang on every word."

"Interesting that you should say that."

"Really? How so?"

"We're very much alike, I think, more than either of us may have realized. I, too, enjoy experimenting with new spells and new applications of magic, and I think you have the makings of a great mage." *Ismerelda's words coming out of me. The student* has *become the teacher.* He smiled. "We'll have to work on this idea of yours and see where it takes us."

"You think it's possible?"

"Did I not write my teleportation spell from scratch?" He thought back to the things that Tavingras had told him of spellcraft. "Anything's possible if you put your mind to it. It took me a long time to realize that, but it's just as true now as it ever was—more so now, perhaps."

"I'm glad that you brought me here and that you started training me. I've never been good at anything, really."

"Nonsense. You're the best archer I know, and you were doing well at your studies, right?"

"No, Lae." She sighed and looked away. "I can shoot a bow, but my days at the university were numbered. I changed my focus from seneschal to lyricist because I had gotten a string of bad marks. I thought writing would be easier than managing finances, but I was wrong."

"Why have you hidden it for so long?"

"Why would you hide something you're ashamed to tell anyone? I'm sorry if I misled you, but I thought you should know the truth."

He folded his arms. "You know something?"

"What?" she asked, her stare fixed on the floor.

"If you hadn't done poorly, you might have stayed in Azura and completed your learning, and if that had been the way of things, you probably wouldn't be standing here with me now." He took her hand. "We would never have known how special we would become to one another. To me, that would have been a tragedy greater than failure in some classroom."

"Do you mean that?"

"I love you, Val, and given the riches of the world, I would refuse them if it meant being apart from you." He grabbed her up in a tight embrace, then pulled away. "Let's go back to the keep, for I wouldn't want to risk staying here with spiders—and who knows what else—crawling the walls and the floors. Besides, I thought coming here might give me a bit of closure, but it hasn't."

"No?"

He shook his head. "No one can ever replace Ismerelda, and I'll always keep her memory in a special place in my heart. Wounds and injuries never completely heal; they seal up and get better, but you always remember what caused them. At times, you'll feel the sting as if it were new, but you move on and try to do your best. It's all you can expect of yourself."

He ascended the stairs, then went into the common room. "One last thing. I'd like to get something to remember her by."

"I'll wait here, Lae. Take your time."

He pushed open the door to Ismerelda's bedroom. The drawers had been left half open, and clothing was strewn across the bed and chair. He spotted a book on the nightstand and walked over to read the title. *Another spellbook written in Nyrethine, perhaps? With the wealth of books she had brought for our journey, I can only imagine what is written in the one she decided to leave behind.*

Sweeping away the layer of dust, he opened the unmarked cover. He noted that the text was indeed written in Nyrethine, but different from what he expected. The first page spoke of a family, gave names of people and places, and detailed relatively minor events. He flipped forward and soon realized the nature of the book. *A journal. Ismerelda's personal journal.*

He flipped to the last few pages and read:

My new pupil has arrived today, a mortal boy by the name of Laedron Telpist. I can see promise in his eyes, but he doubts his abilities, likely a trait picked up from his mother. If he's anything like Filadrena Telpist, I shall have my hands full. I detect a certain tension already, one that I can easily avoid with female students, but the boy seems more nervous than any I've taught. 'What do you think training is for?' I want to ask him, but such a statement could worsen things and inhibit the bond that we must form. This one, I shall have to handle with great care. I think that he has a bounty of potential that he doesn't realize exists.

He closed the diary, stuck it under his arm, and joined Valyrie in the common room. "Ready?"

"What have you there?"

"A little reading material. My teacher's journal."

"She kept a journal? What need would an immortal have for one?"

"The Uxidin are powerful, immortal, and youthful, but with all of those benefits comes a fatal flaw: their memory only keeps details for around half a century or so, unless a particular memory is quite profound."

"They lose their memories?"

"Likely a cause of the rejuvenation, if I had to guess. A spell that constantly refreshes one's body would probably refresh the mind, and in that, I think, lies the problem. The spell could eliminate anything to which the mind doesn't have strong attachment."

"You mean to say that the spell wipes their minds of their experiences?"

"Somewhat, yes, and that is likely the reason why she kept a journal, to have a record of her memories for when they departed." He frowned and stared at the floor. "Can you imagine it? If she had lived to complete my training, it would have been just a matter of time before I was forgotten, remembered only in the pages of some book."

"Some aren't remembered at all, Lae." She looped her arm through his. "I think it's rather charming and thoughtful."

"Charming and thoughtful? What in the world would make you think that?"

"She wrote those things in her journal because she wanted to remember you. Don't you see? Your teacher didn't have to record anything, but she did."

"I suppose you're right. Let's return to the keep. In the morning, we'll head for Morcaine, a city that I could have happily avoided for the rest of my days."

"What's wrong with it?"

"Nothing at all. It's a beautiful city filled with tall buildings, markets, palaces, and churches."

"Then, why wouldn't you want to go there?"

"In Morcaine, I witnessed the attack on the academy, the deaths of my teacher and many of my peers, and the depths of depression to which I plunged. The only good thing I can recall is the moment when Count Millaird sent me to Westmarch to join the Knights of the Shimmering Dawn."

"In that case, we'll have to make a few pleasant memories there."

She kissed him, creating a new memory right then.

❧ Chapter Twenty-One ❧

A Royal Reception

Laedron and his companions, along with Victor Altruis and Meklan Draive, rose and dressed at the dawn's light in their finest garments. They left the safety of Westmarch by stagecoach, bound for Morcaine. Laedron knew the halfway point when he glimpsed the roadside inn where he and Ismerelda had stayed for a night. He and his party slept in the coach, while the drivers endeavored to keep the best pace with respect to the horses' stamina.

High towers and thick walls greeted them when the coach slowed outside the gates of the capital. Everyone stretched and yawned. *I almost feel relieved at seeing the city, for the mere sight of it means that I must wait less time to be reunited with my family.* They passed through the gatehouse after a brief inspection, the guards seemingly unwilling to delay a coach laden with persons of such high regard.

Laedron pointed out places of interest to Valyrie along the way. "We're entering the market now."

"So many people," she said, gawking through the window. "Al'Qarans?"

"Almarians, too, and Gotlanders. You won't be able to tell the Sibelians from the Sorbians, though."

"Why not?"

"Same people, really," Brice said. "People have mistaken me for a Sibelian from time to time because of the way I talk."

"It's not that, Thimble." Marac grinned. "They merely find you alien to the concepts of common sense and tact, traits that can be witnessed in any foreigner who possesses such qualities."

Brice fell back in his seat, his face flushed red.

"Are you always so cruel to your companions?" Meklan asked Marac.

"No... um... I... he knows not to take such things to heart." Marac swatted Brice's knee. "Right? Brice?"

When Brice didn't respond, Meklan said, "It seems that he did take it rather hard. Apologize."

"But, Master Dra—"

"Apologize."

"I'm sorry, Thi—Brice." Marac glanced at Meklan, as if trying to see if his mentor had noticed his slip. "I didn't mean to hurt your feelings."

Brice's lips curled into a grin. "Looks like somebody got in trouble."

Marac rolled his eyes and turned toward the window.

Laedron pointed and said, "The Wardhouse of Morcaine."

"You have Heraldan churches here?" she asked. "I wouldn't have thought Sorbia would allow them."

Victor cleared his throat. "It was closed during the war, for the king was enraged by the actions of the church. He wanted it burned to the ground."

"Someone convinced him not to?"

Victor nodded. "Yes, the engineers. If not for the risk of the fire spreading, the king would have likely set it ablaze himself."

"Not quite what I meant. I thought most of the people here were Heraldan."

"They are, but when the church attacked and killed so many of our people, faith became second to loyalty. The king's own son was murdered."

"He was a sorcerer?"

Victor nodded.

The coach stopped in front of the palace. When the driver opened the door, Laedron stepped out and peered upward at the spires ascending into the heavens. His feeling of homesickness was immediately replaced by intimidation, for no house in Sorbia exhibited such grandeur. Guardsmen with halberds stood at intervals on the steps leading to the palace, their orange and black sashes draped over steel breastplates that sparkled in the sunlight. Climbing the steps, he clutched his stomach, for it churned at the thought of being in the presence of the king. *Calm yourself. He's only a man.* Then, the fear took hold again. *Yes, a man who can order your death with the snap of a finger.* He could tell that his friends were nervous, too, and that made him feel a little better. *At least I'm not alone.*

At the top, Meklan and Victor opened the thick oaken doors, and from the entry onward lay a fine orange and black carpet. Matching Sorbian flags hung from the ceiling some thirty feet above, their ends nearly touching the floor. The line of guards continued along the walls on either side. Seemingly undaunted, Meklan and Victor led them down the hall, then stopped when a steward neared.

"Greetings, Master Draive and Master Altruis," the steward said with a slight bow, his hand over his heart. "Have you come to see His Majesty?"

"Indeed. Advise the king that we have brought his long-awaited heroes: Laedron Telpist, Marac Reven, and Brice Warren."

"And Valyrie Pembry," Laedron said before the steward turned away.

"I'm no heroine, Lae."

"You deserve just as much recognition as the rest of us. You worked with us to defeat Andolis, and we would've never known about Myrdwyer without your book."

The steward returned after a while, then gestured for them to follow. "This way. His Majesty will see you now."

A few halls and a staircase later, Laedron and his party sat in what seemed to be a lounge of some sort. "What is this place?"

"The king's receiving room," Victor said.

"I would have thought he would be on the throne when we met him. A bit strange to meet a king in such a manner, is it not?"

"You've been listening to too many fairy tales. The throne room is for formal audiences with His Majesty."

"This isn't a formal affair?"

"Since we were brought here, I suppose not. He must want to meet you without the watchful eyes of his advisors, nobles, and all the rest." Victor, as if he were at home and unafraid to help himself, held up a hand to one of the servants holding a large jug. The servant approached, poured him a cup of what appeared to be wine, and handed it to him.

Laedron heard a deep voice, then the king and another man entered the room. *Nothing like what I imagined. Pants, a shirt, and an overcoat? I pictured him in flowing robes, scepter in hand, and a crown fixed atop his head.* He stood with the others, except Victor, whose back was to the door.

The king asked, "Is the wine to your liking, Victor?"

Coughing on his drink and nearly spilling it, Victor shot up from his chair. "Your Highness, I—"

"I jest," King Xavier said, offering his hand to Victor.

Victor kissed it, then smiled. "Sire, I would like to present your subjects, recently returned from afar."

One by one, Victor stated the names of Laedron's companions, and in turn, they kissed the king's ring and bowed. Lastly, Laedron did the same when Xavier came to him.

"All of you are so young." The king eyed them. "From what they tell me of your deeds, I expected an army of seasoned soldiers. Please, sit with me a while."

Laedron sat like a dog obeying the command of its master. "Thank you, Your Highness." *It's as if my body obeys before I realize it,* he thought, astonished.

"Tell me, Sorcerer, of your experiences."

What kinds of things would a king want to know? Skip the boring parts. "When we arrived in Pilgrim's Rest, we set upon a plan to go after Gustav. One companion was captured and another..." He paused briefly, preferring not to tell about Brice's resurrection. "... seriously wounded. Vicar Jurgen and I went to the cathedral to face Gustav, and I ended up dropping a chandelier on his head."

"My advisors tell me that Gustav was the priest who perpetrated the attack on our magic academy. When I learned of his death, this grieving father was given the pleasure of knowing that justice had been done, that his son's killer had not gone unpunished. When I was told that he was actually a Zyvdredi master, his death—and his actions—meant even more, frightening me while also giving me even more delight."

"I, too, shared those feelings, Sire, for he killed my teacher and many of my contemporaries."

"Go on, Sorcerer. What of Tristan?"

"We all had a part to play in his demise, Your Highness. Valyrie went with Vicar Jurgen to the consulship to attack his policies and find out where the vicars' loyalties lay. Brice assisted the order knights in Azura with a number of tasks meant to help us, and Marac and I joined the militia."

"What purpose did joining the militia serve?" the king asked.

"Several, Your Majesty. First and foremost, we wanted to be

available if Jurgen and Valyrie needed help. Second, we used the position to learn of any strange happenings, and the information we discovered was invaluable."

"What sort of information?"

"We discovered the presence of Zyvdredi assassins lurking the streets, and we found out Andolis's true family name: Kivesh." Laedron cleared his throat, the mere mention of the name sending chills down his skin. "The militia allowed us a unique vantage point from which to observe the city, and we ended up gaining an ally in Dalton Greathis, the militia commander, who aided us in restoring rightful rule to the country."

"What happened afterward?"

"Afterward, Your Highness?"

The king clasped his hands together. "You were gone from Sorbia for nearly two weeks after that, according to Victor. What, pray tell, did you do during all that time?"

The question caught Laedron completely off guard. "I—" His mouth dried, and he searched for a suitable answer. *Do I lie? What can I say? Think. Quickly!* "We—"

The king sat patiently through the silence.

Finally, Laedron answered, "We traveled to Lasoron."

"Lasoron? What did you do there?"

"I cannot say."

Victor leaned toward Laedron. "Do not anger the king. Answer truthfully."

"I did."

"I mean, answer his question."

"You know," Xavier said, waving his hand at Victor, "there are things that a king must know to rule his country, things that he could never reveal to anyone. Just as this sorcerer knows nothing of the secrets I hold, I may never fully understand the workings of magic. I have one question for you, Sorcerer, which pertains to your dealings in Lasoron, and I expect an honest answer."

"Yes, Your Majesty?"

"Of everything you witnessed whilst traveling in that land, did you come upon anything that would threaten our country?"

Laedron thought long and hard about the things that had happened, then responded, "No, Highness. I can think of nothing that would directly endanger Sorbia."

"Good." The king gestured at the other man who had entered with him. "Kelrick, bring the decree."

Kelrick approached and unfurled a scroll. "By order of His Majesty King Xavier II, the knights responsible for the defeat of the persons commonly known as Andolis and Gustav Drakkar, enemies of the people of Sorbia and the Knights of the Shimmering Dawn, shall be granted the following rewards."

Laedron raised his hand. "You need not give us anything, Your Highness. We've returned safe, and that is reward enough."

"Do you mean to insult me, Sorcerer?"

"N—no, Sire."

"Then accept the gifts."

Laedron nodded, and the king motioned for Kelrick to proceed.

"For Victor Altruis, His Highness grants the right to reestablish a training academy to be known as the College of Mages for the pursuit of magical studies. Although it is customary for the Circle to choose such, he is also elevated to the status of Archmage until such a time as the Circle is capable of selecting its own."

"For Marquis Meklan Draive, His Highness elevates his title to duke and names him Protector of the North." *I never even knew he was a titled noble, and he's elevated to the highest rank in the land?*

Meklan leaned forward. "Sire, is that not the position of your own brother?"

"Indeed, but he has been brought to the capital to aid me here. You shall pick up the banner and carry it forward."

"As you desire, Highness."

"For Laedron Telpist, Marac Reven, and Brice Warren, all shall be knighted and issued as true Knights of the Shimmering Dawn, their lands and titles to carry henceforth to their descendants, and they may demand the address of 'Sir.' By request of His Majesty, Laedron Telpist will, when asked, aid the Archmage of the College of Mages in reforming the Circle."

"And Valyrie, Sire?" Laedron asked.

"It isn't customary to grant titles to foreigners, but... young lady, do you swear an oath of fealty to me and Sorbia this day?"

She bowed her head. "I swear it. I have no intentions of returning to my former home, Your Grace."

The king furrowed his brow.

Victor nearly spit out his wine. "*Grace?* Refer to him as 'Your Highness' or 'Your Majesty,' for he is the King of Sorbia."

"Forgive me, Your Highness, for the way I addressed you. I meant no disrespect." Blushing, Valyrie hid her face with a bow, and Laedron could only imagine how embarrassed she felt. He reached out, took her hand, and squeezed it.

"That's how the Heraldans address the Grand Vicar, isn't it?" the king asked.

"Yes, Sire," Laedron said. "'Tis the highest address in the theocracy."

"No harm done, and she shall be granted the same as you, Sorcerer," King Xavier said, waving his hand. "Kelrick, add that to the decree."

"Yes, Your Majesty." Kelrick left through the hall by which he'd entered.

"I starve." King Xavier stood, and so did everyone else. "Would you care to join me?"

Meklan nodded.

Victor smiled and said, "Certainly, Your Highness."

"Might we be excused, Sire?" Laedron glanced at his friends.

"If it's all the same, we would prefer to return to our homes in Reven's Landing. It's been nearly a month since we've seen our families."

"Who am I to hold you up?" the king asked. "Go, be with your families—Reven's Landing, you say?"

"Yes, Your Majesty."

"How did you plan to get there?"

"By coach, I suppose."

"Go to the docks on the north end of the city. There, you shall likely find a vessel to take you there."

A boat, of course. That would cut our trip into a third. "Thank you for everything." Laedron and his companions bowed deeply, and the king departed.

Before he left, Victor paused long enough to say, "I shall send word for you when we begin, Laedron, and I hope that it'll be no more than a week."

"So, that is that," Marac said, then put on a thick, pompous accent. "Would you care to set sail now, Sir Laedron Telpist?"

Brice waved his hands and spoke in a similar, comical tone. "But, Sir Marac Reven, we could visit the city. Perhaps Dame Valyrie Pembry would like to see the town."

Laedron laughed. "No, Sirs Brice and Marac, I think that we'll return to Reven's Landing posthaste, to be reunited with our loved ones."

"We shall accompany you, Sir Laedron and Dame Valyrie." Brice proceeded through the halls, his hands grasping his lapels, his swagger exaggerated and arrogant, and his nose stuck high in the air.

Not wanting to draw any ire upon himself, Laedron kept his distance from Brice as he followed, but stern glares from the stewards and guards near the main exit seemed to make Brice act normal again. Outside the palace, they turned left, and at the end of the boulevard, Laedron asked around to find a small ship headed north.

He convinced a captain at the end of the row who hadn't actually planned on stopping in Reven's Landing to do so, a favor for which he handed over a gold sovereign. *We'll probably be home in a matter of hours.*

❧ Chapter Twenty-Two ❧

Once Upon a Thimble

The crew tossed out ropes to secure the ship to the little pier at Reven's Landing, and Brice stepped off. He waited for Laedron, Valyrie, and Marac to join him, then walked with them along the dirt path and up the hill. Reaching the crossroads at the edge of the village, Brice turned and said, "Well, it would seem that this is where we part ways."

He stood looking at Laedron and Marac. He'd relied on them for guidance for almost a month, and leaving them with no plan to meet up a little later was a little frightening. "Will I see you again?"

Marac folded his arms. "We live in the same town, you know?"

"Right, yes." He cleared his throat, swallowed, and glanced at the ground. "It won't be the same, though, will it? We're going back to our regular lives, back to the way it was before."

"Can anything ever be the same? I don't think so. Especially not between us." Marac reached out toward Brice. "How could it be?"

Brice eyed his hand as if he were suspicious of Marac's intent. "You won't take it?"

"I... you'll toss me to the ground or something, won't you?"

Marac shook his head, and Brice walked over and took his hand.

"Now, was that so hard?"

Brice raised an eyebrow. "I can never tell with you. One minute, you hate me. The next, we're friends."

"We've been through a lot, and sometimes it's easier to blame someone else than accept the situation for what it is." Marac sighed. "I know I've caused you pain, and for that, I'm sorry."

"Thanks." Brice turned to Laedron. "I know you'll be on to bigger and better things, but can we see each other again someday?"

"It doesn't have to be that way." Laedron swatted him on the shoulder. "Look, we'll meet up tomorrow, at Calvert's side street counter, for drinks and conversation."

"What time?"

"Just after noon. Should be pleasant with autumn approaching." Laedron smiled. "And if you can't see yourself at the loom, you'll always have a place reserved on my adventures."

"I'll hold you to it, Lae." He hoped he wouldn't be standing at the counter, waiting for his friends who wouldn't show. "See you tomorrow?"

"You can wager on it."

Brice walked away, glancing over his shoulder until he couldn't see them anymore. For the first time in a long while, he felt alone. He almost wished that a journey still lay before them, that some monster or madman waited for Laedron's knights to come forward and deal justice. He'd probably be afraid, but his friends would be there to encourage him. *We'd fight it together, whatever the threat. Together, we could do anything.* He wanted to cry, but he kept control of himself, unwilling to disgrace the king or his title should anyone be watching. *Knights don't shed tears, especially not when others might be near.*

His family's house came into view, and he picked up speed. He saw the sheep in the field behind the house, and he remembered his father's favorite speech. *'Brice, my boy, we're fortunate enough in our trade to make our wool from our own sheep. A tailor with an unending supply of thread will never be hungry.'* He chuckled, realizing that he had a pound or more of pure platinum in his pack. *A month of adventuring, and I have more wealth than I could ever spend. It took my father the better part of twenty years to get to where he is, and I could buy a hundred—the man, land, sheep, house, and all—just like him.*

He jogged up to the door and burst through it.

His mother turned, and her jaw dropped along with a bowl. Sliced fruit scattered across the floor. "My boy has come back to me?" Ignoring the mess, she ran to him and, being that he was small and light for his age, nearly lifted him off the floor in a tight embrace. "I thought I'd never see you again!"

"I told you I'd come back, Ma. You never had a reason to worry."

"No reason to worry?" She hugged him so tight he wondered if she would soon cut off his breathing. "How could a mother not worry when her son goes off to war?"

"It wasn't that bad, but you were right."

"How so?" she asked, stepping back. *Ah, to breathe again.*

"Sending me to the knights and keeping me from the front lines."

His father walked into the room, his signature pipe in hand. "Karina, what's all the—Brice?"

"He's come home to us, Geoffrey." She dragged her sleeve across her cheeks to wipe away the tears. "At long last, our son is home."

"I can't believe it. Come here and let me get a look at you."

Brice obliged, and Geoffrey grasped him by the shoulders. "Looks like you came back in one piece."

"Yes, Da. The knights took good care of me. Thank you for putting up the money. I can repay it, and then some."

"Nonsense. Any father with the means would have done the same. A Warren's place isn't on the battlefield, never has been." Geoffrey smiled and pulled Brice toward the living room. "Come, sit a while. Tell me all about your travels."

And Brice obliged.

❧ Chapter Twenty-Three ❧

The Miller's Son

Marac watched Brice tread the road until he disappeared from view, then said, "See you tomorrow, Lae. I'd better get home, too."

"You'll leave it at that?" Laedron asked.

"Leave… what?"

"Brice? The sudden change of heart?"

"I'd never tell him, but I was scared, Lae."

"You?"

Marac nodded, then stared at the ground. "I didn't mean to hurt his feelings, and I would've defended him to the death… but…"

"But?"

"It helped. It's not easy to stop being a big brother."

"You replaced Naettan with Brice? I should've known."

Marac grinned. "I shouldn't have, but it seemed to come so natural. I didn't even know I was doing it until the ride to

Morcaine. When Meklan made me apologize, I thought about how my father had done the same thing when I went too hard on Naettan. Then, it clicked." He snapped his fingers.

"No worries. We made it back home. That's all that matters."

"All except Mikal."

Laedron closed his eyes. "I wonder if they've told his family."

Marac shrugged. "If not, we'll have to."

"We'll go together tomorrow. Let them have one more day of peace."

Nodding, Marac started down the road.

"On the morrow, then. You'd better be there," Laedron said before Marac got out of earshot.

Marac waved over his shoulder without stopping. Heading through the village, he caught sight of Calvert's stall and figured that it couldn't hurt to stop by for a quick drink. *Why wait? A glass of honeysuckle cider would do wonders right now.* He walked over and climbed onto a stool.

Calvert served the man who sat on the other side of the counter, then turned. When he saw Marac, his eyes grew wide. "Marac Reven?"

"The one and the same."

"It's not every day that true, genuine heroes visit my little establishment," Calvert said, grabbing a pint-sized mug. "What would you like?"

"Honeysuckle cider. It seems like it's been ages since I've had the stuff."

"Couldn't find any on your travels? It doesn't surprise me. A closely guarded secret, it is." Calvert paused, his eyes shifty as if he'd remembered something, but he said nothing. Instead, he fetched Marac's drink and served it.

Finding Calvert's demeanor strange, Marac asked, "Anything new going on?"

"No, nothing. Let me know if you need anything else."

"Just the one drink." He pulled out a silver coin. "Then I'll be off."

"That one's on the house."

"Surely?"

"Least I can do to thank you for all that you've done. Enjoy."

He nodded. "Always do. Thanks." He sipped from the stein, trying his best to ignore the sickening aroma of the nearby fish stall. *Just like old times.* When he finished, he stood and walked off toward the edge of town and his family's home. His mind wandered as he went, all of the memories and good feelings of homecoming back to him with each passing step.

First, a stop at the mill to see Da, then onto the house. I hope Ma has something fixed for supper. He followed the road, and when he finally spotted the mill's sails turning in the breeze, he raced up the hill. Pushing the door open, he peered inside. "Da? I'm home. Da?" He entered, took a long look around, and decided that Bordric must not have been there because it was quiet and dark. *Maybe he's at the house. Yes, he must be; it's too late for him to be still up here tending things.*

After securing the door, he jogged toward the house a hundred yards away. Inside, he saw his little brother, Naettan, sitting on a sofa. "Nate!" He rushed over and hugged Naettan.

The boy sat in silence, barely looking up at Marac.

"Nate?" He crouched next to his brother. "Where is Da? Have you seen Ma?"

Receiving no answer, he walked down the hallway. "Da! Ma!"

"Marac?" His mother opened the door of her bedroom. "Is that you?"

"Ma, yes. Finally, someone answers me." He breathed a sigh of relief. "What wrong with Nate? Where's Da?"

"Come with me, Marac." She took his hand, trying to lead him into the room with her.

"Where's Da? Ma, is everything all right?" He hadn't noticed before, but he saw tears running down her cheek. "What's happened?"

She closed the door after pulling him into the room. "Have a seat, Marac."

"Where's Da?" he asked again, having a seat on the edge of the bed. *Why won't anyone tell me anything? Where in the hells… Nate's silent. Ma's crying.* "Ma, where is he?"

"Your father has passed, Marac, while you were away."

Passed. Passed? Passed… He tried to force a breath, his face and neck growing hot, his muscles tense, and his hands trembling. *Dead? No, I won't believe that.* "He was fine before I left. He can't be. Not Da, not now. Impossible."

"We buried him last week, Marac." She sobbed and sat next to him. "It was an accident."

"How?" He shook his head and shot up from the bed. "He was strong as an ox. Two of them."

She followed him into the hall, then to the living room. "An inquest was held by the magistrate, and he determined that Bordric passed from a fall. He'd complained to me about the sails getting stuck, and he went up there to fix—"

"Dead?"

She sighed, bowed her head, and pointed toward the kitchen window. Marac walked over and peered out. He noticed a new stone at the top of the next hill in the family cemetery, a stone that hadn't been there when he left. Then, he turned to look at the dining table, the evening meal prepared and the places set, but where his father usually sat, he didn't see dishes or a napkin. *He's gone? Da's gone...*

Like an arrow, the pain shot through his heart, and he fell to his knees, gasping for air. *Why him? Creator, why has this come to pass? If I had stayed, this wouldn't have happened. I would have helped him with that damned mill.* His vision cloudy from tears, his throat sore, and his body shaking, he couldn't do anything. *We should've come home when we were done with Gustav. Why did we have to stay gone so long? A week might have made a difference. We've saved so many, but I couldn't save my own father!* He was paralyzed, powerless to do anything but cry. Emotions overtaking him, he fell to his side and rolled into a ball. *All the opportunities you had to claim me, and you take him? Creator, why are you punishing me? Why did you take him instead of me?*

He lay there for some time, and the sun hung low on the horizon by the time he stopped crying. Ma came over—apparently waiting until he'd calmed down—and touched him on the shoulder, but he reeled away.

"Your brother and I are still living, Marac. We need your love, too."

He rose to his knees, then to his feet, and stared at her.

"It's my fault. I should've stayed."

"No, Marac, no." She pulled him to her shoulder. "Have you forgotten? He sent you to the knights to save you. You would've been conscripted if he hadn't. There was nothing you could do."

Marac took a deep breath. "I need some time to think. I've got to go... somewhere." His mother nodded, and he walked out the front door, bound for the village. *Calvert's should still be open.*

He paused when his feet hit the bottom step and imagined the night ahead. *I'll be drunk and out of control, washing away my worries a pint at a time. No.* He turned around and stared at the door of his house. *The drink didn't stop Andolis or Gustav, and it didn't help anything else. I'm strong enough without it.*

He climbed the stairs and opened the door. His mother and brother looked up from the sofa. Marac sat next to them and took his brother's hand. "I'm back, Nate. Come, hug your brother."

Naettan smiled and held Marac tight. "I prayed all the time that you would come home. Every day."

"You decided not to go?" Ma asked.

"My place is with you, not at a side-street counter. I don't want Da to be disappointed in me."

"I don't think you could disappoint him, Marac. Even when you were drunk and jailed in Westmarch, your father blamed everyone but you. 'It had to be the guards picking on him for being a country boy,' he said, or 'They must be lying. My son wouldn't do those things.'"

Marac shook his head. "Today, that tradition ends. I

have only myself to blame for the things I've done."

She smiled, then looked away.

"What's wrong, Ma?"

"Oh, I've been trying to decide what to do. We still have some money from the last shipment to Westmarch, but it won't last. I don't see you running the mill on your own, and Naettan's too young to help."

Naettan waved his hands. "I'm not too young, Ma. I can do it."

"No, Nate. I can't work in the place where Da…" Marac closed his eyes. "Too many memories. We'll sell it."

She looked surprised. "Sell it? But this land's been in our family for centuries. We can't sell it."

"Things change, Ma. If my adventures have taught me anything, that lesson was painfully learned."

"It's not even worth what we've put into it, though. If we sell the land, we won't have enough—"

"Money is no longer a concern, Ma."

"Not a concern? Of course it is."

He reached into his bag and produced a hunk of platinum.

"Silver? That'll help, but I still don't think—"

"Not silver."

"No?" She leaned forward and squinted. "What is it?"

"Pure platinum."

Her eyes widened. "Where'd you get that? Are you in trouble?"

"No, nothing like that," Marac said, shaking his head. "I have more than enough. More than we'll ever need."

"This is all happening so fast. Let me think about it,

would you?"

Marac nodded. "We'll talk about it later, then. Whenever you're ready."

She stood, walked into the kitchen, and pulled a pot from the stove. "I didn't make much, but we'll spread it around."

"We'll make do." Marac joined her in front of the stove and put his arm around her. "Revens get by however we can. Always have, always will."

❧ Chapter Twenty-Four ❧

The Comforts of Home

Laedron and Valyrie started down the road, then walked the perimeter of the village. *Little more than a few steps lay between me and my family*, he thought, seeing the old oak by which he'd spent so much of his childhood. He stopped, smiled at Valyrie, and ran over to the tree.

He drew his scepter, pointed it at the bark, and chanted, and by the time she'd joined him, he had finished. "What do you think?"

"A sweet gesture, Lae." She smiled. "Is it a tradition of some kind?"

Brushing his hand over the inscription, he made certain that he'd formed the heart shape and their initials, "L T" and "V P," so that they were legible. "Somewhat, yes. Your people don't do sentimental things like this?"

"You would have a hard time finding a tree so big in the city, and even if you did, the law prohibits marring them."

"A shame." He grinned. "It doesn't surprise me, though. The theocrats seem to prefer their perfect shrubs, pristine lawns, and impeccable buildings."

"Your people just let things go without care or regard?"

"Not exactly. We maintain things within reason, but we tend to avoid absolute perfection. It's unachievable, and in Sorbia, we've learned that beauty can be found in letting things be as they are."

"I thought I knew most everything there was to know about you. It would seem that I have a lot more figuring to do."

He took her hand, then continued toward his home. "We have a lifetime ahead of us."

* * *

Rounding the last bend of the road, he saw his house on the rise. Ma stood on the porch, her broom in hand, toiling away at the dirt. *That woman will never learn. What am I saying? She's a Telpist. Stubborn and willful as the day is long.* A sudden wind came, and when it reached his mother, she clenched her fists. "Blasted breeze fouling up my hard work!"

"I'll never understand why you don't use a spell and be done with it." He stepped onto the porch.

Ma dropped the broom. "Lae?" She rushed over to him and gave him a big hug, then picked at his hair. "I'll have to cut this—"

"Ma..."

"What? You've gone this whole time without grooming? Your hair looks much better when it's short—"

"Ma..."

"Let me grab the scissors—"

"Ma!"

She stopped, then turned to Valyrie. "Oh, I apologize. I didn't

274

see you had a guest."

"Ma, this is Valyrie Pembry."

"A pleasure to make your acquaintance," Filadrena said, offering her hand. "I can't say that Laedron has ever mentioned you. Are you from Reven's Landing? No, I would've heard the name of your family, at least. Westmarch, perhaps?"

Valyrie gently shook his mother's hand, and Laedron could tell she was nervous. "No, madam."

"I see. Well?"

"She's from Azura, Ma, and I've asked her to come home with me."

"Azura?"

"And I love her."

"Love...?" Filadrena paused, her eyebrows high. "The capital of the theocracy? You've brought a Heraldan girl home, Lae?"

Overbearing and to the point, as always. Sometimes, Laedron wished he wasn't related to his ma because she seemed to treat only her children in such a haughty way. Although he knew that she meant well, was sometimes uncomfortably blunt. "I did."

"Let me get a look at her, then." Filadrena squinted and circled Valyrie as if examining a farm animal prior to purchasing. "Tall, slender build, and beautiful—"

"Ma, enough." He slapped his hands against his hips.

"I'm kidding, Lae." Filadrena took Valyrie in an embrace. "If you don't recall, I married a Heraldan, your father, so I can't hold too much prejudice. She seems like a fine, upstanding young woman."

"She is, Ma." He put his arm around Valyrie's waist. "We've been through a lot together."

"That's good. If you can stay together through the tough bits, you stand a better chance of lasting." She gestured for them to enter. "Come, I need to check on my tea. Would you care for some?"

He nodded, then led Valyrie inside. *The same, yet so different.* The living room hadn't changed, but he felt awkward at seeing it. The place didn't feel quite like his home anymore, probably because he had been on the road for so long. Almost a solid month of camping, renting rooms, and—for a brief while—staying with Ismerelda had lessened the draw of hearth and home that he was certain he would have felt upon returning.

Filadrena poured three cups of tea and dropped pinches of sugar and cuts of lemon into each. Laedron and Valyrie sat opposite her at the counter.

Handing out the cups, Ma smiled. "I'll wager that you've never had a cup of tea so fine west of the Great Winding."

"I've never had one at all," Valyrie said, then sipped it. "It's amazing, ma'am."

"You can call me 'Ma,' Valyrie. Everybody else around here seems comfortable with it."

"In that case, call me 'Val.'"

"All right, Val." Ma set her tea on the counter. "Did you two have a good journey home?"

They bobbed their heads at the same time.

"Good. Show her around the house, Lae. Make her feel at home."

His eye twitched because he had expected Ma to say something else entirely. "You don't want to hear about our mission?"

"What's to know? I know the beginning and the end, the two most important parts for me. The middle—the journey—is for you to know." Taking the empty cups to the basin, she glanced at them. "You're surprised?"

"I only thought you might be interested in hearing about it." He sighed. "Ismerelda is dead, Ma."

She nodded, turning back to the sink. "I know."

"You do? How?"

"We heard about the attack on the academy, and a few days later, Laren and I set out to Westmarch to find you. When we got to Ismerelda's house, you weren't there. Fearing the worst, we went to Morcaine to learn the details—the names of those killed, where the survivors had gone. They took us to the rows of unidentified dead, and there, we found Ismerelda. Since we knew her—I told them I was her aunt—they allowed us to take her body, and we laid her to rest here in Reven's Landing."

"But you didn't find me there." He smiled.

She lowered her chin and grinned. "But not you, my son. It gave me hope, and that hope grew stronger as time went along. 'If we've had no news,' I would tell myself, 'that's good news indeed.'"

"Where'd you go after that? Marac said you vanished without a trace."

"We went to Cael'Bril, one of the few neutral countries left when the war started. Throughout the conflict, we heard rumors of a sorcerer and a handful of knights deep in Heraldan territory, and when I found out it was you, I prayed for your safe return. And now, my prayers have been answered."

"Where is Laren, anyway?"

"She's been spending more time by the creek of late, for she's had mixed emotions over the last week on account of Bordric Reven's passing."

He blinked. "Passed? Marac's father?"

"Indeed. An accident in the mill—a fall, if memory serves—claimed him. Did… his son survive?"

"Yes, he's probably been home for an hour or more by now." He glanced at the window. "I need to see him."

"He needs his family right now, Lae. Give him some time to adjust, to grieve with his loved ones."

"Perhaps you're right, Ma. I'll go this evening when he's had some time to take it in."

"Good." She wiped her hands on a linen hanging from the stove. "If I'd known you were coming, I would've planned a feast. I'll fetch something at the market; there's still time yet."

"We'll go, Ma. It's no trouble."

"No, no, you rest and show Val the house. The walk and the fresh air will do me some good." She took her traveling shawl from the rack, wrapped it about her shoulders, then walked out the front door.

"A shawl? In this heat?" Valyrie asked.

"A woman must always be proper and dress according to her status," he said, laughing at the end. "Sorry. We posed the same question to her a number of times, and that's what she always told us."

"Is she nobility?"

"Gentry, I would say, but not by royal decree. The people of this village respected my father, and when he passed, they held the rest of us up in the same light, and it wasn't just because his title had been inherited by my mother."

"He must've been a good man."

"The best, so they say." He stood and gestured invitingly. "Care to see the place?"

She nodded and took his hand.

* * *

After Laren returned, and they'd enjoyed the fine meal that Filadrena cooked, Laedron stood from the table. "I think we'll head over to the Revens' house now."

"Why not wait until tomorrow, Lae?" Ma asked. "It's nearly dark."

"No, I'd rather see him this evening. I can only imagine how hard it'll be for him to sleep tonight, and I just want to assure him that his friends are there if we're needed." He kissed his mother on the head, took Valyrie's hand, and promised his ma to be back soon.

Once outside, Valyrie asked, "How far is it, Lae?"

"Not far. A few minutes' walk if we go by the old path." He pointed out the variety of flowers and trees as they walked.

They passed the mill and approached Marac's house, and he immediately noticed that only a single lantern had been left to burn in the kitchen window. "Strange."

"What?"

"It would seem that they're asleep."

"Perhaps they don't want to be disturbed. Should we turn back?"

"No. It's Marac," he said. "I can think of nothing that would make him want to be apart from me, but if he tells us to leave, then —and only then—will I do so." He stepped up onto the porch and knocked.

After several minutes, Marac's mother opened the door. "Yes?"

"My condolences on your recent loss, Mrs. Reven."

"Thank you for your kindness."

"I wanted to see if Marac was all right. Could we see him?"

"Yes. Would you care to come in?"

"Thank you." Laedron stepped through when Mrs. Reven stepped aside.

"I don't think I've ever met your friend before," Mrs. Reven said.

"Valyrie," she said, extending her hand.

Marac's mother embraced it. "Gloria Reven."

"A pleasure to meet you."

Laedron turned when he heard footsteps approaching from the hall, and he saw Marac come into the living room.

"Oh, Lae," Marac wiped his hands and face with a towel, "I didn't expect to see you today."

"I heard what happened. I just wanted to see how you were doing."

"As well as could be expected, I suppose. It's still hard to believe." Marac rubbed his eyes, obviously concealing a tear, then joined them near the door. "How is your ma?"

"She's well. Do you need anything?"

"No, nothing." Marac glanced at his mother. "I have everything I need."

"If you should change your mind, you need only to call on me."

Marac patted Laedron on the shoulder and opened the door. "I will."

"Good." Following Marac onto the porch, Laedron smiled. "We'll see you tomorrow afternoon, right?"

"Of course, but I doubt I'll drink anything."

Laedron stared at him with curiosity, then started down the stairs, but he stopped when he saw someone walking up the path to the house. "Is that... what's he doing here?"

Brice waved. "Marac, I just heard what happened. I'm so sorry."

"It'll be all right," Marac said, holding up his hand. "We'll have to find a way to make it through."

"Well, my folks told me, and I had to come straight away. Are you well? Do you need—"

"No, no. Thank you for the offer."

It's good to see those two finally getting along. Laedron smiled. "See you tomorrow, my friend."

"Until then."

Laedron and Valyrie started down the path, and Brice asked, "Mind if I walk with you a while?"

"I've never objected before," Laedron said.

Brice grinned. "So, I was thinking—"

"Oh, dear."

Brice raised an eyebrow.

Laedron laughed and said, "Just kidding. What's on your mind?"

"Are you going back to Westmarch soon? To help Victor?"

"I should think so."

"When?"

"A week, maybe less. Why do you ask?"

"I want to go," Brice said, then ducked his head. "That is, if you wouldn't mind."

"You do? Why?"

"I'm not cut out to be a sheep herder. My destiny lies somewhere on that horizon." Brice gestured toward the distance. "I've tasted the adventuring life, and I want more."

"Truly? I imagined you would've wanted to stay here, in safety."

"No, it's not the same now." Brice stopped at the fork in the road. "And I promise not to complain or be afraid… well, I won't tell you if I am, anyway."

"All right. You can come with me if that's what you want, but we're all afraid sometimes. It's nothing to be ashamed of."

"Not Marac, though. He doesn't get scared. Bravest man I ever knew."

Laedron nodded. "Just as a knight should be. Brave and bold."

"All the way until the end," Brice said.

Casting his gaze toward Marac's home in the distance behind them, Laedron smiled. "And after."

❧ Afterword ❧

If you're reading this, you've been good enough to purchase and read all three of the books of *The Mages of Bloodmyr* series. For that, I am eternally grateful. You've shared in the journeys of Laedron, Marac, Brice, Valyrie, Jurgen, and so many others with me. Without me, the stories wouldn't have been told, but without you, the stories wouldn't have truly lived. They live because readers like you take the words on the page and change them into an image. That image is unique to you and it is priceless to me as a writer.

Readers have asked if this is the last book in this series, and they've asked it with some measure of disappointment. Yes, this series is now complete, but there will be other books in the *world*. Some may include the characters we've come to love and know and some shall be totally new, but the world of Bloodmyr—and books within this setting—are far from finished.

On the next page, you'll find a list of ways to stay in touch. Please do. My Facebook fan page tends to see the most updates, but major releases will be listed on all of the places I haunt.

I only hope that you have enjoyed the series and the world thus far, and I hope that you are as excited about all of the adventures we shall have together over the coming years.

Thank you for liking the books enough to keep reading.

—Brian

❧ Connect with the Author ❧

You can easily reach author Brian Kittrell by the various methods described below.

On Twitter:
> **@Brian_Kittrell**
> *http://www.twitter.com/Brian_Kittrell*

On Facebook:
> *http://www.facebook.com/author.BrianKittrell*

On the Web:
> *http://www.latenitebooks.com*

On YouTube (author interviews, discussions, and more):
> *http://www.youtube.com/user/LateNiteBooksDotCom*

Through eMail:
> *brian@latenitebooks.com*

Through the Mail:
> **Late Nite Books**
> **Attn: Brian Kittrell, author**
> **P.O. Box 321**
> **Brandon, MS 39042**

Books By Brian Kittrell
Released and Coming Soon

The Mages of Bloodmyr Series
The Circle of Sorcerers
The Consuls of the Vicariate
The Immortals of Myrdwyer

The Survivor Chronicles
The Dying Times
The War of the Dead
Prisoner and Survivor
A World Forsaken

The Panacea Series
Cure
Stasis
Blight

CPSIA information can be obtained at www.ICGtesting.com
Printed in the USA
BVOW01s1406261113

337404BV00007B/158/P